MARINA R.B

CRANTHORPE
MILLNER
PUBLISHERS

First published by Cranthorpe Millner Publishers (2022)

ISBN 978-1-80378-031-3 (Paperback)

www.cranthorpemillner.com

Cranthorpe Millner Publishers

To my grandad

à mon Papi

Contents

PROLOGUE

What is my purpose in life? Will I be happy? Will I be someone's happiness? Should I worry about these things knowing that I cannot do anything about it? These are questions that most people ask themselves, but I never thought I would. Life always seemed so dull and boring... I never wanted to know what the future would be made of. But on the day I met him, my perspective shifted; I did not know what my fate would be, but I knew that he would be a part of it. My life before that moment felt like it had never happened; like it had been nothing more than a dream. My past felt imaginary, non-existent, because meeting him brought so many new feelings and experiences.

One encounter after another led me to where I was supposed to be; led me to my fate. Fate... I had never considered that someday this idea would be looping over and over in my mind. Yet, ever since that first

1

encounter, everything seemed to have been written for me. I was not in control of anything; regardless of how hard I tried to do the right thing, I always failed miserably. I wanted to please everyone; I wanted everyone to be happy, even if it meant pushing my own happiness aside, but it did not happen, perhaps because it was not meant to happen.

My life felt like a circle, going round and round. Finding happiness; losing it; finding it again; losing it again. I found myself wondering when that circle would end. Would I ever find my happiness, and keep it?

CHAPTER I - FRIENDSHIP

My eyes were still shut. I was afraid to open them, for as soon as I did, I knew that everything would change, and it would all be too real. But I had no choice; I had to face it and accept that, even if nothing made sense, it was still reality. I took a deep breath, opening my eyes wide.

White snow appeared in front of me, each flake sparkling diamond-like as it fell to the ground, before settling down onto the wide, silvery expanse before me. The snow was so flawless that the ground appeared to be covered in an endless silk sheet, extending beyond the horizon. I took a deep breath of the clean, cold air, and as I did so, the wind gently stroked my face, like a caress from the sky.

The freshness of the air only enhanced the beauty of the breathtaking landscape, and my senses were both overwhelmed and enraptured. I had never thought that I could feel well in such cold, but I felt more than well;

every cell in my body was tingling with life.

I placed my hand gently onto the ground beside me and realised that my eyes had been right about this perfect place. Touch was as useful as my other senses. The white, powdery snow froze my fingers, vanishing into the air like thousands of shining crystals as the wind softly lifted it out of my hand. I had never seen snow so vibrant. How could it be lighter than air?

"Fada, look at this land. This is your world, your kingdom, and from now on, you will live here with us."

Angel's tone was grave, and as I looked up at him, he bent his head to meet my eyes. I did not know where I was, or how I had ended up here; everything seemed perfect, but the seriousness of his voice confused my elated spirit.

"What can I say? Everything is so magical..." I managed to utter. I was bewitched by this enchanted garden. It felt like home.

"You should not judge a place by its appearance. Soon, this will be your nightmare."

I shuddered. I did not understand his words. "But how? Can't you see this snow? A place like this could never be anything but peaceful." I smiled. The snow made me happy. But Angel's near constant good mood appeared to have vanished. "What's happening? Why are you so serious?"

"Fada, I repeat, you should not judge a place by its

4

appearance."

"Oh, Angel, please. Look at this snow… look at this landscape. How could anything be dreadful in this place?"

Angel took my arm and we began to walk. His behaviour was so different to usual that my initial delight at the beauty before me was quickly replaced by curiosity and confusion. What was this place? Should I be afraid?

I remember the first time I met Angel, a couple of months ago. Back then, I was living and studying in London, and spent my free time going to museums.

The day started just like all the others, and as usual, I was not expecting much. I left my flat early, reaching the museum just as the front doors opened, though a crowd of people were already standing outside. It was such an amazing museum; there were so many things to discover, and it was impossible to see everything in one day. On that day, I intended to visit the Egyptian section, my favourite part of the museum. The Egyptian jewellery was particularly fascinating to look at; the pieces were all so delicate and precise, and I loved to imagine a magnificent queen of Egypt, like Nefertiti or Cleopatra, wearing them.

That day, I discovered a new exhibit, which included

the most beautiful piece of jewellery I had ever seen. It was an arm bracelet in the shape of a golden snake – designed to encircle the wearer's arm three times – set with beautiful rubies and other gems. Overwhelmed with a desire to draw it, I took my pencil and sketch pad out of my backpack. After a couple of minutes spent frantically sketching, I heard a deep, melodious voice coming from behind me.

"Your artwork is exquisite."

Turning my head, I realised that there was a man standing right behind me. My gaze instantly settled on his mesmerising aquamarine eyes. I had never seen such a bright blue. He smiled, revealing straight, white teeth hidden behind his fine lips.

"I'm sorry; I didn't mean to intrude. I simply wished to praise your work; I have never seen anyone depict this bracelet so beautifully."

I continued to scrutinise him. The man exuded charisma, and he had fine features: his jawline was so straight that it could have been carved from marble, and his short, straight hair was black as ebony, like mine. He had a presence, an aura unlike any that I had ever encountered before.

"Thank you…" I managed to mumble, before I was rendered speechless. I tried to concentrate on what he was saying, and the responses forming in my head, but my limbs were shaking uncontrollably. It was as though

I had been hypnotised by this man; I could not understand what was happening to me. I was trembling so much that I dropped my pencil on the floor. Bending down, the stranger plucked my pencil from the ground, handing it back to me with a flourish.

"You seem nervous... am I mistaken?" he asked, looking into my eyes.

"Well..." I stuttered, before my voice was stolen again.

The stranger chuckled, introducing himself as Angel. Strangely, he did not ask for my name.

"Are you studying at art school?" he asked, smiling.

"No... I'm a history student," I succeeded in saying.

"Oh, I see. You must really like history then?"

"Yes, I love it; it's my passion."

He gave a melancholy half-smile that I did not understand.

"This may be a little forward of me, but would you like to have a coffee in one of the cafés nearby? You see, I'm currently writing an article about the influence of historical events and technologies on modern day life; given your apparent knowledge and interest in ancient history, I would be interested to hear your take on it. It's always useful to include different perspectives in articles such as this, and there is only so much you can research." He smiled benignly, his eyes pleading.

I looked at him, astounded. We had only just met; we

had barely spoken, and yet he wanted us to go and have a coffee together. Not only that, but he wanted me to talk to him about history. I have always found it difficult to refuse when someone asks me to share my knowledge, and I reasoned that potentially having my name on an article might be good for my career. Besides, I was curious; I wanted to find out more about this strange man. I had never cared much for men, or friends in general, yet he intrigued me. I needed to understand why he made me feel this way.

We made our way to a café in front of the museum, and once we had found ourselves a table, he began to ask me questions about Egypt. He seemed genuinely interested, so I assumed that I was making sense; despite trying to concentrate on what was coming out of my mouth, I could not take my eyes away from his face... his eyes. His pupils looked like jewels... real jewels.

We were still chatting when I realised that a couple of hours had already passed. Time had flown by; I had spent most of my morning with a stranger yet had not once felt uncomfortable in his presence.

"I've really enjoyed talking to you, but I should be going now. I have to catch the train soon," I explained politely, reluctant to leave him.

"I understand. Is it a long way from here?" he asked in his rich, sophisticated voice.

"No, not really. It's only a twenty-minute walk."

"Then allow me to come with you."

I did not know what to say. He was extremely polite and seemed like a good person, but I had only known him for a few hours. I could not put my trust in someone so quickly. At the same time, he felt special; once I had got over my shyness, he had been easy to talk to. I felt more relaxed around him than I had ever felt around anyone else. Pausing for a moment to think it through, I reasoned that it was safe to let him accompany me. After all, it was the middle of the day, and he was only walking me to the station, not to my house.

On the way, we continued to talk.

"Tell me," I asked. "Why did you decide to come and talk to me earlier? What made you choose me?"

"Well, you seemed really intent on what you were drawing, and your work was beautiful, so I wanted to compliment you."

He gave me an angelic smile and I felt my cheeks grow warm.

After a few more minutes of walking, we arrived at the station.

"Thank you for sharing your knowledge with me."

He took my hand and kissed it gently. Raising his head, he smiled warmly.

"I hope to see you soon at the museum."

"Yes, me too. Bye, Angel," I murmured softly.

"Goodbye, Fada."

I stared after him in shock as he walked away, my mouth trapped in an O of disbelief. How did he know my name? I was certain that I had not given it to him. Maybe I had said something without realising it? I had been staring at his face for most of our conversation... yes, I must have told him my name, or referred to myself while we were talking.

As I walked towards the train, I thought back on my morning with Angel. I had really appreciated his company, and he had been polite and courteous; he was nothing like the other men that I had met before. There was something powerful about him; something that drew me to him, but I could not put my finger on it. I wanted to see him again, and I was fairly certain that my wish would be granted. After all, he had promised to see me again. With other people, conversation was always flat and monotonous, but with Angel, I felt understood.

Why was I feeling this way about him when I had never felt the need to make friends with others? The change in myself scared me. I did not want to change. I wanted to stay who I was. To be friends with someone implicated suffering. The best way not to suffer was to have no feelings. Solitude was, and had always been, my only friend. Yet I wanted to see this man, Angel, again. It felt like I had finally found someone who I could talk to; someone who I could be myself with. I could not let him go.

10

For the next few months, I met Angel by the rock bench in front of the museum a couple of times a week. We stayed there for hours, talking; he was clever and loved to learn, but he seemed to know nothing about history, which was strange given that he seemed to be so well-educated. Still, he had an incredible way of speaking, and his presence and charisma more than made up for his lack of knowledge.

I always looked forward to seeing him, and day by day, we grew closer, and I began to trust him. It was a new feeling. I had never trusted anyone before. I suppose I was what one might call a misfit, though not in the conventional sense. I was not out there doing wild, crazy things; everything about me was quite plain. I was a history student, living in London, who visited museums for fun. But my mind did not seem to work like the minds of people of my own age. I was quite happy in my own company; friendship did not attract me because it felt like nobody understood me. I could not explain what it was, but everything in my life seemed dull. I always felt forced to be sociable; I had to pretend to care about parties and other things that a twenty-year-old should be enjoying. I found my happiness in fiction books and history. Whenever I was reading, nothing else mattered. I would let my mind wander through the pages, and imagine myself living the lives of the characters, even though I felt that my path was already written: I would finish my studies; get a job in a museum or a library; get married to a man who I would pretend to love... it felt so wrong, and yet I could see no other options.

But my encounter with Angel in the museum changed my outlook on life, and my perception of myself. I finally realised that I could feel understood; that I could have conversations without faking interest; that I could smile without pretending. Little by little, I grew increasingly fond of him, and I began to believe that he liked me too. He was such a gentleman, and always so courteous. As the days went by, my connection with him grew stronger, and even though I hated it, he was always on my mind.

Despite my blossoming affection for Angel, there was a niggling feeling in the back of my mind that something was not right. He had an accent, but I could not pinpoint which country it was from, and when I asked him, he answered vaguely, saying that it was a small country and that it was unlikely I would ever have heard of it. I should have found his evasiveness suspicious and instantly stopped seeing him, but my trust in him overrode any doubt; I could do nothing but accept his vague answers to my questions.

In contrast, I was very open with him about life; my

family; my childhood and teenage years. He seemed fascinated by everything I said, and we would talk for hours about all manner of things. I did not understand how I could get on so well with someone. Before meeting Angel, I had assumed that I would live out my life without ever really connecting with anyone, but here I was, enjoying a conversation with another human being. The more time I spent with him, the more I felt like someone had lit a torch inside my chest, the flames burning ever brighter the more time we spent together.

He became closer to me as well, but he never held me in his arms; when he greeted me, it was always with a nod or with a gentle kiss on my hand. Yet I still felt that there was a connection between us, and I could not help but hope that he had feelings for me. He was constantly in my thoughts, and I found myself wanting to feel his lips on mine. It was such a strange sensation for me, and I struggled to accept it. I had always assumed that I could not love; could not feel that physical pull towards another human being. At twenty years old, I had never hooked up with anyone, or been in a relationship. Love and sex were entirely unknown to me, and I had always assumed that things would remain like that for a long time; I had never been attracted to anyone enough to consider those possibilities. But being with Angel was intoxicating; I had never felt so many emotions and sensations all at once, and I wanted our meetings to go on forever.

After the first few weeks, Angel began to accompany me back to my flat after our meetings, and each night, I asked him whether he wanted to come inside, but he always courteously refused. Nevertheless, my brother, who I shared the flat with, saw him often, though Angel was always so quick to leave that they never had the chance to talk. Over the coming weeks, my brother bombarded me with questions about this mystery man, as did my father when we visited him at the weekends. Neither of them had ever seen me laughing and joking with another person before, so they were rather surprised, but both clearly overjoyed that I had finally found myself a friend. Little did we know that the greatest surprise was yet to come.

"Angel, where are you taking me?" I asked.

"I don't know. My task is to take you to Netis' palace, but I don't really want to…" he answered, his voice grave.

"Netis? Who is Netis?"

"Someone you would be better off not meeting."

I had no idea what was happening, or what Angel was talking about. We were still walking through the empty snowfield; it felt like we were going nowhere.

"What are you talking about?"

"I have to take you to him, Fada. I have no choice."

"What do you mean you 'have no choice'? That's ridiculous."

Angel turned to face me, gripping my shoulders with his hands. I could feel him trying to control his emotions. I had never seen him like this before.

"Fada, please do not make light of this matter. You are not safe here."

"What? If I'm in danger, why did you bring me here?"

"You don't understand… I had to. At first, bringing you here was not a problem for me; it was simply a mission I had to accomplish. But now that I know you… I feel responsible, Fada. It's like I'm taking you to your end."

"My end?" I stammered.

"Netis is full of wrath and hate. If I take you to him, you could get hurt…"

I tried to concentrate on what he was saying and not lose myself in a sea of emotions. I needed to analyse the situation logically. I did not know where I was, or how I had come to be here. Two seconds ago, I had been in London; now, I was in a strange land, and Angel was talking some nonsense about taking me to my end and delivering me to a man named Netis. He seemed to be afraid of this mystery man, so why was he taking me to him? I put my hands on Angel's face.

"Angel, where are we? Who is Netis? Why does he want to see me? How does he know who I am?"

Angel took my hands off his face and looked down.

"This place is called Hagalaz—"

"Hagalaz? What are you talking about? I've never heard of it."

"Hagalaz is not on Earth, Fada. It exists elsewhere. This is where we live—"

"We?"

"Creatures like me." He looked deep into my eyes. "I'm not human, Fada. No one who lives here is. They are like me. Like you."

"Like me? Angel, that's crazy. I'm human. I live in London. I'm not some creature, and neither are you!" I was completely confused.

"I suppose you could call us human beings, we're just not from planet Earth…"

This was a joke; it had to be. There was no other explanation.

"Ha, I almost believed you. You really do have a gift for making up crazy stories!" I laughed.

"Fada, this isn't a joke. I'm from this planet, and so are you."

His face and voice were so serious that I stopped laughing and stared at him. He had to be messing around; it was such a ridiculous statement. But his eyes

16

told me otherwise.

"I can't tell you more, that isn't my role. I'm Netis' slave, nothing more."

His voice was mournful, his expression bleak. I could see his lips trembling as he spoke. It was unbearable to see him this way; he was usually so confident, so charismatic. I could not just keep denying his claims. I had to try and believe him.

"Okay, I understand that you can't answer my questions. But you must realise how confused I feel right now. Is there anyone who can explain to me what is going on here? You're scaring me, Angel. I need to know," I muttered, trying to keep calm.

"Netis will explain well enough."

His tone was final, but he seemed to pause for a moment, as though debating whether to say something.

"No," he mumbled. "I can't take you to her."

"Who? Take me to who? I'm so confused, Angel." I wanted to remain calm, but I could hear my voice rising in panic.

"I can't, Fada. If I take you to her, Netis will never forgive me."

"What are you talking about? Who is she?"

"Maheliah... Netis' sister. They are at war, Fada. I can't take you to her. I would be betraying him."

"Can't you just send me through a portal, like the one we used to come here?"

17

"No, I can't use the power Netis gave me to betray him."

"The power he gave you? What do you mean?" I asked.

"Not everyone in this kingdom can open portals; only those who belong to the royal family. It's an ancestral technique, which only the people who govern Hagalaz are allowed to master. But Netis taught me because he knew that I would need it to get to you and bring you here. That's why I can't use it against him; it would be yet another betrayal."

Angel was looking at me with sadness. I knew that what I was doing was unkind, but I needed answers. I did not want Angel to be in danger, but I had to understand the truth behind this impossible situation.

"I don't want you to get in trouble, Angel. But please... you must understand that I need answers. If you can't give me answers, just take me home—"

"I'm afraid I can't do that. You deserve the truth, Fada. You deserve to know who you are."

He smiled, but I could see that it required a huge amount of effort. Desperate to offer him some comfort, I hugged him tightly, hating how cruel I felt. When I left his embrace, his face remained close to mine, and I could feel his breath caressing my cheek. His two sparkling aquamarine eyes gazed into mine, and time seemed to stop. The emotions flickering behind his pupils were a mess.

"It's okay, Angel. You can take me to Netis—"

"No."

His voice was thick with emotion.

"Then what?" I asked gently, my gaze fixed on his eyes, staring into his soul.

Eventually, he came to a decision, releasing me and holding out his hand for me to take.

"I will take you to Maheliah. I could not live with myself if I took you to Netis knowing that he might hurt you. You mean more to me than my loyalty to him. And you deserve answers."

We walked side by side through the snow without speaking; by some miracle, I managed to keep a lid on my burning curiosity. I wanted to ask Angel so many questions. London had changed into Hagalaz: a kingdom on another planet. I was too confused. I loved to read fantasy novels and ancient myths and legends, but I had never imagined that anything depicted in those stories could be real. They were just wonderful fictions, invented by humans. Finding myself on what was supposedly another planet, inhabited by a magical, humanoid race, was strange beyond words.

Not only was I curious about Hagalaz, I was also

intrigued by the man Angel had spoken of: Netis. He seemed to possess a huge amount of power, not only over Angel but over this land in general. I wondered what he wanted from me, and more importantly, how he knew who I was. Angel had always seemed so nonchalant, yet whenever he spoke the name of this man, his behaviour changed. I was not sure that I wanted to meet Netis after everything Angel had said about him, yet he also fascinated me. I wanted to understand what a man like him could possibly want from me.

My day had started so normally, yet here I was, in a kingdom called Hagalaz, following Angel to meet a woman I knew nothing of; fleeing a mystery enemy that I had not known existed, and I was supposed to believe that none of this was a dream? Nothing made sense anymore, but I was determined that, by the end of the day, I would be at least one step closer to knowing the truth.

CHAPTER II - HAGALAZ

After my morning lectures, I travelled to the museum to meet Angel. I liked that he was part of my routine now, and it felt like today would be another great day spent sitting on the bench by the museum and chatting. But when Angel arrived, he seemed lost in his thoughts, though as soon as his piercing, ice-blue eyes met mine, I forgot about his distractedness. He greeted me brightly and asked me if I fancied a change of scenery for once. I asked him what he meant, and he explained that he would like to spend some time in nature, since it was such a lovely day. He suggested that we go for a walk in Richmond Park, and I gladly agreed, happy to follow his lead.

We rode on the bus for just over an hour, chatting animatedly all the way, though I noticed, yet again, that Angel looked tense. Something was clearly troubling him; usually, he looked into my eyes when he spoke to me, but today, he seemed distant. Perhaps something had happened at home? He had never been especially forthcoming about his personal life, so I simply assumed that whatever had upset him must be something he did not want to talk about.

Once we arrived, Angel asked me if I was happy to walk around the wooded area of Richmond Park. It was thoughtful of him to ask for my permission every time he suggested something, but I did not understand why he always treated me with such care; there was no need. As per usual, I agreed with his suggestion, and we headed into the woods, walking until our surroundings felt nothing like London at all. The trees were densely packed, the light was dim, and there was no one else around. I looked at Angel to find him staring at the ground with empty eyes, grinding his teeth so much that his jaw never stopped moving.

"What's wrong with you today?" I asked, positioning myself opposite him. Angel looked up and stopped walking.

"I don't know what you mean," he answered in a low voice, avoiding my gaze.

"Angel, please, don't lie to me. I can tell that something is off with you today. What is it? It's okay, you can talk to me."

Angel did not answer immediately, fixing his gaze firmly back on the ground. Then, taking a deep breath, he looked up again, opening his mouth as if to speak.

But he did not say anything. Instead, he looked behind me and stopped moving. I frowned, confused by his behaviour, and turned around to see what had captured his attention. A young fawn stood in our path, gazing curiously at us, its tiny head cocked to the side. The little creature was so beautiful that I promptly forgot my anger towards Angel. It was hard to stay upset when staring at something so sweet and innocent.

I moved towards it slowly, trying not to scare it, but a few seconds later, a doe, clearly the fawn's mother, arrived. She did not seem happy to see a human standing so close to her baby, so I quickly stepped backwards, fearing that she might decide to attack us. The doe's eyes grew fiercer as I moved away, and she began to kick her hind legs into the soil, a sign that she was about to charge.

As the deer began to run towards us, Angel appeared in front of me, and let out a guttural shout. The deer instantly stopped moving, its once strong legs trembling in fear. I looked at Angel, but he was standing between me and the deer, so I could not see his face. The deer was still looking at him, and I could see terror in the creature's eyes as it lay on the ground, still trembling. I was shocked; I could not bear to see an animal suffer like that.

"Angel? What are you doing? Enough!" I shouted, pulling him closer to me.

Feeling my arms around him, he closed his eyes, and the doe immediately leapt to its feet and sprinted off into the forest with its baby by its side.

I had no idea what had just happened. What had Angel done to the deer to make it stop moving? I looked at him, frowning. He looked at me too, his face a mask of confusion. After a moment of tense silence, I snapped, breaking our eye contact and walking back towards the park entrance. I needed to leave this place. I had put my trust in this man from the day I first met him, but this was the first time I had doubted that trust; the first time I had considered that, maybe, he was not the man I thought he was. He looked dangerous to me now, and it angered me more than it scared me. Was I not allowed to have friends? Was a normal life too much to ask for?

Angel ran after me and grabbed my arm, begging me to stay.

"No! I won't stay here with you. What just happened? How did you do that?" I shouted, looking at him with anger.

He did not answer, staring at me with confusion. This behaviour was so unlike him... perhaps this was who he truly was? I hated myself for thinking that I had finally met someone great, and I hated myself even more for feeling so deeply for a man I barely knew.

I pulled my arm away from his hand and walked

briskly in the opposite direction, but Angel ran in front of me, gripping my shoulders to prevent me from walking any further.

"Why did you bring me here?" I spat.

"Fada, please calm down," he stammered gently.

"Leave me alone, nobody tells me what I can or cannot do."

"I'm sorry, but I have to."

I opened my eyes wide in shock. His words froze me, and I was suddenly afraid.

"What do you mean, Angel?"

"Fada, you have to know who you really are. The time has come," Angel murmured.

"What are you talking about?" I was trying to keep calm, but I could hear the tremors in my voice.

He did not answer; he simply held out his hand. Seconds later, a shimmering, orange-sized sphere appeared, which swiftly grew to the size of a doorway. It looked like a mirror made of water, but as I gazed upon it, I noticed that the shining doorway depicted a completely different landscape. My eyes grew wide with awe; what was happening? Was this a dream? Befuddled, I grasped Angel's hand firmly and closed my eyes, waiting to see what would happen next.

I could barely believe that the whole episode in the forest had only just occurred; it had been such a confusing, complicated morning, yet now, here I was, walking through an unknown land towards the residence of a woman named Maheliah. Everything that had happened since entering the woods that morning seemed like something out of a folktale. I was still wondering why I had followed Angel through the portal. Part of me had been terrified by the impossible, shimmering doorway before me, but another part had been intrigued by it, and it was that curiosity that had compelled me to follow Angel blindly through the strange portal.

Sick of my own thoughts and confusion, I decided to quiz Angel some more.

"Angel, why was that deer so afraid of you? It looked like she had been paralysed or something."

There was a moment of silence, broken only by the sound of our footsteps in the snow. Angel sighed.

"When I'm angry or stressed, the adrenaline coursing through my veins stimulates my optic nerve, causing my eyes to emit a sort of electric charge. As a result, people or animals within my immediate vicinity experience the sensation of being electrocuted. But this only happens when I am extremely on edge, or when something important to me is at risk."

I stood there, gaping at him for a moment, before

plucking up the courage to ask, "How did you get this… power?"

"Netis taught me, so that I could protect you if needed. It is an ancestral technique from another kingdom, so I'm not sure how, or when, Netis mastered it."

Angel's voice was calm throughout the whole explanation, seemingly unfazed by the absurdity of the topic we were discussing. The fact that he had this kind of power was incomprehensible, but then… he had said so many incomprehensible things today that I could only assume that I must be dreaming.

"What triggered your anger, Angel? What were you stressed about?"

Angel did not answer.

"Were you angry that I was asking you too many questions? Were you afraid that I would discover your… our secret too soon?" I asked.

"No, Fada, that's not it. Don't think about it anymore."

Shrugging, I decided to move on to something else, asking if we were still far away from Maheliah's. Angel informed me that we would be there soon, and the silence resumed. I was sick of it. I did not want to stay like this, walking without speaking. I had too many questions. Besides, if this world was real, if Angel was truly from this strange land, it meant that he had been

27

lying to me this whole time. I had the right to know why.

"Why did you lie to me, Angel? Why didn't you tell me about all this when we first met?" I murmured, tears threatening to spill from my eyes.

"I'm so sorry, Fada. I never wanted to hurt you. I wish I could have told you the truth from the beginning. But be honest with me, would you have spoken to me again if I had said that I was from another world and had come to take you home to your kingdom?"

He had a point. I would have assumed that he was a lunatic and would have run for the hills; I would probably have avoided the museum too for a while, just in case I bumped into him again.

"Pretending that you were writing an article was a good way to get close to me…"

"I wasn't sure it would work, but I knew that you visited the museum almost every day, and when I watched you, you always studied the exhibits so carefully, reading everything. You seemed so interested… so passionate."

"Wait, you spied on me? For how long?"

Angel bent his head in shame.

"About five years. But ever since your birth there have been spies watching you. Netis always ensured that his men were close by at all times, to protect you if necessary."

"To protect me? Why?"

"Netis wants you alive; he wants to train you, so that you can help him bring peace to the kingdom. He made sure that you stayed alive and healthy, because he knew that he would one day find a way to bring you to Hagalaz. There have always been people watching you."

I was astounded. He could not be speaking the truth... it was impossible. I had been spied on since my birth? People from another world had been watching me all my life? It was ridiculous, it had to be a lie. Or a dream... yes, this was a bad dream. I just needed to wake up.

"If what you say is true, how did they spy on me for so long without me noticing? Without my family noticing? And why? Why not just kidnap me when I was a baby? Why wait till now?"

Angel placed a finger over my lips, his eyes pleading.

"Slow down, Fada. Please. I don't know exactly how the other spies alluded your notice. I assume they were well trained, like I was. And Netis did try to kidnap you when you were a baby, but a force stopped him; it was as if a magnetic field was protecting you. Then, when you were a child, too many humans knew you. If you had vanished without explanation, it would have alarmed those around you. They would have tried to find you and could have discovered us. We couldn't take that risk, so Netis decided to wait for you to become an adult, so that your disappearance would look less suspicious. He told me to make sure I was seen with you by several people who know you, so that they would assume you had left to live with me in another country."

My heart was thumping fast. Netis had planned everything from the beginning. I should have been angry with Angel for lying to me; for spying on me for so many years, but instead, I felt sorry for him. He had been a pawn in Netis' game, and now, he was willing to risk everything, risk the wrath of his master, so that I could learn the truth. Angel was not to blame. It was Netis who deserved my anger and my hatred. He had forced others to do his dirty work for years, and if Angel's apparent fear of him was anything to go by, he was a cruel, heartless, despicable creature. Part of me wanted to meet him, so that I could give him a piece of my mind. But Angel was right; there was no knowing what he might do to me. I was better off knowing the truth before I confronted him.

We continued to walk, both lost in our thoughts, until we reached an enormous mountain, surrounded and covered by snow.

"This is Maheliah's palace," Angel explained, as I stood there in awe, my mouth hanging open.

The mountain was not particularly wide, but it was tall. Just in front of me, I could see what looked to be the main entrance, or perhaps the only entrance. Two vast, white columns, set into colourful, gem-studded granite, stood on either side of a large, iron gate. Two women were stationed beside the gateway, dressed in long, black garments, the fabric billowing in the gentle wind. Each of them held a long, fearsome looking spear, and as we drew closer, I could see that they were both tall and strong.

Angel grabbed my arm, stopping me from walking any further.

"Fada, wait. I can't go any closer. This is Maheliah's part of the kingdom; no one associated with Netis is allowed here."

"I can't go there alone, Angel. Those guards look terrifying!"

"Don't worry, they won't hurt you. All you need to do is tell them your name; they will know who you are."

I looked at him desperately, but he just smiled and squeezed my hand reassuringly.

"I know it's hard, especially after everything that has happened today, but you need to trust me, Fada."

I gazed up at him. There was only kindness in his deep blue eyes. I was certain that he cared for me, and despite everything that had happened, I trusted him still.

"When I have my answers, how will I find you?" I

31

asked.

"I will find you, don't worry. Now, go and speak to Maheliah. She will give you all the answers you need."

I glanced up at him again as he released my hand, slowly turning me back to face the palace. Gently, he pushed me forward, and I hesitantly began to make my way towards the imposing gateway. I had never been so scared in my life. I was in the middle of an unknown world, all by myself, walking towards a place I knew nothing of, to speak to a woman I had never met before. It was a lot to come to terms with, and I wondered how I was still standing. But Angel had promised me that he would find me, and he had sacrificed enough to lead me here; I could not run from this now. I had to know the truth, and why, of all the girls Earth had to offer, Netis had chosen me.

When I arrived in front of the two women guarding the palace, I was rendered speechless. The two of them were identical; somehow both elegant and formidable, with hard features. But it was their eyes that had drawn my attention. Like Angel's, they glittered like crystals, but instead of aquamarines, the twins eye sockets held amethysts, shimmering with so many shades of purple that it took me a moment to drag my own eyes away from their gaze. As I shook my head, gathering my thoughts, they looked at each other, then at me.

"Hello, I'm Fada," I murmured, feeling ridiculous.

How could they possibly know who I was?

They looked at each other once again, smiling, then bent their heads in reverence.

"Princess," they uttered simultaneously, their voices deeper and more accented that I had expected.

Looking up, they forced their spears into the ground, opening the gates to the palace. I stared again, stunned, and more than a little confused by how they had addressed me. What did they mean, 'princess'? The two women smiled again, ushering me inside, and though my entire body was trembling, I obeyed.

Inside, everything was magnificent. The main hall was carved from white marble, and stalagmites lined the walls, drawing a path which led to a grandiose staircase. At the top of the staircase was a raised platform, lined with great spears of ice that soared up to the ceiling, and ornamented with large, white feathers and hundreds of coloured gemstones. As I marvelled over this magnificence, my gaze fell onto the striking silver throne, positioned atop the raised platform, and the woman who sat upon it.

The woman's elegance and confident gaze suggested that she was certainly older than me, though she was probably no older than thirty-five. She wore a white, flowing gown, the bodice of which was decorated with delicate silver ribbons, and dozens of silver bracelets encircled her wrists. Most of her wavy, bronze-tinted hair was gathered on top of her head, except for the few loose curls that hung around her face and her neck, bouncing around her long, silver yarn earrings. She was probably the most enchanting woman I had ever met, and I wondered how someone could possess such elegance and grace.

Her emerald eyes stared questioningly at me, her face an ever-changing canvas of confusion, disbelief, desperation and delight.

"Maheliah?" I asked shyly, hoping that this queenly figure was the person I was looking for.

The woman leapt to her feet.

"It's impossible… are you…?" she asked in a melodic voice.

"Fada," I answered.

She walked towards me slowly.

"Fada? Is it really you?" she asked again, gently cupping my cheek with her hand.

"I mean, I guess so? Fada is my name… why does everybody know me here? What is this place?"

She took my hand and began to lead me towards her throne, but I pulled away, suddenly frightened. The woman turned to face me again.

"Fada, I never imagined that you would come to me one day—"

"I don't understand, how do you all know me? How do you even speak English? Can someone please explain to me what is going on here?"

"It's okay, Fada, I'll tell you everything. But before I do, tell me how you got here."

"Angel brought me here. He said that he had to take me to Netis because it was his duty, but he decided not to. He said that I would be in danger if he took me there, so he showed me the way to you instead and told me that you would answer my questions."

Maheliah smiled.

"Angel? I don't know this man. But no matter. What he told you was the truth, Fada."

"But I don't get it. Who is Netis? What does he want from me? What is this place? Why does everybody seem to know me when I've never been here before? And how did I get here? One minute we were in Richmond Park, the next, Angel created some kind of portal and we found ourselves here. I'm so lost…"

My voice broke. I had tried for so long to control my emotions, but I was overcome with fear and confusion. I just wanted to go home to London, back to my normal life, and forget about this whole strange day forever.

Maheliah took my hand again and squeezed my palm reassuringly.

"Let me explain. First, you have to know that this man, Angel, took a great risk bringing you to me. If, as you say, he is in Netis' service, then he has just betrayed him."

35

I tried to concentrate on what Maheliah was saying. I wanted to remember every word.

"Fada, I've been waiting for you for twenty years, and so has Netis. We both tried to bring you here, but he seems to have done a better job. Though I'm sure he never intended for his servant to fall in love with you."

My face flushed. Hearing that Angel could be in love with me warmed my heart.

"Thanks to Angel, you are by my side at last, and for that, I am grateful. But before I explain to you what your future role is here, I have to tell you the past... your past."

Maheliah looked at me questioningly, as though asking me whether I was happy for her to continue. I nodded solemnly.

"Twenty-one years ago, Netis and I were on good terms; we were raised together, as siblings. We had always been close, and when another war against the kingdom of Othalaz started, our bond only grew stronger. There have been many wars between our kingdom and Othalaz over the years, for they envy our treasures and our wealth. You see, Hagalaz is the only place in our world where you can find Anam stones; when Hagal people die, their eyes mineralise, forming beautiful, coloured crystals, which we call Anam stones. Such gems fetch a high price when traded, so over the years, the Hagal people have gained great wealth from

36

them. The people of Othalaz have always been jealous of this wealth and have tried to acquire some of it for themselves on many occasions, even resorting to killing our people and storing their corpses.

Luckily, during this particular war, we had Netis in our arsenal. At the time, he was the bravest and strongest warrior in the kingdom, and thanks to him, we won many battles. Women and men fought together, led by Akaoh, the king who raised Netis and I. During the war, his wife, the queen, died on the battlefield, and I became Queen of Hagalaz. Upon his wife's death, Akaoh decided to become High King, leaving the throne to Netis so that he could rule by my side as king during this difficult time.

Akaoh trained Netis to become strong and pitiless, and as a result, he never stopped fighting for our kingdom. But the battles became bloodier and bloodier, and little by little, our side weakened, and Othalaz grew stronger. We lost too many warriors, and though we trained more as quickly as we could, eventually, there were too few of us to face up to the countless numbers of Othal warriors. Sadly, there were no opportunities for us to create more Hagal people—"

"What do you mean? How do you create other people?" I interrupted, fascinated.

"Oh, yes, sorry, let me explain. You see, the men and women of Hagalaz are infertile. I can't tell you all the details of it now, it would take too long, but it is said that Hagalaz was cursed thousands of years ago, and for that reason, we cannot conceive. Back in the day, everybody thought that our people would be doomed, and that the Hagal people would soon be extinct. But one day, some of our more curiously minded discovered something. They found that each of us would occasionally hear a voice echoing in our minds; a tiny voice, calling out to us. After following these voices, they discovered that the voices were coming from within the bodies of human embryos, on Earth.

From then on, every Hagal who heard such a voice resonating in their mind would request for a portal to be opened, like the one Angel used to bring you here, and they would go down to Earth, following the call until they found the woman who was pregnant with their embryo. After the child was born, they would take the child, and bring it back to Hagalaz. After a while, the Hagal people realised that only women heard female souls, and only men heard male souls. From that day forward, our people decided that women should be raised by women, and men by men. That is how we conceive in Hagalaz. It has been this way for generations, and it will remain like this until the curse is broken. Do you understand, Fada?"

I nodded. I was unable to speak, too shocked by what she had just said. I began to feel afraid; could it be that

I was one of those babies? Was I a Hagal woman? It made sense, based on what Maheliah had said about the Hagal people being infertile. I had never had my period, and it had always concerned me – on Earth, I knew that most women experienced menstruation at some point in their lives, even if they were infertile – but I had never spoken about it to anybody because I had been too afraid to say anything. I had always lived with my dad and my brother, and I had never felt like I could talk about it with them. But now, I had an explanation.

"As I was saying, we were fighting, losing many warriors, and we could not train more people. Then, one day, I heard a strange sound in my head. At first, I didn't understand what it was, but eventually, I realised that a soul was calling for me: I had to go to Earth and find the baby. Wartime was not an ideal time to have a child, especially for me, as the Queen of Hagalaz. I had to fight and lead my people; fighting and raising a baby at the same time was not the idea of motherhood I had in mind. I did not know what to do, but this call resounded in my head so strongly that I struggled to walk.

I went straight to Netis and told him of the call, and he told me that the exact same thing had happened to him. A soul had called to us at the same time. Netis was absolutely bewitched by the soul's call, and from that day forward, he stopped fighting, focusing entirely on the call. It haunted him, and he was desperate to find the soul.

A week later, Akaoh signed a peace treaty with the High King of Othalaz, and though it seemed strange that he would not tell us what this treaty was about, I was just happy that there was peace again, and that we would be able to raise our prince and princess properly. That day, Netis and I travelled to Earth, in search of our embryos. But when we reached the source, we discovered that the same soul was calling us both. We had both been drawn to the same woman, and she seemed to be pregnant with only one baby. Nothing like that had ever happened before; we did not understand what was going on.

We swiftly journeyed back to Hagalaz and proceeded to argue almost every day over who would keep the baby. Netis was obsessed with keeping the child; he insisted that this soul was different, that it was stronger than the other souls and should be trained to be a great warrior. Though I disagreed with his intentions for the child, he was certainly right about the power the soul seemed to possess; the force with which it called to us was immeasurable.

For nine months, the soul continued to call to us, and the bigger the baby grew, the stronger the sound became. After a few months, the call became so strong that I had no choice but to rest in bed until the baby's birth. Netis, on the other hand, did not seem to suffer;

he behaved as though the soul had stopped calling to him, yet he affirmed that the voice was still present, and suggested that I was only adversely affected because I was weak.

After nine painful months, the baby was born; the woman who gave birth to her sadly died in the process. I suppose I don't need to tell you what the name of the baby girl was…"

I was staring at Maheliah, astounded. This was not my story. There was no way. She had the wrong person. I could not be the soul that had tortured her for so long.

"When you were born, both Netis and I ventured to Earth to visit you. I was delighted that you were a girl, so that I could keep you and raise you as my own, but when I told Netis that I would take you, he wouldn't listen to me, arguing that you needed to be educated by someone who could give you a military education and turn you into a redoubtable warrior. He wanted you by his side and refused to compromise.

I tried to take you then, to save you from him, but a force stopped me from touching you, pushing me away. Netis tried to grab you, but he was forced back too, by the same force. You started crying then, and we heard the human who raised you walking towards the room, so we had to leave. I tried to take you many times following that day, but every time, the force stopped me. I could not understand what it was, though I supposed

41

that you were protecting yourself, somehow.

As the years went by, I regularly sent people to check on you, to see that you were safe and well. I had to stay in Hagalaz to rule, so I could not go myself, however much I wanted to. We knew that we would find a way to get you to Hagalaz eventually, so Netis and I both agreed that we would pretend that I was raising you away from the Court, hence why nobody could meet you. Sadly, this agreement was our last. After spending nineteen years living with Netis' anger and snide comments; living with him constantly telling me that you would never belong to me, I decided that I could not take it anymore. He had changed too much; our bond had broken, so I moved out of the palace, taking the people who wanted to follow me, and we came here, to the place where we had trained our warriors during the war with Othalaz.

Since that day, Netis and I have been at war, though we have yet to fight any battles. We never talk anymore, and over the past year, I have only seen him a couple of times..."

Maheliah paused and looked over at me. My mouth was agape.

"There are still many things I haven't told you yet, but I sense that you have probably been given enough information for today."

I stared at her, my mind a mess. This could not be my

42

story. I was just an ordinary human, living in London, not a strange princess from another world. I felt confused and upset and angry. I did not want to be a strange being. I just wanted to go home and live my life.

"Fada, are you okay?"

"No…" I sobbed, tears threatening to spill from my eyes.

"Fada, I can only imagine how hard it must be for you to understand and accept all of this, but this is your story. This is who you are. You are a princess of Hagalaz."

I looked up at her, desperate to cry but too angry to let the tears escape.

"No, I'm not a princess. I'm not one of you. I'm an ordinary human being, nothing else. I want to go home."

"I'm sorry, my dear, but that's impossible. You're one of us. You can believe whatever you want, it won't change anything. You are meant to live in Hagalaz. I know how much of a shock this must be for you, but it's the truth. You can't change that."

I glared stubbornly at Maheliah. I was desperate to believe that she was lying to me; that this was all just some strange, made-up story, or a dream that I would soon wake up from. But I could not deny the sincerity in her voice; I knew that she was telling the truth. Her story explained so many things. I had always felt like I was different, and I had always struggled to connect

43

with people, but then Angel had come along, and I had clicked with him instantly. It all made sense now. But a part of me still did not want to believe her; it was too painful to accept. I had lived for twenty years without knowing who I was, being spied on by people from Hagalaz, who had tried to kidnap me on multiple occasions.

"My whole life has been a lie," I sobbed, the tears now freely flowing down my cheeks. "I struggled through life, never being understood; I have spent years feeling out of place... odd... different. And why? Because a queen and a king from another world couldn't decide who I 'belonged' to, so instead of finding a solution, they just left me to live in a world which was not mine..."

I burst into tears as the realisation that I was from another planet and had never truly belonged finally hit me. I realised that I had to live here now, in Hagalaz, with these people that I did not know; I had to learn a new culture; a new language; how to fight... I had to leave my brother and my father forever. No. I could not live without them. They had raised me; loved me; cared for me for twenty years. I could not just walk away from the life they had built for me. Yet, from what Maheliah had said, it seemed that I was no longer in control of my own life. I had no choice but to follow the path before me. At this moment, I understood the words Angel had said to me, when we had first arrived in Hagalaz.

'Soon, this will be your nightmare'.

CHAPTER III - FAREWELL

Once I had dried my tears and collected myself, Maheliah offered to show me around the palace, and to introduce me to the rest of her people. I thanked her for her kindness but begged her to let me return to Earth first, so that I could collect some of my things and say goodbye to my family. She frowned, but after a moment of contemplative silence, she agreed to let me visit Earth one more time, understanding that leaving behind a world that had been mine for twenty years would not be easy.

Maheliah wanted to open a portal herself, but I asked her if Angel could take me back instead. She hesitated once again, but relented, understanding that my trust in this man would make me more inclined to return to Hagalaz with him afterwards. Unfortunately, neither of us knew how to contact Angel, or where he was, so we headed down to the palace entrance, hoping that he might be hiding somewhere nearby. Maheliah began to speak to the gate guards in a strange language, and they replied in kind, their gestures suggesting that they had not seen him. Then, one of the guards suddenly turned to the left and shouted.

All of us turned to see Angel approaching the palace. He looked different; I was used to seeing him in t-shirts and denim jeans, but the Angel walking towards us wore dark brown leather trousers with matching leather boots and was stripped to the waist. Seeing his naked torso did strange things to my body. I was already attracted to him, not only because of his beautiful aquamarine eyes but also because of his charisma and personality. But seeing his half-naked body made my heart beat rapidly in my chest. He was breathtakingly beautiful.

As he drew closer, I noticed that his lips were pursed in a thin line, and his jaw was tense. I could not see his eyes, for his gaze remained affixed to the ground as he walked towards us, but I could tell that he was anxious. Once he was within speaking distance, Maheliah ordered him to open a portal to take me to Earth, before turning to face me.

"I'm so glad that you are by my side now," she said in her liquid silver voice. "I'm sure that you will be a wonderful queen. I know that I am just a stranger to you, but I really hope that you will be able to feel at home in my palace."

She hugged me warmly before ushering me towards

Angel. I was overjoyed to see him again, but he was still looking down at the ground, his muscles tense with stress.

"Angel, are you okay?" I asked softly.

"Yes, don't worry about me, Fada. I'm fine," he answered, even though I could see clearly that this was not true.

Once we had walked a little way from the palace entrance, Angel silently held out his hand, opening the portal. After a few seconds, the portal was as large as a gate, and hand in hand, we passed through it, returning to the place I had once called home.

The sun was setting over the London skyline as we walked through the city streets. Everything was the same, but the familiarity gave me no comfort. All too soon, I might never see these streets again. This morning, I had been sitting in a university lecture; now, I was about to say goodbye to the only family I had ever known, and embark on a new life in a strange, magical world. I would miss this city, and Earth too; I had never felt like I belonged but knowing that I would never see this world again made me realise that I should have appreciated it more when I was able to. Soon, it would be time to say farewell to my everyday life on Earth; a life that would no doubt rapidly become nothing more than a vague memory.

"You should call your brother now, so that he gets here sooner," Angel advised me sorrowfully, as we approached my flat. "I'll wait here so that you can spend some time alone with him."

It was the first time that I ever heard sorrow in his voice, and it made me feel even sadder than I already was. I wanted to hug him tight, and tell him everything was going to be okay, but I had my own problems to worry about. Even though I wanted to make him feel better, I knew that I had to think about my own situation first. I took a deep breath, then called my brother, asking him to hurry back home but without giving him any details.

I walked up the stairs slowly. My flat seemed so dingy and commonplace now. I had lived here only a few months, yet it was strange to think that I would never see it again. I looked at my bed; my desk; my bedside lamp... all of these things that were not mine anymore. I could not take everything with me; I had to choose what was most important to me. It felt like no material thing could possibly help me to deal with this situation, but at the same time, I knew that I would regret not having anything from my past life.

As I searched through the drawer of my bedside table, I found exactly what I was looking for. Before I had left for university, my father had given me a pendant, shaped like a silver rose, and inside it, there was a photo of my father, my brother and me. I held it tightly to my chest, then fixed it around my neck, before looking back down at the open drawer. A warm wave of nostalgia hit me as I spotted my little music box: a birthday present from my brother. Even at a young age, I had expressed a passion for history, and so, for my eleventh birthday, my brother had gifted me a nineteenth century music box, which he had found in a charity shop. It played a beautiful, gentle melody, which always reminded me of him.

Looking around the rest of my bedroom, I pondered what else I should take. My clothes and shoes would stay here, as would my jewellery and electronics; I had no idea whether they even had electricity in Hagalaz, so it seemed pointless to take my mobile and laptop. Opening my desk draw, I found my sketchpad and pencils staring back at me. I wanted to take them all, but I doubted Maheliah would be happy if I turned up with a suitcase full of drawing materials, so I restrained myself, picking up only my most recent sketchbook and my two favourite pencils, reasoning that they probably had paper and pencils in Hagalaz anyway.

Finally, I turned to my bookshelf. This would be the most difficult decision of all. I adored books, and for many years, they had been my only source of companionship. But I knew that I could only take what I could carry, which meant choosing only a few. I gazed nostalgically at all the titles: The Dangerous Liaisons, Tess of the D'Urbervilles, Don Juan... all wonderful novels that I would never read again. Feeling so heartbroken about leaving my books behind felt foolish – more important things would soon be missing from my life – but the connection I felt with so many of these stories and characters made it difficult to imagine my life without them. I simply hoped that I would be able to speak and read the language of Hagalaz soon, for I knew that I would not be able to cope without having books in my life.

Choosing three of my all-time favourites, I packed them into my backpack and sat down on the bed, waiting for my brother to arrive home. As I sat there, staring at the whitewashed walls, I tried to rationalise everything in my mind. I had to admit that I was lucky: I was leaving behind my dad and brother, no one else. I would only miss those two people, and they would be the only people who would miss me. Things could have been much worse. My life on Earth had never felt right, and I had rarely felt happy. If I was to be realistic about this whole situation, it was a blessing that I had such a life; it made leaving and starting over so much easier. Still, I would miss my family desperately, and I could feel the tears beginning to well-up in my eyes at the thought of leaving them for good.

Wiping viciously at my eyes, I tried to stem the oncoming torrent; I did not want to be crying when my brother arrived home. Frantically, I tried to think of something else, and began to methodically go through everything I had learned today. Both Angel and Maheliah had mentioned Netis, and I had to admit, I was truly intrigued by him. He seemed magnetic and powerful, and part of me was eager to meet him and form my own opinion of this king. I needed to hear his version of Maheliah's story and understand why he yearned for me to be by his side.

It was so strange, the way Maheliah had spoken about me... it was like I was a good that she and Netis were fighting over. I vowed to myself that I was going to show everyone in Hagalaz that I would never belong to anyone or listen to any of their stupid rules. I understood that I had to go and live in this new land, but that did not mean I would change who I was. I would not let anyone tell me what to do, and I was determined to make everyone understand that I was not to be manipulated. This king would be no different; he would soon learn that I would not be a pawn in whatever game he was playing.

I began to wonder what my life would be like, living in Hagalaz. I would have to learn how to live among them; learn a different culture and language, and most importantly, I would finally understand my purpose in life. I thought about Angel and what role he might play in this new life. I had grown incredibly fond of him, and I knew that I needed him in my life. Regardless of what type of relationship we ended up having, I needed him by my side, and I hoped that him living with Netis and me living with Maheliah would not make things difficult. It was insane to even think about. It felt like I was already making plans and adjusting to this new life all too quickly. I had been in Hagalaz for only a couple of hours, yet I had felt more alive there than during my entire life on Earth. Perhaps, deep inside, I was glad that something like this was happening to me. My life finally had meaning, and it was exciting to start from the beginning.

My thoughts immediately returned to my dad and my brother, and this time, I could not stop the tears. I realised I would not have time to say goodbye to my dad, and it struck me that I might never see him again. If I had known that last weekend, when we had gone to visit him, I would have hugged him tighter; told him I loved him over and over again; focused on his face and tried to remember every little detail. My heart felt like it was shattering into a million tiny pieces.

At that moment, I heard the door open. My brother stood in front of me, his eyes wide.

"Fada, are you okay? What's going on?"

Seeing his face was so strange to me now; I knew that this might be the last time I would ever see him, and it hit me even harder than before. But I could not go back; I had to face him and say my farewell.

Breathing deeply, I mumbled in a tiny voice, "I have to go."

"What? Where?"

"I can't tell you. It's just the way it is. I have to go."

My brother did not answer. He just stared at me, frowning.

"Are you in trouble? Do you want to talk about it?"

"No, I'm not in trouble. I'm just leaving, that's all…"

"That's all? I don't understand, Fada. Where are you going? For how long?"

I did not know what to say. I couldn't very well tell him that I was leaving forever to live in some magical kingdom and would probably never see him again. My heart was broken. I hated having to leave him with such vague answers.

"I have to leave for… for some time," I whispered.

"What for? What will you be doing?"

Learning to become the future queen of Hagalaz, but I can't tell you that because you would never believe me, I thought bitterly. Then I remembered that he had seen Angel several times. I had to make use of that fact.

"I'm leaving with Angel, the guy I've been hanging out with recently. I'm going back to his country with

53

him, but once I'm there, it might be hard for me to come back to London…"

It was the perfect excuse, and fairly close to the truth.

"Are you crazy? You can't leave for a foreign country with a man that you've only known for a few months. You haven't even finished your degree. Why the rush to leave now?"

"I won't need a degree in his country. Angel is kind of a big deal over there. I'll live like a real princess; you don't need to worry about me."

"You've changed, Fada. What's happened to you? You were always so smart, so focused on your studies, and now you're willing to throw it all away for a man you barely know…"

"But what if I've changed for the better? What if the life I was living before wasn't a life at all? Now, with Angel, I finally feel like I belong somewhere. I have no choice; I have to go. Tell dad that I love him more than anything. I promise that you will both stay in my heart forever. I'll never forget you…"

My voice broke. Tears were rolling down my cheeks now and I threw my arms around my brother's neck, squeezing him tightly as I sobbed into his shirt. I could feel his heart racing in panic. I felt so cruel, leaving him like this. But what else could I do? Pulling away, I kissed his cheek tenderly, then grabbed my bag of memories and headed towards the door of the flat. As I opened the door, I turned back to my brother's shocked, grief-stricken face.

"I will always love you and dad, and you will be in my heart, always. This is something I have to do; you have to trust me. I am doing this for a reason. You may not understand, but you have to believe me. I love you."

I shut the door, leaving my brother, and my old life, behind.

As I ran down the stairs, blinded by my tears, I heard the door to my flat opening and my brother running after me, shouting my name. I had no choice but to launch myself down the stairs and race outside to where Angel was waiting for me. I could not believe that I was running away from my brother, but I knew that, if he caught me, he would never let me go, and Angel would be forced to hurt him. It was a situation that I wanted to avoid at all costs. Arriving in front of Angel, I broke down in his arms.

"Why me? I don't want to leave my family. It's not fair..."

Angel gripped me tightly and kissed my head softly. I could not see the expression on his face, but I could feel his heart beating fast and strong. Snuggling deeper into his chest, I shut out the outside world, consumed by my sorrow. I did not even notice that Angel had opened a portal until an icy breeze touched my face. Angel began to walk forwards, and without realising what I was doing, my body began to copy his movements, trudging slowly through the snow whilst still firmly attached to Angel.

I was so numb to my surroundings that I could not tell whether it took us days or minutes to reach Maheliah's palace, not that I cared. My mind was too chaotic right now to care about such a trivial thing as time.

With the palace now in sight, Angel stopped, looking deep into my eyes.

"Fada, before I take you to the palace, there's something I want to show you. There's a place I always go to when I'm feeling at my lowest or when my mind is a mess. I know that what you're going through right now feels like a nightmare, so if this place can offer you a moment of solace, even just a moment, then it will be worth the visit."

I looked at him, sceptical. I could not concentrate on anything but my sorrow, how would visiting another strange, new place help me? But I reasoned that delaying my return to the palace was probably a good idea; I needed to gather my thoughts before meeting with Maheliah again. Wiping away my tears, I nodded, and we started walking again. I let Angel do most of the work; my mind was not in the right place to focus on the world around me, so I clung to Angel and trusted my body to place one foot in front of the other.

Eventually, we stopped, the sudden change in motion jolting me out of my thoughts. In front of me was a circular lake, about the size of a football field. A magnificent bridge rose above it, carved from shining white rock, and engraved with images of roses encircled by brambles. In front of the lake was a rock bench, featuring the same designs as the bridge. Combined with the glittering snow that coated the surrounding landscape, the vision before me was like nothing I had ever seen before.

"Do you like it?" Angel asked quietly, as we stood side by side, staring out at the lake.

"I can't quite believe it's real," I whispered, my eyes wide in awe. I was bewitched by the place, and for an instant, I forgot my pain, my mind too focused on the mesmerising view before me.

"I know. It's beautiful, isn't it? I hope it helps you feel better—"

"Why does my happiness interest you so much?" I interrupted, not quite sure why I had asked the question.

Angel did not answer, turning his face aside and fixing his gaze on the snow beneath our feet. Suddenly overcome by an unfamiliar boldness, I took a step towards him, turning my body so that our chests were facing. A strange sensation had come over me. I wanted him to hold me. I needed to feel his body on mine. It was such an unusual feeling for me; I had never felt the need to be in the arms of a man. But when I was with Angel, the thought always burned its way into my mind, breaking through my defences like a battering ram of desire.

The entire day had been insane, and saying that I was not feeling like myself was an understatement. I was another person. This behaviour... this need to be in Angel's arms... it was all so sudden and unusual. Perhaps this was growing up? Regardless, I was certain that I wanted to listen to my heart. Somehow, I knew that I was doing the right thing.

I drew closer to him and tentatively placed my left hand on his shoulder. He looked up instantly, his eyes like blue fire, both breath-taking and bewitching. I did not know where I was anymore; I barely knew who I was anymore. All I knew was that I was standing before this magnificent being, and I wanted him.

Absentmindedly dropping my bag to the ground, I placed my other hand on his other shoulder, trembling, before moving my fingers towards his neck, without stopping to look into his eyes. Slowly, I moved my face towards his, and unbeknownst to me, Angel was doing the same. Moments later, our lips touched. It was like someone had scorched my mouth with a delicious flame, and I ached for more, caressing his lips with mine until he grabbed my waist and drew me into him, his mouth pressing firmly down onto mine. Snowflakes began to fall all around us, but they did nothing to calm the fire raging through my body.

Eventually, Angel removed his lips, meeting my eyes with another burning stare. My whole body was on fire, and my heart felt like it was trying to leap out of my chest. I gazed back into Angel's eyes, knowing that my desire must be painted on my face.

"Are you sure this is what you want?" Angel murmured softly. "You're a princess, Fada. You deserve better…"

In response, I moved my face closer to his and whispered in his ear, "No, I'm not a princess. I'm just Fada. Nobody tells me what to do."

Brushing my lips against his cheek, I found my way to his mouth again, kissing him softly. We stayed like that for some time, entwined in each other's arms, savouring our moment of bliss in the knowledge that, all too soon, we would both have to return to our realities. It was a terrifying prospect, beginning a new life as a princess in a strange kingdom, but knowing that Angel would be close by soothed my anxiety. He would keep me safe, no matter what happened.

CHAPTER IV - LEARNING TO LIVE

I was standing in front of Maheliah's palace, watching as the grand gates opened. Angel had already left for Netis' palace, not wanting to risk being seen again, and I felt his absence like an open wound. It was hard to be away from him, especially now that we had both realised our feelings for each other. But I had no choice. I had to face my new reality, and I had to face it alone.

Maheliah greeted me with a warm hug, which felt odd considering that we had only met a few hours previously. But I did not want to insult her by rejecting her affection; I was going to be living with her for the foreseeable future, so I tried my best to hug her back. Admittedly, it was not difficult. She was a likeable person, and she had already shown that she was kind-hearted and caring by letting me return to Earth and by placing her trust in Angel almost instantly. I could not have asked for a better tutor to guide me through this strange learning experience.

Maheliah led me upstairs and through an open door. The walls, carved from the mountain itself, had a calcareous tint to them, and the floor was covered in panels of grey wood. On the wall just in front of me was a massive window, made of either glass or ice, I could not tell, and underneath it was a decorative wooden bench, covered by a white fur throw. There was another, much smaller window adorning the left wall, and beside it stood a short, wide chest of drawers, carved from white wood and decorated with silver handles, shaped like lilies. To my right, next to the door, was an identical chest of drawers, topped with a large mirror. A wooden chair stood in front of them, covered in the same kind of white fur throw as the bench. In the centre of the room was a magnificent baldachin bed, which looked like it could easily fit four people, covered in several white duvets and pillows. I had never seen such a wonderful bedroom.

"This is your room," Maheliah announced with enthusiasm.

"It's gorgeous, I've never seen such a beautiful room. Is it really mine?" I asked, dropping my bag on the floor by the door.

"Of course. You are a princess, Fada. It is only right that you should have a bedroom fit for one."

Before I could respond, someone knocked on the door, and we both turned to see two beautiful women standing in the doorway. I could only assume that they were twins, for they looked almost identical, the only difference being the lengths of their straight, ebony hair: one sister wore hers down to her hips, the other wore hers shorter, down to her waist. Both sisters had startling almond-shaped pink tourmaline eye, and they were both dressed in white, figure-hugging dresses, which fanned out at the knee like a fishtail, the fabric kissing the floor. They were impressive to behold and made me feel very unattractive.

Maheliah smiled, ushering the two women into the room.

"Fada, may I introduce my dear friends, Nalhya and Lilhya. They will attend to you every morning and evening, helping you dress and fix your hair. Girls, may I present the future queen of Hagalaz, Fada."

"Welcome princess," chorused the two women. They shared the same accent as Maheliah.

I felt deeply uncomfortable being called a princess, especially by two such stunning young women. I did not feel worthy, or prepared, to hold such a position of power.

"We brought the dress," the twins continued, reaching behind the door to retrieve a floor length garment.

Maheliah took the dress from them and handed it to me.

"Before I introduce you to the others and show you around the palace, you must be dressed appropriately. Your earthly clothes will not do here. Girls, if you will…"

The twins drew closer to me and Maheliah left the room, closing the door behind her. The dress was immediately taken from my hands by one of the twins and placed delicately onto the bed, while the other twin took hold of the white screen that lined the righthand wall, pulling it towards me.

"Your Majesty, if you could undress yourself…"

"Oh, call me Fada, please. There's no need for any of that princess nonsense," I exclaimed.

The twins looked at each other for a few seconds before looking back at me. They nodded hesitantly.

"As you wish. If you could please get undressed, Fada, and give your old clothes to us, then we can attire you properly."

My heart beating fast, I began to undress myself as requested, until I was standing in only my underwear. Reluctantly, I handed my clothes to Nalhya and Lilhya.

"You must remove all of them, Fada," one of them whispered, smiling sympathetically.

I had no desire to be naked in front of two strangers, but their voices were so gentle and kind that I felt my resistance waning. Besides, I had no way of returning home; I might as well try and fit in. Making sure I was hidden behind the screen, I removed my underwear and handed it over to one of the twins. The other twin handed me a silky bodysuit in exchange. Looking down at the elegant, sensual garment, I protested.

"Don't you have anything like my normal underwear?"

"No, I'm afraid not. We don't wear that kind of thing here."

I looked down at the bodysuit again. It was unlike anything I had ever worn before; I was not used to wearing such delicate lingerie, but I did not have the energy to argue. Once I was no longer naked, the twins removed the screen and helped me into the dress, spending a long time adjusting the ties at the back. I felt uncomfortable having people do things for me, so I decided to try and chat to them as they worked. If I was going to see them every day, I needed to at least try and befriend them.

"I'm sorry, umm… could you tell me which one of you is which? I don't want to get your names wrong."

"I'm Nalhya," said the twin with the longer hair.

"And I'm Lilhya," said the shorter-haired twin.

"Oh, okay, thanks. Umm… well, Nalhya and Lilhya, it's lovely to meet you."

"It's lovely to meet you too, Fada."

"How is it that you speak my language? Does everyone in Hagalaz speak English?" I asked.

"No, we learned it, along with Maheliah and a few others. Ever since she knew that you weren't going to grow up in Hagalaz, she decided to learn your tongue, and taught us too, so that you wouldn't feel alone when you finally came to live with us," Nalhya answered.

"I believe Netis and some of his people learned as well," Lilhya continued.

They spoke about it so nonchalantly, as though learning a language from another world was not a big deal. This world and its people were truly incredible, and I was grateful for their intelligence. It was a relief to be able to communicate with the people around me without having to rely on hand gestures.

Once the twins had finished adjusting my dress, they came and stood in front of me.

"We should do your hair as well. Would you please sit down in front of the mirror, Fada?"

Nalhya opened one of the drawers and took out a silver brush and several hairpins, passing a handful to her sister. Then, standing on either side of me, they started to style my hair, twisting and pinning my black curls, somehow gently coaxing my crazy hair to comply with their intentions. After only ten minutes, they had finished, and I could not help but marvel at my reflection in the mirror. My curls had been pinned to form a thick serpent of hair, following the curve of my spine down to my waist. Most of the wayward curls that usually framed the sides of my face were now piled up on the top of my head, the ends of them merging with the ebony serpent, except for several curls that had been left resting against my cheeks. My hair had never looked this glamourous, and had I not watched the twins style it I would have been convinced that it was a wig and not my own hair at all.

Once I had recovered from the sight of my hair, I stood up to admire the rest of my reflection. They had dressed me in a white, floor-length, strapless gown, made from a linen-like material, featuring two strips of fabric that crossed in the centre of my chest to create a beautiful and delicate bodice. Two transparent pieces of fabric lined the sides of the skirt, running from my ribs down to the floor, beneath which were strips of tulle, preserving my modesty. At the back of the dress, several pieces of fabric were tied together in intricate knots, and I quickly discovered that they moved hypnotically with every movement I made. Suddenly, I was no longer jealous of Nalhya and Lilhya, for I now looked just as stunning as they did.

"Thank you for doing my hair, and for this dress. It's beautiful. I never imagined that I might wear a dress as gorgeous as this one day."

Lilhya shrugged. "These are the kind of clothes we

wear in Hagalaz. Earth clothes are very strange."

"I guess you're right, though it would have been difficult to wear such dresses with the type of life I had on Earth."

The twins looked at each other for a few seconds, as if they were talking by telekinesis, before looking back at me.

"Please forgive us if this sounds impolite but… can we ask you a favour?" Nalhya asked.

"Go ahead…"

Lilhya piped up. "We were just wondering whether you would be willing to tell us about your life on Earth? Your world is entirely unknown to us; it's so intriguing. We would love to hear more about it."

"Of course, that's not impolite at all. I would be very glad to tell you about Earth. It would give me a chance to relive some of those memories."

I had been so busy since coming back to Hagalaz that I had forgotten my grief, but talking about Earth reminded me of the family I had left behind and how much I missed them. Nalhya and Lilhya looked at me, confused.

"Fada, are you okay?" they asked in unison.

"Yes, I'm fine. Don't worry. I was just thinking about my family."

"We're sorry, we didn't mean to hurt you."

"It's okay, you didn't hurt me. Everything's fine."

It was so strange. Back on Earth, I had always tried to find excuses to get out of conversations; they had always made me feel anxious and uncomfortable. But here, I felt so at ease talking to the twins. The two of them were so kind and genuine; I already felt close to them, and I was certain that we would become firm friends. I did not understand how I could have changed so quickly. Then again, I had felt the same with Angel, relaxed and at ease. Perhaps it was simply the people: I had never fit in on Earth, but Hagalaz was my true home. It made sense that I felt comfortable here.

As I was pondering this sudden change in myself, Maheliah returned, clapping her hands delightedly at the sight of me in my new attire.

"Fada, look at you! You're absolutely gorgeous."

She proceeded to walk around me, complimenting my appearance and the twins' hard work. I was not used to being the centre of attention, yet here, after only a few hours, I had become a princess. It made me feel uncomfortable, being scrutinised like that. It had all happened too fast, and I was not sure I could handle much more. Wearily, I asked Maheliah if I really had to see the rest of the palace and meet everybody today. All I wanted to do was rest and be alone for a while, to come to terms with everything that had happened. Maheliah looked at me sympathetically, assuring me that everything could wait until tomorrow.

"You should rest now, my dear. Would you like something to eat? You must be famished."

I thanked her kindly for the offer but politely refused; I was too overwhelmed to contemplate eating anything right now.

Maheliah gestured to the twins, and after smiling at me kindly, the two of them left the room, walking in sync as though they were one person.

"They're really sweet. I've never seen two people so close to one another," I told Maheliah once the twins had gone.

"I know, they have such a strong bond, though it's hardly surprising. It's fairly common for twins to be close."

"But there's something different about them. I've met twins before, and they had a strong bond, but it's nothing compared to the bond between Nalhya and Lilhya. They are like one person in separate bodies."

"That's because the relationship between twins is stronger in our world than on Earth."

"What do you mean?"

"Our folklore tells us that we are not one, but two entities. Every soul has a partner, a complementary soul, and when you meet the soul that complements your own, there is no turning back. If you become separated, your soul will cry out for the other, and vice versa. More often than not, twins are one another's partners. They

69

are soulmates, in a way; that's why twins have such a strong connection. Sadly, it also means that they will never experience true love, since their soul belongs to their sibling."

"Does everybody have a soulmate, or is it only twins?" I asked, intrigued.

"We believe everyone has a soulmate. It is said that as soon as you meet your soulmate, you experience the sensation of having met that person before. Everything feels natural with them; you feel simultaneously at peace and wide awake, like you have awoken from a deep slumber. But you might not realise that person is your soulmate straight away. In fact, at the beginning, it is very common to not feel attracted to them. But the two souls will call for each other, as if a force drives them together, and it is not unusual for this connection to turn into love. Sadly, it usually brings nothing but pain and sorrow."

"Why?" I asked, confused.

"As I said, once you have found your soulmate, it is impossible to live away from them. Yet the two souls often end up being in the bodies of two people who cannot be together. It is believed that there were many times in the past when princes or princesses met their soulmates, but their other halves were not royalty; sometimes they were common folk, or even slaves. A prince or princess cannot marry a slave, so they were forced into a marriage with someone they were not connected to, suffering day after day because they were not allowed to share their life with the person they were supposed to be with. They had to live with a person that they did not love, away from the one their soul desired."

"Have you met your soulmate, Maheliah?"

"No, I haven't, and I think it is much better this way. As I've just told you, it usually ends tragically. Besides, my soulmate might not even have been born yet."

"What do you mean?"

"Our folklore speaks of a special kingdom on our planet, called Eihwaz: the soul kingdom. No one knows where this kingdom is, and it does not appear on any of our maps, but we believe that it is the home of the souls that do not have a body yet. Sometimes, these souls leave Eihwaz, and wander into our kingdom, watching and waiting to be reincarnated. Our lore states that, from the moment a soul enters a new body, it forgets everything about its past lives, though it is said that some people do experience flashes of memory. However, such flashes can only occur if the new body is experiencing something similar to what its soul has already experienced, or if the body goes to a place which its soul has a strong connection to, such as the place where one of the soul's previous bodies died."

I stared at Maheliah, trying to take in what she had told me. It was quite a story, but it did not seem at all plausible. I struggled to believe that soulmates and reincarnation existed, especially since that would mean I probably had a soulmate myself. Then again, I had just discovered that not only was I a princess from another realm, but that realm was not even on Earth, and was only accessible via a magic portal. Considering everything that had happened today, the concept that soulmates and reincarnation might be real should not have been at all surprising.

Maheliah kissed my cheek, laughing at my perplexed expression. I still needed to get used to her kissing and hugging me. She told me to rest, and informed me that the twins would come by in the morning to get me dressed for the day.

"Also, just so you know, a snowstorm breaks out every night in Hagalaz. Don't worry, the palace protects us very well, but I thought I ought to warn you. It can be quite loud."

I nodded, thanking her for her courtesy. Maheliah smiled, squeezing my hand warmly, before turning and leaving the room.

As soon as the door closed behind her, I walked over to the bed and collapsed onto the soft linen, letting out a huge sigh. I was finally alone. The bed was warm and comfortable, soft and velvety to the touch, and I let myself sink into the sheets, trying to empty my thoughts. My mind was a whirlwind; there was too much information swirling around my head. Unable to relax, I began to unpack my rucksack, but the night was falling fast, and though I searched for a candle or some other light source, I could not find anything. I made a mental note to ask Maheliah about that in the morning.

Carrying my books to the chest of drawers, I placed them in the bottom draw, deciding that I would store my drawings in the top drawer, just like I had in my bedroom on Earth. I placed my music box on the dressing table and fixed my pendant around my neck, holding the photograph compartment tightly in my hands.

The sun was nearly completely set, and the storm was now raging outside. It did not seem to be snowing yet, but I could hear the strength of the wind; any trees that had once been standing must surely have been flattened to the ground by now? Walking over to the fur-covered bench, I sat beneath the giant window, holding my pendant in my fingers. The night sky was magnificent: hundreds of stars twinkled in the darkness, and just in front of me, a multicoloured aurora performed a mesmerising dance, snaking through the sky like a sea serpent. As I looked closer, I noticed a series of planets suspended in the blackness. One had a purplish tint to it and looked about the size of the Earth's moon; another glowed a vibrant, ethereal blue, reminding me of the blue planet I had now left forever.

After several minutes spent staring into the vastness before me, I began to yawn, and decided that it was time to try and sleep. Walking over to the bed, I gently removed my dress and bodysuit, laying them carefully on one of the chairs so as not to damage the delicate fabric. Nalhya and Lilhya had forgotten to take my normal clothes with them, so I put on my shirt and pants, not knowing where my Hagal pyjamas were, or even whether they wore any. Finally, I carefully removed the hairpins from my hair, knowing that I would never sleep if I kept being stabbed every time I turned over.

Crawling into my bed, I snuggled beneath the warm, soft duvets and promptly fell asleep, my emotional and physical exhaustion finally wiping me out.

I could not say what time it was when I woke up. The twins had yet to arrive, so I stayed snuggled up in my warm bed while I waited for them to appear. It still felt like I was dreaming, and I was not eager to leave my bed, knowing that reality would strike as soon as I got up.

I heard a knock on the door, and without waiting for an answer, Nalhya and Lilhya entered the room.

"Good morning, princess. How was your first night in Hagalaz?" they asked in a same voice.

"Please, just call me Fada. Princess is so formal."

"If that is an order, we will do as you ask."

"No, it isn't an order, but I would feel more comfortable if you would treat me as a friend."

They nodded solemnly, but as I stood up, they began to laugh.

"What are you wearing?" Nalhya exclaimed.

"I didn't know what to wear for the night, so I put on my old clothes."

They laughed even more, and Lilhya swiftly walked towards the chest of drawers, pulling out a long linen nightshirt.

"We sleep wearing these, not your strange clothes."

I forced a smile. I knew my made-up pyjamas were not fancy, but I always slept on my own, so it had never bothered me before. But with the two gorgeous twins smirking at me, I felt ridiculous.

Coaxing me out of bed, the twins dressed me in my stunning outfit from the day before and re-styled my hair. Just as they were making the finishing touches to my hairdo, Maheliah entered, greeting us all warmly, before asking how my first night in Hagalaz had been. I answered that I had slept very well, which was not a complete lie, for the bed had been very comfortable. But my sleep had been plagued with nightmares; I would have preferred a dreamless night.

"Once you're ready, we'll go downstairs so that I can

75

introduce you to everyone and give you a tour of the palace. Life here is very different compared to what you are used to. It may take some time for you to adjust."

Once Nalhya and Lilhya had finished doing my hair, we all headed downstairs.

"We'll start with the washing plant. I can't remember if I told you this, but everyone here only has a couple of outfits, as our fabric supply is limited; I'll tell you why later. Every evening, Nalhya and Lilhya will bring your dress here, to be washed and dried. Then, every morning, they will bring it back to you. As such, you must be careful with your dress, for until we can get another one made, this will be your only item of clothing."

The washing plant was a vast room, buried deep within the mountain, featuring a few large basins that had been dug into the floor and filled with water. I nodded in greeting to all the people who were sat doing their washing; not only did I have no idea how to say hello in their language, but I also did not know whether there was a specific form of greeting that I should be using. They all greeted me by saying a word in their language, simultaneously moving their left hand from their heart to their forehead. I should have felt happy to have been acknowledged, but their greetings seemed less than friendly, and they all looked at me blackly as we turned and walked out of the washing room. I wondered what I had done to invite such a reception. I had never even met them before; how could they hate me already?

Unfazed by the looks of the people in the washroom, Maheliah breezily continued to show me around the palace, taking me next to the kitchen. It was a big room, again carved from the rock of the mountain, and was bustling with activity. Huge cooking pots, suspended from iron rods, hung over a vast hearth, and the room was humming with the sounds of people busying themselves with tasks.

"This is the kitchen. We don't really use this place to its full potential: we mostly eat soup or vegetables, and fish when possible. Meals happen only three times a day."

"How do you manage to get through the day with so little to eat?"

Maheliah shrugged. "We're at war with Netis, Fada. His people have food coming in from other kingdoms, and the farms of Hagalaz, but he does not allow us access to these provisions. We have to make do with the plants that we can grow in our caves. In the past, we used to feast, but now we must be content with what we have access to. From time to time, we send some of our workers down to the coast to catch fish, but we can't do that every day. I need everyone by my side at all times, in case Netis decides to attack us."

I was shocked and angered by Maheliah's words. How could Netis be so cruel, letting his own people and his sister starve like that? It did not make any sense to me, and I despised him even more than before. I wondered how I would react to meeting someone like him. He seemed truly despicable.

Maheliah introduced the cooks and the farmers who worked in the caves, and they greeted me exactly like the people in the washing plant, giving me a dark, disapproving look. Maheliah did not seem to notice though, so I began to think that I must be imagining these black stares... perhaps they were just solemn people?

Despite my concerns about being disliked, I enjoyed my little tour of the palace. I had been afraid that Maheliah would introduce me to everyone at once, but visiting the palace room by room and meeting everyone little by little was far less overwhelming. I just had to hope that they would change their opinion of me once they got to know me. After all, it was only my first day.

Leaving the kitchen, we headed outside, exiting the mountain from the opposite side to where I had entered the day before. In front of us lay a vast reservoir of hot water, the steam evaporating from it soaring skywards.

"This is where we wash ourselves, in that hot spring. I believe these kinds of things exist on Earth?"

"Yes, they do, but most of them are too hot to bathe

in."

"Well, not to worry. The temperature of this hot spring is just perfect, and I'm sure you will enjoy your daily visits. Everyone usually bathes every two days, as there are too many of us for every person to bathe daily, but as queen, I must be present at both bathing sessions, in order to be viewed as being one with all my subjects. You must do as I do, and come to the hot springs every day."

"Does that mean that we have to be naked in front of everybody?"

"Yes, is that a problem?"

"I'm not sure that I would feel comfortable, to be honest."

"Don't worry, Fada. You will soon become used to it. Besides, the men and women bathe separately, so you and I are only required to be present for the women's bathing sessions."

We kept on walking to the left of the mountain, eventually arriving at what looked like a very small arena.

"That's the training court, where our veteran warriors train new, young warriors to fight. Nowadays, everyone has to be ready…"

Maheliah frowned and bit her upper lip, her eyes pained. I understood her distress. Because of me, war was waging in the kingdom, and everyone had to be ready to fight against their own kind at any moment. I felt saddened by the trauma I had inadvertently caused these people, but I had to remind myself that it was not my fault. This war was between Netis and Maheliah: I was just the catalyst.

After watching the warriors train for a few minutes, we headed back inside, and Maheliah finished showing me the rest of the palace. The dining room was more decorative than any of the others had been, complete with silver chandeliers hanging from the ceiling and a long glass table, around which were positioned many chairs, of the same style as the bench and chairs in my bedroom.

"This is the dining room, as you can see. As with bathing, we take turns to eat, for we are too numerous to all sit here at the same time. For each mealtime, we have an early slot and a late slot, and we rotate who eats in which slot. You must be starving by the way, let's sit and have a meal before we finish the tour. We're just in time for late breakfast. Come, sit next to me."

I sat down and about twenty people appeared, all greeting me with the same word and hand gesture as the others I had met. Yet again, they seemed to be forcing themselves to greet me, and it was clear from their body language that they did not like me being here.

The cooks carried in a large cooking pot, filled with soup, and some of the other kitchen workers brought in silver bowls and spoons. Each bowl was filled with soup and then passed down the table, until everyone had been served. Dipping my spoon into the soup, I tasted it hesitantly, afraid that I might not like it. Fortunately, I was pleasantly surprised; it tasted not dissimilar to leek and potato soup, which had been a university staple of mine back on Earth.

After taking a few more mouthfuls, I decided that this moment of quiet was the perfect opportunity to ask Maheliah some more questions, since I had so many.

"Maheliah, I was wondering... how does time work here? I mean, are days twenty-four hours, like they are on Earth?"

"Yes, we measure our days in a similar way to yours, but unlike you, we only ever have eight hours of daylight. Everyone wakes at dawn, and we all make sure that we are back in the palace by twilight. As you now know, there is a snowstorm every night in Hagalaz, which varies in strength depending on the day. But even when the storm is not so strong, it is still impossible to go outside during the night, the temperature drops too much. Never stay outside overnight, Fada. You'll be killed for sure."

I was listening to her diligently, aware that everything she was telling me was important. I was certain that this snowstorm was probably not the only thing I had to be wary of here.

81

"I understand, I'll make sure I stay inside at night. On the subject of night-time, how do you light your rooms when it gets dark?"

"It's complicated. Before the war, we used to have beautiful candles that we imported from other kingdoms, but we don't have access to those anymore, so we have to make do with makeshift oil lamps. One of the plants that we grow in our caves can be used to be produce oil if you extract it carefully enough, so we usually pour a little of that into a dish and light it. It's not much, but it's just about bright enough to see by."

"Why don't you light up a fire?"

"For the same reason. This part of Hagalaz is a broad expense of snow. There is nothing: no animals, no trees, nothing. We depend on the other kingdoms for most commodities, and since the war broke out, we can't access wood anymore. It's the same with fabric. When the other kingdoms supplied us, we made the most beautiful garments; the people of Hagalaz have a reputation for being talented seamstresses, and the outfits we made were in high demand throughout the surrounding kingdoms. But that time is over now, at least for my people, and we have to make do with only a few outfits per person."

It saddened me to hear how hard life had become for Maheliah and her subjects since the war had broken out between her and her brother. I could not believe a person could be so despicable. How could Netis keep everything for himself and give nothing to Maheliah? The war had to stop. These people deserved their lives back, and besides, I wanted to experience the lifestyle these people had lived before the war, and I wanted to visit the other kingdoms. But I needed to learn more about Hagalaz and its people before I could figure out how to end this war, so I tried to concentrate on my questions.

"Maheliah, how come I can breathe here like I can on Earth?"

"I'm not sure... I suppose the composition of the atmosphere must be the same. It's the same kind of air, just in a different place."

I felt a bit stupid, realising that the answer to my question was so straightforward. But everything was so strange to me; I knew that this would probably not be the last stupid question I would end up asking.

The cooks had reappeared while Maheliah was answering my question and had cleared away the bowls at rapid speed.

"Why don't you have a rest for an hour? We can continue the tour afterwards. I can imagine all this new information is overwhelming for you, and I'm sure you have many more questions, so it's probably best if you take a break now. We can start afresh in an hour once you've had time to process everything."

I understood Maheliah's reasoning, and though there were a million questions I wanted to ask, I decided to take her advice. Standing up from the table, I nodded politely to everyone, before making my way back to my room. From what I had seen and heard so far, it seemed that life in Hagalaz was not easy, at least, not as easy as it had once been.

As I walked up the stairs, I began to daydream about the time before the war, when Hagalaz had been a peaceful, magical place. I wanted to know that world, that version of Hagalaz, and I decided that it was my duty to help restore balance to my new home. I was the reason the war had begun; it was only fitting that I should be the one to end it.

CHAPTER V - AN ICE-HEARTED BEING

A fierce, icy wind shocked me out of my daydreaming as I opened the door to my room. For a moment, I was blinded by my hair swirling around my face in the wind, but once I managed to push my curls behind me, a strange sight met my eyes. The main window had completely melted; all that remained were a few icy fragments, lying on the bedroom floor. A stranger stood in front of the gaping hole where the window had been. His bearing was regal, and he held himself gracefully, but his gaze was dark and brooding. He was looking at me like I was an object, a good to be taken, and as I met his eyes he smirked, as though convinced that he had almost achieved his aim.

Despite his unsettling gaze, I could not look away. His eyes were absolutely bewitching, his pupils like two polished onyxes. He looked at me like he was scrutinising my soul, his gaze piercing mine with ease. His dark brown hair was tied loosely at the nape of his neck, and several wayward strands delicately caressed his face. He was wearing dark leather trousers and boots, as well as an oversized linen shirt, too loose to cover his chest entirely. A silver ring glimmered on his right forefinger.

Many times, I had tried to envisage what he would look like, but he was unlike any of my imaginings. I had expected him to look rather odd and unattractive, yet he was handsome and elegant, though despite his pleasant appearance, he looked more intimidating than I had anticipated. I could not stop myself from looking him up and down in silence, petrified that he was here, in my room.

"I have a feeling that I don't need to introduce myself," Netis remarked in a tenor voice, smirking.

Looking deep into my eyes, he came closer to me. I moved back immediately, trying to give him my darkest stare whilst feeling like my heart was about to leap out of my chest in terror.

"I knew you were dauntless," he continued.

"I know exactly what you want… but I'm not coming with you." I spoke through gritted teeth, trying my best to sound fearless.

He chuckled darkly, looking me up and down.

"You're as beautiful as I thought you would be."

"Complimenting me won't work, Netis. I'm not coming with you. Go away."

He stepped towards me again, but this time, I did not move. I wanted to face him; he had to know that I was not afraid of him.

"I'm not leaving without you."

I hated his air of self-assurance.

"Get out now, or I'll call for Maheliah and you'll be forced to leave."

He chuckled; his body was now so close to mine that I could feel his breath on my face. I remained fixed to my position, trying desperately to control my limbs and stop them from shaking.

"Do you really think that I fear Maheliah? She has never been able to do anything. She even failed to bring you here. If that traitor, Angel, had not brought you to her, you would be mine now. Maheliah is no threat to me."

His words stabbed at me, fuelling my rage. How dare he speak ill of Maheliah and Angel.

"Perhaps if you had shown me the same kindness that Maheliah and Angel have, I would have come with you gladly. But you're a monster; despicable and cruel. You don't even know what kindness is anymore. I'd sooner die than be by your side. Now get out."

Netis' face screwed up in an expression of rage, and he bent his head, clenching his fists in anger. I stumbled backwards, afraid that he was going to hit me, but as soon as I moved, he unclenched his fists, seizing my left arm right under my shoulder and gripping it fiercely. I let out a scream of agony. His hand burned my skin, like I had just plunged my arm into a furnace. The pain was so strong that I collapsed onto the floor, my arm still in Netis' grasp. I closed my eyes tightly, tears trickling down my face. The burn was so intense that I could feel it raging through my entire body.

On the edge of consciousness, I felt Netis release my arm and place his hands on my back, lifting me into his arms. I could still feel the burn, and had no strength left to resist. I felt my body rocking as he carried me to the window, the icy wind on my eyelids waking me just long enough to see the landscape passing before my eyes at rapid speed before the pain claimed me again, and I succumbed to unconsciousness.

I was woken by a dull, throbbing pain, coming from my arm. Confused, it took me a few seconds to realise where I was. Netis had taken me… kidnapped me. As I slowly returned to consciousness, I realised that I was lying in a bed, in the centre of a room, which looked not unlike the rooms in Maheliah's palace.

Turning my head to the left, I looked at my arm: there

was a bandage around my wound, where Netis had burned me. I touched it with the tips of my fingers but instantly recoiled in pain. Taking a few deep breaths, I decided to try and sit upright, and slowly pushed myself up using my uninjured arm. That was how I discovered Netis, sitting in the corner by the door with his arms folded, his head nestled in the crook of his elbow. He was staring at me.

Panicking, I tried to escape, but my legs refused to obey me; I was too weak to move. Netis stood up and began to walk towards the bed, his gaze fixed on my eyes. I clutched the duvet, drawing it towards me like a cotton wool shield, shifting backwards until my back was flat against the bedhead. Netis kept coming closer, all the while looking deep into my eyes, scrutinising my soul. Sitting on the bed, he leaned towards me, his face so close that I could feel the heat of his breath on my lips.

"Am I making you uncomfortable?" he murmured.

I turned my face to the right, breaking his gaze. What could I say? Yes, he was making me uncomfortable. I knew that he was dangerous, and I had no idea what he had planned for me. But, at the same time, part of me enjoyed being this close to him; if I was uncomfortable, it was more because I felt strangely attracted to him.

Furious with myself, I tried to get out of the bed again, reaching for the wall and using the solidity of it to help me drag myself away from Netis, towards the door. But as I slid away from him, Netis stood up and immediately pinned me against the wall, placing his hands gently on either side of my head. My back was flat against the wall, and my face close to his chest, as he brought his face closer and closer to mine, still looking deep into my eyes. I knew that I should be trying to run, but my body refused to listen, transfixed by how close we were to one another.

His behaviour confused me. I had assumed that he wanted me by his side to train me, so that he could use me as a weapon. But in this moment, he seemed to want me for entirely different reasons, his face now so close to mine that I was unable to move. Was he going to kiss me? Did I want him to? Why was I even contemplating that? I hated this man; despised him. He had taken me against my will.

"Don't be afraid of me. I mean you no harm," he murmured, lifting his face up a little, away from mine.

"And yet you burned my arm," I answered gravely.

He took my chin delicately between his fingers, his expression suddenly sorrowful.

"What do you want from me?" I whispered.

"I want you, Fada. You shall be by my side, eventually…"

I was so confused; I could not keep up with his constantly changing narrative. I wanted to push him away and to run towards the door, but just as I tried to do so, someone entered the room and called out something in the Hagal language. I recognised the voice. Angel.

"Angel, please, help me," I cried.

Netis muttered something in a grave and threatening voice and Angel took a step backwards, bowing his head. I stared at him in horror. Why was he not doing anything to help me? Was he really so afraid of Netis? I looked up at Netis and felt my blood boiling. I would not let this man control Angel anymore, and I would not succumb to my body's traitorous desire for him.

Mustering all my courage, I shoved Netis backwards, kicking him in the crotch. As he collapsed in on himself in pain and surprise, I ran towards Angel, grabbed his hand, and ran from the room. As we fled downstairs, I could feel my adrenaline wearing off, and my body began to shake. Fortunately, now that he was away from Netis, Angel took charge, pulling me through the castle and out of the back entrance. Maheliah was waiting outside for us, a portal still shimmering behind her.

"Fada, are you all right?" she exclaimed anxiously, pulling me into her arms.

But I could not answer, for all I could hear was Netis, his voice thick with hatred and fury as he shouted Angel's name. I looked at Angel. He was biting his lower lip anxiously, clenching his fists. I imagined the worst. Netis' voice seemed so furious; I was afraid that he might kill Angel. I could not let that happen.

Suddenly, Angel lifted his head, his expression determined. He took a deep breath, then, slowly, he began to make his way back towards the palace.

"No, Angel! You'll be killed."

He ignored me and continued to walk to his death. I wanted to stop him, but Maheliah grabbed my right arm and pushed me through the portal, following after me as the portal closed behind her. Stumbling forwards, I found myself back in front of Maheliah's palace.

"I was so anxious, Fada," Maheliah exclaimed, as she emerged from the portal. "I knew that this moment would come eventually, but I did not expect him to discover that you were in Hagalaz so soon."

I was barely listening to her words, my thoughts fixed on Angel and the fate that awaited him. All I wanted to do was go back and rescue him, but Maheliah had just spotted my bandage and did not give me a chance to vocalise my concerns.

"Fada, what happened to your arm?"

Without waiting for me to respond, she removed my bandage, causing me to cry out in agony. I looked at her, expecting her to apologise, but Maheliah was simply staring down at my arm with a horrified look on her face. Following her gaze, I could see why. My arm looked hideous; the skin where Netis had touched me was red as blood and ragged with blisters, all of them oozing a viscous, yellow liquid.

"He will pay for this…" Maheliah murmured viciously. "How dare he touch you. How dare he…"

I was too horrified by the state of my arm to respond. It looked as though it had been corroded by acid. I started to tremble. How would I ever recover from this?

Maheliah swiftly led me into the palace, calling out commands as she guided me up to my room. Two women entered the room shortly after we did, and Maheliah carefully showed them my burn; I could only assume that she was explaining to them what had happened. They left immediately, returning swiftly with various ointments and plants.

"These two are some of our best healers. They will treat your wound in no time. I must get your window repaired as well. I can't believe he had the audacity to come here…" Maheliah paused. "I shall leave you now. The healers will attend to your needs."

"Wait! Please, before you go… how was Netis able to burn my arm with his hand? Is it a magical skill? Like the portals?"

Maheliah sighed, looking down as she wrapped her arms around herself. Closing her eyes for a moment, she took a deep breath, before coming back to sit next to me.

"It is an ancestral technique from Othalaz, that kingdom I told you about who we were once at war

93

with. Netis was always fascinated by this power when we were children, but he was not permitted to master it, not only because he was not from Othalaz but also because our kingdoms were at war. But, when the war came to an end, his wish was finally granted…"

"Is it a power you can learn, then? Or did someone give it to him?" I asked, intrigued.

"Nobody knows, not even me. I never saw him receive any training, but I think it unlikely that such a power can simply be bestowed upon someone. It has always been quite a mystery to me, and to the royals of Othalaz. They were very unhappy when they discovered that the heir of Hagalaz had mastered their ancestral technique, though it is not the first time that Netis has mastered an ancestral power from another kingdom. He is the only person I know of who has managed to acquire such skills from other kingdoms, which is yet another reason why you should be careful around him. His powers make him obnoxious and proud. He thinks he's invincible."

"Does he?"

Maheliah paused for a few seconds, looking down with a blank look. She then shook her head slightly and answered in a quieter voice.

"I'm sorry, I was just thinking out loud. I don't know if he believes himself invincible. He just comes across as being arrogant enough to believe something like that.

He's always been so proud of his powers."

I was astounded by her story, but also perplexed. If Netis was so powerful, why had he allowed me to escape? He was such a strange, mysterious being, and knowing that he had somehow gained all these powers piqued my curiosity. Maheliah just seemed to accept that he had acquired them, but I wanted to know how. I wanted to understand.

"Anyway, it doesn't matter what he can or cannot do. I don't want to talk about him anymore," Maheliah continued, shutting down our conversation. "I need to leave now. I must find some workers to repair your window."

Once she had left the room, I looked at the two healers, who were busy covering my arm in plants and ointments. I did not understand what they were doing, but they seemed professional, so I stayed still and silent, allowing them to get on with their work. They looked similar in appearance, but they were not twins like Nalhya and Lilhya. They appeared to be in their late forties, and both of them had straight, dark brown hair, tied neatly in a bun. Like everyone else in this kingdom, their eyes were incredible: both a dark, lapis-lazuli blue.

Maheliah came back a few minutes later, followed by several people carrying big blocks of ice, who promptly walked straight to the window and began to repair it. Maheliah, meanwhile, came over to inspect the healers' hard work. My arm had been covered with dried leaves, plants and ointments, to the extent that my wound could no longer be seen, and had been wrapped in a fresh bandage.

"They'll come back tomorrow morning to take the bandage off, and to dress your wound again if necessary," Maheliah explained.

"Surely it will take more than a few days to heal, considering the depth of the burn?"

"Don't underestimate the power of our medicine," Maheliah answered, smiling.

Once the healers had left, after gesturing to me and Maheliah in the customary Hagal manner, Maheliah came and sat closer to me.

"Angel's outside," she whispered gravely. "He would like to speak with you."

I stared at her in shock. I had completely forgotten that Angel had been forced to brave the wrath of Netis. I remembered the rage with which Netis had pronounced his name, and I felt guilty that I had not been thinking about him. At least the fact that he was here meant that he was alive, though I could only imagine that what he wanted to tell me was not going to be good news.

Leaping to my feet, I rushed down the stairs and hurried outside to where Angel was waiting. Strangely, he had no wounds or burns; I had been frightened that

Netis would beat him to death, but there was no sign that they had fought, physically at least. He smiled painfully at me, asking if I would walk with him to the frozen lake.

"Of course. Angel, are you okay? What did Netis do to you? What did he say?" I asked anxiously.

Angel did not answer; he just stared blankly at me and nodded his head in the direction of the lake. Understanding that he was not ready to talk, I followed him in silence, the only sound being the crunch of our footsteps in the snow. Once we arrived by the lake, Angel took a deep breath and looked into my eyes.

"I'm not going to lie to you and say that Netis has been kind to me," he told me in a weak, battered voice. "He punished me harshly, but I deserved it. He could have been more violent."

"What are you talking about? You did nothing wrong, Angel. You don't deserve to be punished."

"Fada, I brought you to Maheliah when my duty was to bring you to Netis, and I helped you run away too. He had every reason to punish me. I'm his slave, Fada."

"No, you're not, Angel. You're not a slave, okay?"

"Oh really? Then what's this?"

He grabbed a necklace from his pocket and thrust it in front of my face. I had never noticed it before; I assumed he must have kept it hidden under his shirt when we had met on Earth. The necklace was a simple leather cord, upon which hung an onyx as large as a pupil. I touch the gem hesitantly.

"I don't understand," I murmured.

Angel held my hand, the one that was touching the gem.

"This necklace means that I belong to Netis. But he ordered me to take it off…"

"Doesn't that mean you're not his slave anymore? Surely that's good news, right?"

Angel bent his head and I stopped smiling.

"Not really. It means that I'm not Netis' slave anymore, yes, but it also means that I can't live in his palace anymore."

I looked at him in confusion.

"Why is that a problem? You can just stay with us. Maheliah has a huge palace, I'm sure there'll be room for you somewhere."

"Fada, I'm a traitor. There's no way Maheliah or her people would accept me."

"Of course she will accept you, Maheliah is one of the kindest people I know."

"It doesn't matter how kind she is: I chose Netis, Fada. She can't accept me."

"Where will you go then?"

"Nowhere. After tonight, I won't exist anymore, the snowstorm will make sure of that. It's impossible to survive a night out in the open in Hagalaz."

I felt my heart shattering as he spoke those words. It was my fault that he was in this situation. He had disobeyed Netis twice because I had asked him to, and now, he was going to die... alone... in the cold. There had to be a solution; it was unbearable to imagine someone dying because of me, let alone someone I cared so much about. We had only just accepted our feelings for one another... I could not let that first kiss be our last.

"No, Angel, please, you can't die. You have to stay here, with me," I sobbed, flinging myself into his arms.

He held me tightly, like he was saying goodbye, and as I looked into his perfect, aquamarine eyes, all I could see was sorrow. I moved my face closer to his, kissing his lips before burying my face into the hollow of his neck.

"Why did you take so many risks for me? You didn't have to. I don't want you to die because of me..."

Angel brought his mouth close to my ear.

"Because I love you, Fada."

It felt like my heart had stopped. I pulled away slightly and looked into his eyes again, not quite believing what I had heard, but his gaze was sincere. My emotions descended into chaos: I wanted to feel elated, but knowing that this might be the last time I would ever hear him say those words tore at my soul. Heartbreak and joy battled for supremacy in my mind, and not wanting him to see how torn I was, I buried my face into his neck again.

"I love you too, my Angel…" I murmured softly, brushing my lips against his skin. "Please, come with me. You can't die." Speaking those words aloud bolstered my determination, and I looked up at him. "I will speak to Maheliah. She will agree to put you up, I'm sure of it."

Pulling away, I grabbed his arm and began to walk towards the palace, trying to drag him behind me. But he would not move.

"No, Fada. She'll never agree to it. She won't accept a traitor in her palace."

"I don't care. I'm the princess, she has to listen to me. You can't stay outside tonight. I forbid you to leave me…"

Angel pulled me back into his arms and held me close, laying a gentle kiss on the top of my head.

"It's okay. I'm right here, Fada."

As I clung to him, I felt Angel sigh heavily.

"Maheliah won't accept me in her palace, I know that. But if you think you can convince her otherwise… I suppose we might as well try."

Relieved that he had agreed to my request, I half dragged him back towards Maheliah's palace, but as we approached the entrance, he stopped me.

"Fada, wait. I can't go inside. I'll wait for you here

while you go and speak to Maheliah."

I looked at him, unsure whether leaving him was a sensible decision, but his expression was adamant. Forcing him inside was not an option, so I nodded reluctantly and entered the palace alone.

Once inside, I sprinted up the stairs to find Maheliah sitting on her throne, apparently lost in thought. I ran towards her and knelt.

"Maheliah, please, I'm begging you. Help him!"

She stood abruptly, clearly shocked by my behaviour.

"Fada, what are you doing? Stand up. Who are you talking about?"

"Maheliah, please help him. Netis banished Angel and he can't go back to the palace anymore. But if he stays outside tonight, he'll die."

"What do you want me to do? He chose Netis. I can't accept him in my palace."

"You can't say that! It's thanks to him that I'm by your side now. Without him, I would be with Netis."

Maheliah bent her head. She knew that I was right; she owed Angel many things. He had betrayed Netis numerous times now, and she had taken advantage of it. He had brought me to her palace and had helped me escape from Netis' clutches. She owed Angel a debt of gratitude, and I was hoping that she would respect that.

"You're right, Fada. It is thanks to Angel that you are with me, and I can see that you are very fond of each

101

other. I can't host him in my palace – my people would never forgive me – but we have a cave outside the palace that we don't use. He can sleep there tonight."

It was not what I had expected, but a cave was better than nothing. I just hoped it would be warm enough to protect him from the storm.

Maheliah and I walked outside to find Angel still standing there, waiting for me beside the guardians of the palace.

"Dear Angel," Maheliah declared, in a voice worthy of a queen. "I know what has happened to you, and though I cannot accept you into my Court, I cannot deny that you have done many things for me. It is thanks to you that Fada is by my side now, and for that, I am grateful. You shall sleep in one of the caves adjacent to the palace for the night. Tomorrow, you will have to find another place to stay."

"I am most grateful to you, Maheliah. You are a most wise and gracious queen. Netis should treat you like one."

Moving his hand from his heart to his forehead, Angel made the same gesture that the others in the palace had done when they had greeted me earlier. For two people who were supposed to be enemies, Maheliah and Angel had been nothing but courteous to one another. It made me realise how lucky I was to have convinced Angel to take me to Maheliah's Court when

I had first arrived here. I could not imagine Netis behaving in such an understanding manner.

The cave was situated on the side of the palace, just beneath my now-repaired bedroom window. It was quite small but seemed to provide shelter enough for one person, though the solid floor did not look especially comfortable. Angel thanked Maheliah once again for her hospitality and then gestured for me to leave with her. Reluctantly, I complied, spending the walk back to the palace contemplating how I could make the cave more comfortable for Angel.

Upon re-entering the palace, I headed straight to my bedroom, picking up two of my three duvets and one of my pillows. As I made my way back downstairs, Maheliah stopped me.

"Fada, what are you doing?"

"I'm taking these to Angel. I am grateful to you for hosting him in this cave, but the floor is hard and cold; I don't want him to catch a chill."

"What about you? What will you sleep with?"

"I still have a duvet and a pillow, so I'll be fine. Don't worry, Maheliah, I know what I'm doing."

She looked at me quizzically for a moment before waving me on, telling me to make sure I was back before nightfall. Thanking her, I ran towards the cave, to find Angel sitting cross-legged on the floor, contemplating a bracelet that he was holding. He stood up when he saw me.

"Fada, what are you doing?"

"Could everybody please stop asking me that? I'm bringing you some duvets and pillows. I hope it'll be enough. The floor doesn't look very comfortable."

He thanked me warmly, layering the duvets on the floor, before pulling me into his chest and kissing me softly. I stayed there in his arms for a few minutes before pulling away, conscious of Maheliah's warning. Angel held me back, encircling my fingers with his.

"Fada, wait. I've got something for you."

He showed me the bracelet that he had been looking at. It was an arm bracelet… an arm bracelet that looked strangely similar to the one I had been drawing all those months ago at the museum, the first time that I had met Angel. He handed it to me, and I held it gently, mesmerised and overwhelmed.

"Is it really for me?"

"Yes. Netis ordered me to give it to you, to hide your wound…"

A present from Netis? How bizarre. Why would he offer me a present, especially one designed to hide a wound that he had caused me? And how had he created such a bracelet so quickly? He must have owned it for a long time… that was the only logical explanation. But why? Did it belong to someone?

My mind was brimming with questions, but I could

hear the snowstorm coming and I knew I had to go. Angel kissed me once more before hugging me tightly; I did not want to leave his embrace. Reluctantly, I left the cave and dragged myself back to the palace, leaving Angel alone to deal with the frozen night...

CHAPTER VI - HIM

The day was barely dawning when I left the palace the next morning, with the last of the snow from the night before still falling softly from the sky. I did not care; I was too anxious to check on Angel. I had spent all night in my bed, but I had barely slept, my mind preoccupied with Angel and whether the cave and duvets would be enough to keep him safe from the glacial storm. I had felt the chill of the night air under my one duvet, so I could only imagine how cold Angel must have been. I knew that I was frailer than he was, being used to London temperatures and not the freezing Hagal nights, but still... there was only so much a person could take.

As soon as I walked inside the cave, I knew that I had been right to be concerned. Angel was huddled in the left corner of the cave, almost hidden beneath my duvets, but his face was just about visible. His lips were a terrifying shade of blue; his skin was white as snow, and his hair glistened with water and ice. He was shivering uncontrollably, the sound of his teeth chattering sending waves of panic through my body.

I ran towards him, realising as I drew closer that the duvets had frozen solid, trapping him in an icy cocoon. I frantically touched his face. It was cold as ice, but my touch seemed to wake him from his unconsciousness. He raised his eyes without moving his head and his lips tried desperately to form words between shivers.

"F… Fada… I'm f… fine… don't wor… worry…"

I did not answer, running my fingers over his face as my eyes brimmed with tears. It was unbearable to see him in such a state.

Slowly, my initial panic subsided, and was replaced by determination. He was still alive, just. I had to make sure he stayed that way. Pulling myself back to my feet, I ran towards the palace and sprinted straight into the kitchen. Trying to make the cooks understand what I wanted was a challenge, but after many repeated signs and hand gestures, they finally understood, and lit up a fire ready to warm some soup. I knew that soup alone would not be enough to warm him, but I needed to feel like I was doing something to help. I could not comprehend how this had happened to him; with the cave and the bedding I had given him, he should have been protected. I began to fear that I had yet to understand just how dreadful Hagalaz could be.

When the soup was finally warm, I grabbed a spoon

and several towels and ran back outside towards the cave. The guardians of the palace stared at me with a black look; they clearly disapproved of me giving our soup to 'a traitor', but I did not care. I could not let Angel die.

"Eat this, Angel. It's soup. It will warm you up…"

"This is… useless, F… Fada… tomorrow… it will… be the s… same…"

"No, it won't be the same. I'm going to speak to Netis at once. He'll take you back, I'll make sure of it. I can't let you die."

"No, F… Fada… don't. He could… harm you…"

Ignoring him, I left the soup beside him on the floor and ran back towards the guardians. Once I was close enough for them to hear me, I shouted 'Netis', hoping they would understand that I wanted to know where his palace was. They looked at each other, confused, then looked down. I shouted 'Netis' again, pointing in every direction to make them understand what I wanted. They stared at each other and exchanged a few words; it was frustrating not being able to understand what they were saying. After a minute or so, they finally looked back at me and pointed straight in front of them.

I nodded, grateful for their help, and began to run as fast as I could. I had been in such a hurry that morning that I had got dressed on my own, so my gown was not tied up properly and I had to keep pulling it up every so often. I should have felt cold, but I did not, my mind too preoccupied with running as fast as I could towards Netis' palace. Angel's frozen face haunted me and I knew that I had to find a solution, otherwise he would die. I could not beg Maheliah to host him in the cave every night, then spend every day trying to revive him. A temporary shelter was not enough in Hagalaz. Angel needed a home again.

Ten minutes later, I arrived in front of Netis' palace, panting great clouds of frozen air. Slowing down to a walk, I tried to regain my breath, taking in my surroundings. I had left in such a hurry the day before that I had not realised how massive Netis' palace was; I had never seen such a building. The palace was entirely white, and unlike Maheliah's mountain palace, it was vast in width, not height, though I reasoned that high towers were probably impractical given the nightly snowstorms. The main structure was a long, narrow, rectangular building, surrounded by a wall which seemed to extend for miles, and at each corner of the rectangle was a short, stumpy tower. That was all I could see from where I stood, but I guessed that there were more buildings around the other side; there was no grand entrance as far as I could see, so I assumed that I must be at the back of the palace. The whole aesthetic was rather plain – a contrast to what I had expected Netis' domain to look like – and the building looked

109

undeniably practical, like a shelter rather than the home of a king or queen.

After walking for some time, I finally arrived in front of the only door I could see on this side of the palace; the same door that I had assumedly escaped through the previous day. I took a deep breath and pushed, hoping that the door would be unlocked. To my surprise, it was, which seemed rather careless considering that they were at war, but I was not going to complain. Behind the door, a long corridor stretched out in front of me, and to my right were a set of narrow, white stairs. I remembered running down them with Angel, so I reasoned that, if I was lucky, they would lead me to Netis; I just had to hope that I would not run into anyone on the way.

As I reached the top of the stairs, I looked around me. To my right was nothing but a wall, and to my left was yet another long, narrow corridor. A heavy-looking white door stood in front of me. Not wanting to risk the corridor, and hoping that this was the room I had fled from the previous day, I took a deep breath and knocked. I felt like such a fool, throwing myself into the lion's mouth, but I had no choice. Angel would die if he had to stay another night inside the cave, I was sure of it. I had to convince Netis to take him back; I would endure a thousand painful things if it meant saving Angel.

A shout came from inside the room: Netis, speaking in the Hagal tongue. My heart was thumping fast in my chest, and I hesitated, the anger in his voice dissuading me for a moment. Then Angel's icy face flashed through my mind, and my resolve hardened again. I had to do this.

Opening the door slowly, I found Netis sitting in front of his desk, holding some papers. When he saw me, his eyes widened in surprise.

"Sorry to bother you, but it's important…" I murmured, before my courage left me again.

Netis stood and began to walk towards me.

"Why did you leave in such a hurry yesterday, if you intended to return so early in the morning?" he questioned.

"I'm not an object that you can steal, Netis. I will come to you if I want to. You can't force me to stay here," I answered in a grave voice, still trembling.

He came closer to me and looked at my arm, where my wound was.

"Hasn't Angel given you the bracelet?"

"He has, but the wound is not yet healed, so I can't put anything on it. I should thank you for the bracelet, but I'd rather say thank you for the burn. Surely you must know how thrilled I am to have such a beautiful scar on my arm that I will have to cover up for the rest of my life?" I answered in a sarcastic tone.

His eyes darkened; I had expected to see anger in his gaze, but the tortured look that flickered across his onyx eyes surprised me.

"Why are you here, Fada? Do you finally accept to be by my side?"

"You're joking, right? You banished Angel."

"Oh, that's why you're here. Did you find his body on the ground?"

I tried to stay calm. Shouting at him would only make him angry. I needed to remember why I was here. He would never take Angel back if I responded to him with bitterness and spite.

"No, Angel isn't dead. Maheliah hosted him in a cave by the palace."

"No matter. One more night and he'll be gone forever."

I tried to concentrate and not let my anger control me; I did not understand why Netis was being so unpleasant. Angel may have betrayed him, but he had been loyal to him for years, and was one of the kindest people I had ever known. I could not understand why anyone would want to harm him.

"That's why I'm here. I was hoping that you would consider taking him back."

Netis did not answer, scrutinising my eyes with his emotionless gaze.

"Who do you think I am?" His voice was calm but firm. "Did you really think that you could just walk in here and convince me to alter my decision? I raised that

112

boy; I trained him; I made him the man he is today, and this is how he thanks me? Betrayal is not something I can tolerate."

"But it wasn't his fault. I made him take me to Maheliah's palace; he brought me here from Earth, just like you asked him to. And can you blame him for wanting to help me when you hurt me? You were the one who told him to get close to me; it is only natural that he would want to help me."

"He's weak; he should have brought you straight here. Do you really expect me to feel pity for someone so pathetic as Angel?"

"You're a monster!" I snapped, his words finally cracking my mask of calm. "You're heartless and cruel; Angel was right to take me to Maheliah's when I first came here. How dare you speak about Angel like that."

Netis frowned and gritted his teeth.

"Is that so?" he growled, throwing his fist against the wall behind me.

I instinctively moved my body closer to the wall, flattening my back against it. My heart was thumping in my chest, and I felt tears coming to my eyes. I should have been afraid of what he might do to me; of being injured again, but I was more afraid of seeing him act this way. I knew that I had hurt his feelings, even though he pretended to have none, and much that I hated to admit this to myself, I felt sorry for him. Why was I

113

thinking about his wellbeing when he could not care less about mine?

Confused by my feelings, I curled in on myself, ready for whatever damage Netis intended to inflict on me. But when I looked up at him, his reaction was unexpected. His face relaxed, little by little, and he slowly moved his hand down from the wall above my head. I could see pain in his eyes, but I did not understand why. He moved his body closer to mine, and I closed my eyes, turning my head to the side, thinking that he was about to hurt me. But he did not. Gently, ever so gently, he slid his fingers around my waist, taking my chin delicately in his other hand. Turning to face him, I opened my eyes, and stared directly into his. Pain. All I could see was pain and regret, as his two onyxes gazed into my soul.

"I'm sorry, Fada. I mean you no harm. Please, forgive me..." he murmured softly, without breaking our connection.

I did not know how to answer; I was too confused. Why was he suddenly acting like this?

His face slowly came closer to mine, and I could feel his hand on my waist, but I could not stop looking into his eyes. I did not understand what was happening to me. I hated this man, yet I could not leave his embrace; somehow, his arms felt safe, felt right. I should have been terrified, being so close to him, but his touch was

114

soothing.

I felt his other hand move from my chin to my waist, and his gaze shifted down to my chest. I looked down too and realised that the top of my dress was gaping open, exposing a good portion of my breasts. I had forgotten that my dress was not tied up properly, but the panic I should have felt never came; I felt too content in Netis' embrace.

After a few seconds, finally managed to convince myself to pull away, clearing my throat and pulling up my dress as I did so.

"Please, take Angel back. I don't want him to die. I'm begging you, Netis. Don't be heartless…" I murmured, trying hard to avoid his gaze in case I lost myself in his eyes again.

"I'm sorry, Fada. I won't change my mind unless you accept to be by my side."

"I can't… I can't betray Maheliah, and I don't want to be used by anyone. I want to stay with her, and I know that you won't keep me in your palace by force."

"What makes you think that?"

"Maheliah would notice my absence if you kept me here, and she would come looking for me."

"You think I'm scared of her?"

"No, but I know you don't want to hurt me… not anymore."

"How can you be sure?"

"It's just the way I feel. Am I wrong?"

He looked down at me silently, a complex expression on his face. Then, finally, he closed his eyes, moving away from me.

"If you only came here to discuss Angel's fate, then you can leave. This conversation is over."

He turned around and walked towards his window, his silhouette outlined by the faint morning light coming through the glass.

I looked at him, confused, before turning back to the door and leaving him. I had failed. I had spoken to Netis in vain, and I had no idea what else I could do to convince him. I knew that I could have agreed to live with him, but it felt wrong to give up so easily, and I knew that it was not the right path. Besides, it would mean betraying Maheliah, and although I had only known her for a couple of days, I could not do that to her. She had shown me more kindness in those few days that most of my 'friends' on Earth put together. There was something more though, something I could not put my finger on. I could not explain it, but every inch of my body was telling me that I should not agree to live with Netis. It was the strangest sensation; it was as if a force was pushing me away from this decision.

Sighing, I tried to think of how else I could convince Netis to take Angel back. He did not seem like the kind of man who would care about how much I loved Angel, or how much he loved me, so bringing that into it would not help matters. I needed to remember that he was a warlord and a king. He had spent his whole life debating and making important decisions based on logic; my arguments on love would not make any difference to a man like him.

I arrived in front of Maheliah's palace, lost in my thoughts. I wanted to see Angel and check on him, but I was distracted by Nalhya, who was standing outside next to the guardians. She walked fast to get close to me, her expression anxious.

"Fada, Maheliah orders you to come to the throne room at once. She seems quite furious."

I took a deep breath, preparing myself for the royal telling-off I was about to receive, before following Nalhya inside. The faster I explained things to Maheliah, the sooner I could go and check on Angel.

Lilhya was standing beside the throne, while Maheliah paced up and down, her expression anxious and frustrated. As soon as she noticed me, she stopped, frowning.

"I can't believe you went back to see Netis, especially on your own. How irresponsible of you."

"I'm sorry Maheliah, but I had to speak to him. He needs to take Angel back. I don't want him to die…"

"Did you speak to Netis, then? Did it work?"

I bowed my head in shame. She was right, speaking

117

to Netis had been no use.

"That's what I thought," she concluded, her voice harsh.

She gestured for me to follow her upstairs, and as we walked into my room, we were met by the two healers from the previous day, who were standing waiting for me. They swiftly got to work, sitting me down and removing my bandage, wiping away all the ointment and plant material. I stared in amazement. All that was left of my wound was a fully healed, hand-shaped scar. How had it healed so quickly?

"I'll get an arm bracelet made to cover that scar," Maheliah insisted.

"Oh, it's okay, I have one already. Angel gave it to me… from Netis."

I opened one of the drawers and took out the bracelet, showing it to Maheliah.

"I've seen this bracelet before… I think Akaoh gave it to him, many years ago. I can't believe he kept it all these years…"

This bracelet had been a present from Akaoh? I remembered what Maheliah had told me about him. He had been the High King of Hagalaz and had raised her and Netis. But why had he given Netis a bracelet? It seemed like such a bizarre gift.

Placing the bracelet over my scar, I looked at myself in the mirror. Though it was only there to hide a scar I could not help but admire how gorgeous it was. Such a bracelet must have cost a fortune to make... and as a gift from his mentor, surely it was precious to Netis? Why had he decided to give it to me? I could not imagine someone as insensitive as Netis being motivated by guilt alone, but then why else would he have given it to me?

Nalhya and Lilhya, who had followed us into my room, looked me up and down and laughed brightly.

"It seems you do need our help to get dressed in the morning..."

Maheliah smiled softly, her spirits lifted by the twins' jibe, and promptly left the room, giving the twins a chance to fix my dress and hair.

While they were getting me ready, I tried to think of how else I might be able to persuade Netis to take Angel back. It was useless trying to speak to him; he would never back down, no matter how many times I begged. But he must have a weakness of some kind... nobody was flawless; not even the stoic king of Hagalaz could be that powerful. I tried to remember his behaviour during the time I had spent with him. He had been conceited, angry, but... there was something else. When he had held my waist in his hands and brought his face close to mine, he had looked at me, at my body, like he wanted me. Was that his aim? I had assumed from what Maheliah had told me that he had wanted me by his side to use as a weapon, but maybe he wanted more than

119

that?

I did not know much about men, especially men on this planet, but I knew that they always seemed to be driven by sex, regardless of the situation. I had experienced my fair share of men staring at me like I was a piece of meat, and it was one of the reasons why I had never let a man touch me. I was afraid of them; the desire I saw in those men's eyes was frightening, because I knew that they did not care about my own pleasure, or my wellbeing, or my feelings. They had a way of creasing their eyes slightly while looking up and down at me; it always felt like they were undressing me with their gaze, and in that gaze I could see all the things they were thinking of doing to me, and none of them were ever gentle or caring.

The way Netis had looked at me was different. There had been desire in his eyes, yes, but there had also been something else. He had looked at me, not just my body; he had stared deep into my eyes, scrutinising my soul. His gaze had been passionate, intoxicating, and I had not wanted him to stop. The way he had run his hand down from my chin to my waist; the way he had gently placed his hands on me; the way he had looked at my breasts… he may have wanted me by his side to fight, but he also desired me, that much was clear.

I began to tremble. Netis was drawn to me; he wanted to kiss me; to touch me. No matter how cruel Maheliah and Angel seemed to believe that he was, he was not one of those monsters who would touch a woman against her will. He could easily have taken advantage of me without my consent, but he had chosen not to. I knew it was stupid of me to put my trust in a man who had scarred me for life and cast out the man I loved, but I could not deny the sense of safety and security I had felt in Netis' embrace. I knew that, deep down, Netis was a good man, and I trusted him not to hurt me.

Lilhya's brush caught on a knot in my hair, and I was dragged back to the present. It was so strange: here I was, getting my hair done in Maheliah's palace, whilst thinking over and over again about Netis' behaviour towards me and how his desire might be the weakness I was looking for. I shivered. I had made a decision, an insane decision, but irrevocable. To save Angel, I would give myself to Netis.

CHAPTER VII - A HEART HIDDEN UNDER THE ICE

I shivered again. Giving myself to Netis was terrifying, but my love for Angel was strong; I was willing to pay any price to save him. Besides, it was my fault that he did not have a roof over his head. He had put himself at risk for me; sacrificed his once comfortable life for my sake. Now, it was my turn to sacrifice myself for him. Having sex with another man to save the life of the man I loved seemed totally illogical, but I had seen how Netis had looked at me. I hoped that his desire for me was greater than his hatred towards Angel.

Once Nalhya and Lilhya had left, I cautiously made my escape, trying to avoid being seen, before hurrying back to Netis' palace for the second time that day. As I walked, I tried to imagine what Angel's reaction would be if he discovered what I was about to do. I knew that he would never accept my decision, and I hated myself for having to make this choice. Ever since I had met

Angel, I had always hoped that he would be my first and only; the only man who would ever touch my body in that way. But this desperate decision had reduced my hopes to naught.

I was still lost in my thoughts when I arrived at the back entrance of the palace, and almost bumped into the two guards who were stationed outside the gate. I had assumed that the entrance would be unguarded, as it had been earlier that morning, and had not prepared myself to meet anyone. My body started trembling in fear. The guards were staring at me, surprised, but when I tried to enter the palace, they stopped me.

"Where do you think you're going?" one of them uttered, in a very strong accent.

"You clearly don't place much value upon your life," the second continued.

That last sentence made my blood run cold. The guards were imposing, and I knew that they could easily kill me if they wanted to. I tried to explain that I was here to see Netis, but I did not have time to finish my sentence; one of the guards had taken my arm with violence and lowered his face close to mine.

"Fucking a royal is something I've been wanting to do for a long time…" he murmured, savagely.

"… and I'm sure we're not the only ones who would love to have a taste of your royal body…" his friend continued.

The first guard moved his hand from my arm to my bum, and his friend came closer to me, trying to put his hands on my hips. Instinctively, I spat in his face, slapping the other one with my now free hand. The first guard released me, touching his face where I had hit him, and gave me a black look. I was getting ready to defend myself, though I feared I would not be strong enough to do much against them. I wondered how these men could possibly find pleasure in touching a woman against her will. My breathing was heavy, my heart thumping fast. I was terrified, but I tried not to show it. I knew that my fear would only give them more satisfaction.

As they came closer to me, the sound of someone clapping, slow and sharp, broke the tension. The guards turned around and immediately stopped moving. I looked behind them: Netis was standing by the door, his expression furious. I could not understand why, but seeing him standing there made my body relax in relief.

Netis spoke quietly but firmly to the guards in their own language, and the two of them rapidly retreated, standing as far away from me as possible whilst still guarding the gate. Netis smirked at me.

"I see that your fierce spirit is not only directed towards me, Fada."

"Indeed… though I have to admit that behaving this way towards you is much more satisfying, Netis," I replied mockingly, regaining my calm.

"Which I am grateful for," he continued, his smirk growing wider. "Tell me, what brings you to me twice in one day? I'm guessing it's about Angel again?"

I immediately grew tense when I heard his words. It was too late to turn back now.

"Yes... I... I would like to strike a deal with you..." I stammered, my voice weak.

Netis looked at me, confused by my sudden change in demeanour, but after a moment's hesitation, he beckoned me inside.

Without saying a word, I followed Netis up the stairs. I felt like such a fool, walking up the same stairs that I had fled down only the day before. Suddenly realising the seriousness of what I intended to do, my pulse sped, and as Netis opened the door to his room, my chest became tight with anxiety.

Shutting the door behind us, Netis turned to face me.

"I'm quite curious to know what this deal is about."

I opened my mouth to answer but nothing came out. I felt so strange: I was anxious... terrified... but at the same time, I was curious to see what his reaction would be when I revealed what I had planned.

"If you want to strike a deal with me, you have to talk to me, Fada."

Once more, I was unable to say a single word, too confused by all the emotions swirling around my mind.

Bending my head, I instinctively touched the bracelet that covered my wound. Netis must have noticed my gesture because he looked down at the bracelet and came closer to me. I felt like someone had sent a wave of electricity through my body, my muscles tensing in response to his closeness. I looked up at him, but his expression was not what I had expected. His eyes were painfully sad; full of regret.

Gently, he touched the bracelet with his fingertips and slowly removed it, being careful not to brush the metal against my burn scar. Feeling his hand on me made me shiver at first, but slowly, my muscles began to relax. Placing the bracelet carefully on the desk behind him, he looked down at my wound, caressing it with the tips of his fingers.

"I know you won't believe me, but I'm really sorry for that," he murmured, his voice full of sadness.

"You're right, it's quite hard to believe you," I murmured, as he raised his eyes to meet mine. I could see the sorrow behind his beautiful black pupils. "And yet, for some reason, I do."

He smiled softly, stilling my fears. This was it. I needed to tell him why I had come.

"I…" Sighing, I took a deep breath and tried again. "I know what you have wanted for the past twenty years."

Netis did not answer; his gaze had drifted back to my

126

wound, but as I spoke, his eyes met mine.

"… me…" I whispered.

Netis immediately let go of my arm, his eyes widening.

"Don't think that I'm going to agree to living here with you and these despicable men," I continued, with more assurance. "I could never betray Maheliah…"

"Then what are you suggesting?" Netis asked in a serious voice.

"You haven't killed Angel, and I suppose I should thank you for that. I can't deny that he betrayed you when he brought me to Maheliah. But now he doesn't have a home anymore, and if he spends another night out in that cave, he could die—"

"I'm well aware that you want me to take him back here, Fada, but guilt-tripping me into it won't work—"

"I know that." It was too late to turn back now. I had to strike this deal, for Angel. My heart was beating fast, and it felt like my entire body was trembling.

"Then why are you here?"

"I… I know that you want me, Netis. I've seen the way you look at me."

His eyes widened again but I kept going, determined to go through with my plan.

"If you want me… I will give myself to you… you can have my body…"

Netis stepped backwards in shock.

"You would give yourself to me, to save Angel?"

"I love him, and I owe him. He sacrificed himself for me. It is only right that I do the same for him…"

Netis closed his eyes and turned to face the window, clenching and unclenching his fists. In that moment, he looked so vulnerable that a part of me wanted to close the space between us and wrap him in my arms. But I remained where I was, the logical part of me standing firm.

"You really do see me as a monster, don't you?" he whispered, still staring out of the window.

"I don't know what to think of you, Netis—"

"But you believe me capable of agreeing to use your body that way?"

I did not know how to answer. Perhaps I had been wrong about him; perhaps he did not desire me after all. I looked down, closing my eyes. I had no plan B, but I knew that I had to do something, and I needed to do it fast. Letting go of my logic, I tried to tune in to my instinct instead. Something was pushing me towards him, and I decided to let it guide me, relinquishing control of my body and allowing my intuition to take the lead.

I walked towards him and touched the nape of his neck with my fingertips. Netis turned around to face me, his expression unexpected. There was a gleam in those beautiful onyx eyes that was hard to understand: a

128

strange mixture of desire and affection. I gazed into his eyes for a few seconds, before slowly grabbing the nape of his neck and laying a kiss on his lips. I had no idea what was happening to me. I was kissing Netis, and for some strange reason, it felt good; it felt right. As soon as my lips touched his, a wave of contentment surged through me.

I felt his hand sliding along my arm towards my face, his delicate touch causing me to shiver, but not in an unpleasant way. He pulled back from me and looked into my eyes, his expression the same strange mixture of desire and affection. I did not know what he saw in my gaze, but after a second or two, he moved his face closer to mine, touching his lips to my own. Suddenly, the energy between us shifted, and he began to kiss me harder, running his hands down my back and pulling me closer to him. My hands grasped the back of his neck, and I began to run my fingers through his hair. I was no longer in control of my own body; I was barely thinking at all. All of me was here, in the present moment.

Netis slid his right hand up my back and started to unlace my dress, his movements gentle and delicate. He moved his lips from my mouth to my cheek, then down to my neck, as I felt my dress sliding down my body. I had been in such a hurry to get dressed that morning that I had not put on the bodysuit, so the dress was the only item of clothing standing between his hands and my

129

naked body. I had never been naked in front of a man before, and I tried desperately not to think about it, distracting myself by kissing him. I did not want to see the desire in his eyes; it would have made the moment all too real, and I was not ready to admit to myself that I was about to have sex with a man.

Netis tightened his hold on me and moved us towards the bed, but my trembling legs prevented me from staying upright, so I ended up collapsing onto the bed. He stood in front of me and took his shirt off, before lowering himself towards me and bringing his face close to mine. I turned my head to the right, still unable to meet his gaze, and he kissed my neck as I slid towards the middle of the bed. Netis followed my movements; the more I moved back, the closer his body was to mine. I felt so stupid because I had no idea what to do with my own hands. I supposed that I should have put them on him, but I was paralysed; unable to move.

Sliding his lips onto mine, he laid me down on the bed, and I could feel his right hand on my left leg as he spread my legs apart. He touched my thigh delicately, his fingers moving slowly towards my crotch. I tilted my head and sighed, shivering from head to toe as my body slowly relaxed, waves of pleasure pulsing through my veins. With that pleasure came guilt and shame: I should not be enjoying this, I was here to save Angel, but I could not help what my body was feeling.

After a moment, the waves of pleasure began to subside, and I felt him taking his trousers off. Suddenly, I was afraid. I knew what was coming, but at the same time, what was about to happen was entirely unknown to me, and I could not stop my body from tensing at the thought. He spread both my legs even more and laid on top of me, his gestures rougher now, though I could feel that he was controlling his strength. He started kissing me, softly at first, then harder, and in that moment, I felt him coming inside me. My head instantly jolted backwards and I had to stifle a scream of pain, thrusting my nails into his back, my breathing quick. The first few strokes were agony, even though he was gentle with his movements, and I grabbed his back tighter, keeping my eyes shut and trying to control my moan of pain. I had not expected to feel like this.

My eyes were still shut but I felt Netis lay a gentle kiss on my cheek. It relaxed me a bit, and I unclenched my fingers that were still plunged into his back. As my body began to relax, the initial pain faded, and I found the strength to finally open my eyes. We lay like that for some time, though I could not say how long. Time had no meaning anymore; I was living entirely in the present moment. I sighed as he began to pulse back and forth on top of me. Feeling him inside my now relaxed body was lighting up a fire in my veins, the flames coming in waves. The stronger his strokes were, the stronger the waves were too. Eventually, his back-and-forth movements became faster, his body almost crushing mine as he buried his face into the hollow of my neck. After a few more strokes, he stopped moving, leaving both our bodies trembling with adrenaline. Withdrawing himself slowly, he stayed on top of me for a moment, regaining his breath, before moving away to sit on the edge of the bed.

I looked up at the ceiling, my thoughts completely empty as I regained my breath. I could not comprehend what I had just done, and I had no idea what I needed to do next. I felt numb, my body and mind frozen in shock. Eventually, I managed to take a deep breath and sit upright. My fingers felt sticky, and looking down at them, I saw they were covered with blood. I panicked, turning towards Netis, but seeing him quickly answered my questions. There, on his back, were the consequences of my fear: deep red scratches, dripping with blood. It looked as though he had fought a wild beast, but it was my hands that had done this to him. I started to tremble, hot tears pouring down my cheeks. Netis turned, shocked by my tears, and instantly drew me towards him, holding me gently in his arms.

"I'm so sorry… I didn't mean to… hurt you…" I stammered between sobs.

His eyes widened in surprise.

"Shh… I'm fine, Fada, don't worry," he murmured,

rocking me softly.

I relaxed into his embrace and lay my head on his shoulder, still crying. I did not understand my own behaviour; why was I so upset by the scars on his back? Perhaps I was simply overwhelmed by everything that had happened, but it still did not make sense that I was thinking about his wellbeing in this way. Eventually, my emotional and physical exhaustion caught up with me, and I fell asleep in his arms.

When I woke up, the light was different; at least one or two hours must have passed. I was lying in Netis' bed, a pile of duvets covering my naked body. Sitting up slowly, keeping the duvets in front of me, I wiped away the salty tear stains from my cheeks. Netis was standing in front of his window, his hands behind his back. He must have sensed that I was awake because he turned to look at me, smiling. He started to walk towards me but I looked at him with shame in my eyes, remembering the scars on his back. A look of pain crossed his face and he looked down, his smile fading.

"You fell asleep, so I took the liberty of laying you down in my bed," he explained.

"Thank you, that was very thoughtful of you," I answered, trying to sound calm.

"You can leave now; I mustn't keep you. The storm will be starting in an hour or so. You need to get back home before then."

I did not understand why he looked so serious. I was afraid that he was angry with me for hurting him, or that he had not experienced as much pleasure as he had anticipated when he had agreed to have sex with me. I had not thought about his pleasure at all. I had been too focused on my own pain; my own pleasure; the bizarre reality of the situation I had found myself in. My muscles tightened with anxiety. What if he refused to take Angel back? What if I had not been enough to satisfy his desires? Worse still, what if he threatened to tell Angel, or Maheliah, about what I had done?

"I would really appreciate it if we could keep this between ourselves, Netis. I don't want Angel to know what I just did," I murmured softly, looking down in shame.

"What did you just do?"

I blushed, not understanding what game Netis was playing.

"The deal we made... and the way we concluded it..." I managed to murmur, looking back at him.

He seemed surprised, and looked like he was about the say something. But he stopped himself, smirking and raising his eyebrows instead. Turning to face the window again, he crossed his hands behind his back.

"You may inform Angel that he is allowed to come back," he stated, looking out of the window. "And you don't need to worry. I will not tell anyone what happened here."

I did not understand why he was reacting this way; he had been so sensitive, so gentle… but now he seemed severe and heartless again. Confused, but not wanting to annoy him further, I climbed out of the bed and dressed myself, before walking towards the door. I stopped there for a second, turning back to face him, but he was still looking out of the window. Strangely saddened by his coldness, I opened the door and left, making my way slowly down the stairs.

Walking out of the back gate in a daze, I barely acknowledged the guards as I left Netis' palace and walked slowly back to Maheliah's Court. I had given myself to Netis to save Angel, but though I had expected to suffer physically and emotionally, the experience had been strangely pleasurable. I had assumed that I would despise being touched by Netis, but feeling his skin on my skin had been soothing, and his behaviour had been the exact opposite to what I had expected. He had been kind, gentle and caring with me, and in his arms I had felt understood and protected. Why?

My mind was in turmoil. Not only was I confused about what had happened with Netis, but I also had no idea how I was going to tell Angel that he had been pardoned. He would probably ask me how I had managed to change Netis' mind, and I had no idea what lie to tell him. What if he was too sick to return to the palace? It had been many hours since I had last seen him, what if his condition had worsened? Suddenly anxious, I started running, arriving outside the cave a few minutes later. Angel was still in the same position as he had been when I had left him that morning, and he did not look well at all. His lips were still a concerning shade of blue and his skin was as white as snow. I ran towards him and cupped his face in my hands, kissing his cheek.

"Oh Angel, I'm so sorry I wasn't with you today."

"No... I understand... I'm not really... very interesting... right now..." he stuttered, his voice weak and broken.

"Don't be silly, that's not the reason at all. I... I talked to Netis. It took me a while, but I finally convinced him to agree to take you back. I hurried here as fast as I could to tell you the good news," I exclaimed, trying to sound cheerful.

Angel looked desperately into my eyes.

"Can I... really go back...? How did you convince him?"

"It doesn't matter, you're safe now. You're going to be okay."

Slowly, I helped Angel to his feet. His legs were

trembling, but he just about managed to stand upright, leaning on me for support. I dared not look into his eyes; I hoped that I would still be able to behave normally around him despite my betrayal. No matter how hard I tried to convince myself that I had only had sex with Netis to save Angel, I could not fail to recognise how cruel my behaviour had been. I had broken the trust of the man I loved. Sighing silently to myself, I tried to put those thoughts behind me. It was too late to regret my choices now. Angel was safe, that was all that mattered.

Picking up my frozen pillow and duvets, I walked slowly back to the main gate of Maheliah's palace, with Angel using my shoulder as a crutch. When we arrived in front of the palace, Maheliah was waiting for us.

"The guardians came to tell me that you had returned. I'm guessing you've once again been to Netis' palace without my permission? I suppose your visit was as useless as this morning?"

"It wasn't, actually. I managed to convince him to allow Angel to return to the palace."

Maheliah's eyes widened in surprise. She knew Netis better than I did, so I could only imagine how unexpected this news was to her. Netis was not the kind of person to compromise.

"How incredible... I am impressed... and delighted for you, Angel, of course. Shall I open a portal for you? You look far too weak to open one yourself," Maheliah asked, looking at Angel.

Angel took my hand in his trembling fingers and laid a kiss on it, before thanking Maheliah for everything that she had done for him. She smiled, swiftly opening a portal, which Angel promptly entered, smiling back at me before he disappeared. With the portal closed, Maheliah and I walked back inside the palace.

"I'm glad Angel is safe now. He's a sweet boy. I can see why you are so fond of him."

"I'm glad too, and forever grateful to you, Maheliah, for looking after him as best you could. You have been kind to him, despite him being a traitor."

"It's thanks to him that you are by my side now; I owe him for that. Besides, I can see that he will always protect you."

We dumped the duvets and pillow in the washroom before heading to the dining room for our evening meal. I ate in silence, my mind still in turmoil. I had saved Angel; I was proud of myself for that. But in doing so, I had completely overturned my opinion of Netis. I had hated him with a passion, but as soon as his lips had touched mine, something had changed. I had felt content in his arms; his gestures had been gentle and caring; he had looked after me. Now that I was away from him, I could not stop thinking about him, and about the scars I had left on his back. I told myself that I was simply concerned for his wellbeing. I just wanted to check that

138

he was okay, and that he had taken care of his injury. But deep down, I knew that I was just desperate for an excuse to see him again. I needed to be close to him again, to gaze into his eyes, into his soul. Thinking about his hands on my body and his lips on mine made me realise that I needed to see him again as soon as possible.

"Maheliah, would you allow me to go back to Netis' palace tomorrow?" I asked quietly.

"Why would you want to go back there? You've already saved Angel. You don't need to see Netis again," she answered, surprised by my strange request.

"I know… I just thought I might be able to reason with him about the war, since I succeeded in helping Angel…"

Obviously, I could not tell her why I actually wanted to see him, though the excuse I had given her was not a complete lie. I could ask him about the war as well, and I reasoned that, since he had been willing to take Angel back, he might be willing to at least consider ending this stupid quarrel between himself and Maheliah.

"I'm not sure, Fada. I don't want Netis to hurt you again. He has such a bad temper, and you never know how he might react to certain things you say."

"I know he can be temperamental, but he didn't hurt me this time. I'm sure I could reason him. It would take time, but it's worth trying."

139

Maheliah gave me a serious look, then sighed, smiling.

"Well, I suppose I can't just lock you up in your bedroom," she laughed.

I smiled, elated that she had agreed to let me see him again. I knew that she was not too happy about me going back there, but she was right. She could not lock me up in my room forever.

Once dinner was finished, I went to fetch some hot water and a towel and brought them up to my room. I needed a wash, but it was too late now to go down to the hot springs. It felt good to be clean, and as I washed the last of the sweat and grime off my body, my mind drifted back to Netis. I could not imagine that he had been satisfied by our liaison; he had surely expected me to pleasure him in some way, but I had just laid there, paralysed, before digging my nails into his back. I was fairly sure he must have realised that it had been my first time, yet I could not stop thinking that he had probably been disappointed by my behaviour. I needed to show him that I could do better, that I wanted to pleasure him. His hands had touched my body with so much care; I felt the need to do the same to him.

It felt wrong to admit that I wanted him, but I could not deny the desire I felt. He was a handsome man, and I liked the way he looked deep into my eyes, gazing into my soul. His touch was soft but intoxicating, and every time he smiled, I felt a wave of wellbeing course through my veins. I was desperate to feel his hands on me again; tomorrow could not come soon enough.

CHAPTER VIII - AKAOH

It felt like a repeat of the previous day as I stood at the entrance to Netis' palace. The same two guards stood by the door, though unlike yesterday, they did not approach me, indeed, they barely acknowledged my presence, keeping their eyes firmly on the ground. I glanced at their faces and noticed that they were both sporting dark purple bruises. I wondered what had happened to them, but not wanting to risk engaging in conversation, I walked through the door, leaving my questions behind. Strangely, they did not say a word, and let me enter without trying to stop me.

Making my way up the stairs, I came to Netis' bedroom door. Everything was the same as yesterday, except that I had no deal to make this time. What was I doing here? Did I really want to see this man again? Why? Taking a deep breath, I knocked and opened the door, pushing my fear and confusion aside. Netis was exactly where he had been the day before: standing in front of his window with his hands crossed behind his back. He turned sharply, angrily uttering some words in his language, but when he realised that I was the intruder, his eyes widened and he stopped talking. I shut the door quietly behind me and began to walk towards him.

"To what do I owe the honour of your visit?" he asked, after a moment of silence.

I did not answer, coming closer to him instead, until my eyes settled on my bracelet, which was sitting on his desk. I had completely forgotten about it, but now I remembered that Netis had taken it off the day before, to look at my scar. He followed my gaze and touched the bracelet with his fingertips.

"I see. You came back for your bracelet. I understand, you don't want people to see the scar I gave you—"

I placed my hand over his mouth and whispered a brief 'shh', looking deep into his eyes. My other hand found his, the one that was holding my bracelet, and pushed the bracelet away, entwining his fingers with mine.

"I'm not here for my wound, but for yours," I murmured.

Netis tried to say something, but I stopped him with a look, moving my hands down to grip the lower part of his shirt. Pulling it upwards, I eased it over his head and

143

arms as he looked at me in surprise. I moved my head to the side, signalling that I wanted him to turn around. The gleam in his eyes was intense and confused, but he turned around anyway. The sight of his back stabbed at my heart. It looked like he had been tortured, though at least the cuts had begun to heal now. It was not as bad as I remembered it being, and seeing all the old scars he already had on his back, I could only imagine how insignificant these new wounds were to him. I slid my fingers over his skin, gently caressing the scars with my fingertips, before placing my hands on his waist and tenderly laying a kiss on his tortured back.

"I'm so sorry…"

Netis turned and stared at me. He seemed lost, and I could understand how strange my behaviour must seem to him. But I could see the desire in his eyes, burning like the embers of a dying fire, and my need for him intensified.

"Your hand hurt me once, but you redeemed yourself by touching my body with kindness. My hands hurt you yesterday, so now I want to show you that they can be gentle too."

I slid my hands around his neck and brought my face close to his, but I did not have time to kiss him, for he instantly laid his lips on mine with passion, his hands sliding around my waist, pulling me towards him. As soon as our lips met, the same wave of wellbeing that I had felt the day before washed over me, and I lost myself in the moment. Desperate to feel his hands on my skin, I guided his fingers towards the back of my dress; understanding what I wanted, he quickly unlaced me, sliding the fabric down my body. It still felt strange to be naked in front of a man, yet the sparkle in Netis' eyes as he looked me up and down sent a shiver of pleasure down my spine. I had never considered myself particularly beautiful, but the way he stared at me made me feel like a goddess.

Once we had reached the bed, I pushed the centre of his chest, forcing him to sit on the edge, and lowered myself onto his lap, moving my hips back and forth over his crotch, on top of his trousers. I could feel that my movements were pleasuring him, and he kissed my neck passionately, running his hands over my back and my breasts. It felt good to see him enjoying this moment, and it was fantastic to feel his hands on me again.

My right hand was still on his chest, and I moved it slowly towards his crotch, unlacing the front of his trousers. My heart was thumping fast, unsure whether I was doing the right thing, as I reached inside and started to pleasure him with my hand. His breathing became ragged, and he gripped my body harder, grabbing my bum and my breasts. I felt a wave of heat roll through my body and I sighed with pleasure. Netis brought his hand down to my crotch and began to pleasure me too,

145

both of us breathing heavily as we touched each other.

Eventually, Netis grabbed my waist and laid me down on the bed. His gesture had been rough but in a good way, and as he grabbed my wrists and pushed my hands above my head, I spread my legs to let him come between them. My gaze met his and it felt like I could no longer move my eyes. I was transfixed by his beautiful onyx eyes, gazing at me with so much desire and care. In that instant, I wished for this moment never to end.

While Netis was still holding my wrists together and looking deep into my eyes, he came inside me, and I moaned with pleasure, my head tilting backwards and my eyes shutting automatically. I opened them again and found Netis smiling softly. He moved his face closer to mine and kissed me passionately, biting my lower lip as I sighed in ecstasy. He released my wrists slowly and slid his fingers along my arms, putting his left hand on the bed next to my head as he grabbed my left breast with his other hand, kissing it in soft, circular movements. It felt like a thousand tiny butterflies were fluttering inside my stomach, and my desire for him grew even stronger. I could feel the weight of his body crushing mine, his back-and-forth movements sometimes soft, sometimes harsh.

After a few minutes, I placed my hands on his waist and moved slightly to the left. Netis seemed to understand that I wanted to move because he stopped thrusting, turning over onto his back as we kissed passionately. I started to move up and down slowly on top of him and Netis began to moan loudly as the heat within me grew more intense. I grabbed his hands and put them on my breasts, looking into his eyes and smiling. I did not understand how I could have adjusted so quickly. The previous day, I could not even look at him, but right now, losing myself in his eyes was all I wanted to do. It was incredible to see the pleasure he was feeling, and it made me happy to see that he seemed to desire me as much as I desired him.

Grabbing my bum and pulling me closer to him, he began to move his hips up and down strongly. I laid my upper body on top of his and bit his chest gently, breathing deeply, waves of pleasure cascading over my body. A few minutes later, I felt his hands gripping my bum even tighter, then, little by little, he stopped moving, both of us breathing heavily. His fingers slid down my legs as I moved to lay on my stomach next to him. The waves of pleasure had not disappeared yet, and it felt like they never would. I was no longer in control of my own thoughts; I barely knew who I was. All that mattered in this instant was that I was enjoying the present moment. Everything felt right.

A couple of hours had passed since I had returned from Netis' palace, and I was sitting in my room, staring out of my bedroom window, lost in thought. As soon as I had arrived back at Maheliah's, the reality of what I had just done hit me. I should have felt ashamed, but I did not. It felt right somehow, when Netis touched me. He made me feel content, complete, and I could not deny my desire for him.

I sighed with frustration. None of this made any sense. I was in love with Angel, that I was certain of, yet I also felt this need to be close to Netis. I tried to convince myself that the only reason I was drawn to him was because I had discovered the joy of sex with him, but the reality was quite different. My connection with him was so much more than just sexual desire; even just being in the same room as him made me feel relaxed. I felt so comfortable, so calm in his presence. Why? I hated the fact that I did not understand my own emotions. I had only known Netis for a couple of days, why did I feel this way?

A knock on the door rescued me from my musings, and I smiled as Maheliah entered.

"Did you talk to Netis today?" she asked.

"Yes… but I'm afraid I don't have anything new to report…" I answered, blushing.

"See, I told you. It's useless to try and reason with Netis, he's too obstinate."

"We just have to be patient, Maheliah. I know I'll succeed eventually."

Talking about Netis made me lose myself in my thoughts again, and though Maheliah was speaking to me, I could not hear her. Talking about Netis' obstinate temper made me think of Akaoh. I remembered Maheliah telling me that Akaoh had raised Netis to be a heartless warrior, and that he had given Netis my bracelet, many years ago. It seemed such a strange gift for a king to give to a young man whom he was training to be insensitive and ruthless. It made me want to understand more about this mysterious High King, and his relationship with Maheliah and Netis.

"Fada, are you listening to me?" Maheliah asked in an irritated voice.

"Sorry, Maheliah, I was just thinking… could you tell me more about Akaoh?"

"Akaoh? What do you want to know about Akaoh?" she asked, her eyes wide with surprise.

"I'd like to understand how he managed to educate two such different people; you and Netis are nothing alike at all. It's intriguing. He must have been incredibly powerful."

"You're right, he is extremely powerful."

"He is? You mean, he's still alive?"

149

"As far as I know, yes. He's more than a hundred and twenty years old now though, and the last time I saw him, he did not look his best…"

"Wait, how is that possible?" I interrupted, confused.

"What do you mean? It's common here for people to live well into their hundreds. Isn't it on Earth too?"

"Not at all. Most people don't even reach one hundred years old. How old are you and Netis?"

"We turned fifty years old a few months ago."

"What? How is that possible? You look like you're in your thirties!"

"From what Akaoh told me about Earth, it appears that we grow at the same pace as humans until we are twenty years old or so, but from then on, we seem to age half as quickly, hence why Netis and I look younger than you might expect."

I stared at Maheliah. Every day seemed to bring with it some new, unexpected revelation.

"So, Akaoh is more than a hundred and twenty years old…" I continued, still confused.

"Yes, if he's still alive. I haven't seen him in a long time. Shortly before I left the main palace, he retired to the ruins of the old palace without explaining why, though I'm guessing he had probably had enough of my constant arguments with Netis. Knowing him, he's probably still going strong, though I have no idea how he gets food over there."

"What do you mean 'the old palace'?"

"The palace where Netis and I grew up. It was built by our ancestors hundreds of years ago; we used to live there before Akaoh and Netis built the new one. During the old times, life in Hagalaz was quite different, and many incredible balls and banquets were held at the palace..."

"Can you tell me more about Akaoh's life?"

"Of course, though I can only tell you what I have heard and read. Akaoh never spoke much about his past."

"That's okay, I'd just like to know more about him, and about the history of Hagalaz. There's still so much I don't know."

"All right then. Five hundred years ago, after hundreds of years of war, our ancestor built a new palace, to celebrate the rebirth of our kingdom. Hagalaz had always been wealthy, but this time was particularly prosperous, as no more wealth was being wasted on war. There were banquets almost every day and distinguished guests came to stay at the palace, dining on the finest foodstuffs imported from all over the kingdom and beyond.

Life was peaceful for many years, until Othalaz once again declared war on Hagalaz. The kingdom of Laguz came to our aid, and finally, Othalaz was vanquished, restoring peace to Hagalaz. However, this aid came at a price, and the princess of Hagalaz was the one to pay it. She was sent to Laguz to marry the prince, as a thank you for their help and in order to unite the two kingdoms. This sort of arrangement between two kingdoms had never been made before, but it was the only way to keep Laguz on our side. That princess was Akaoh's sister, but though he was only four years younger than her, they were not close at all. She grew up understanding her role as a princess and accepting that she might have to sacrifice her own happiness for the good of her people. Akaoh, on the other hand, had quite a different temperament. He was fiercely independent, and though he had many teachers and advisors who could have made him a strong warrior and a great king, he refused to listen to any of them, always learning by himself and making his own rules. Most of his advisors died mysteriously, and some believed that Akaoh was responsible for these deaths.

The king, Akaoh's father, died not long after the princess was sent to Laguz, and Akaoh became king of Hagalaz. It is said that he played a part in the death of both his parents and his sister, but nothing official has ever been confirmed. By the age of sixty, he was the only remaining royal, and decided to marry Heliah, the strongest and most resilient female warrior of that time. She was a fierce woman, and her gaze was harsh and brittle, her eyes sparkling like a thousand tiny fires.

Life was more peaceful and prosperous than ever before, and the other kingdoms envied us. After many years, Othalaz decided to wage war against Hagalaz yet again, mostly because they desired the diamond eyes of the fierce queen. There were many battles, and Heliah killed hundreds of Othal warriors, making her the most feared Hagal warrior in the history of our kingdom. One day, Akaoh heard a soul calling to him, and soon afterwards, Heliah heard a soul as well. Months later, Netis and I were born.

We grew up during wartime, and Akaoh started training Netis at a very young age. When Netis was only ten years old, Akaoh took him out onto the battlefield, and by the age of thirteen, Netis was fighting alongside him. Netis was injured multiple times, but Akaoh never ceased his training, and continued to force him to fight before his wounds had fully healed. Heliah never cared much for me, but then, she did not consider herself our mother. She was more interested in fighting and winning the war than caring for us.

I was left with a series teachers and advisors, who taught me the history of Hagalaz and how to be the perfect princess. Akaoh refused to allow me to become a warrior like Heliah, though I never understood why. Instead, he wished for me to learn the details of our laws and customs, so that I might rule Hagalaz one day.

When Netis and I reached the age of sixteen, the war

finally came to an end, thanks to an agreement between Akaoh and the King of Othalaz. To this day, I still have no idea what this agreement was about; Akaoh kept it secret from everyone, including Heliah. But despite peace being restored, our wartime childhood had shaped Netis and I, and whilst it had made me determined to do everything in my power to maintain peace in Hagalaz, it had turned Netis into a fearless, pitiless warrior, just like Akaoh. Akaoh seemed to have no feelings at all: no hate; no love; no sadness; no happiness. He was permanently stoical, and nothing seemed to affect him. I was terrified of Netis becoming like him, for although our education had been different, we had grown close to each other over the years, and I feared that he would not care for me anymore if he became like Akaoh. But thankfully, many peaceful years passed, and even though Netis was stoical and pitiless towards everyone else, he was still caring towards me.

During these peaceful years, Akaoh and Netis built the new palace, and we all moved there once it was finished, leaving the old palace behind. That same year, we heard your soul calling to us, and Othalaz once again decided to wage war against us. Heliah was killed by the king of Othalaz during the first battle, and I remember Netis telling me that Akaoh had calmly watched the king of Othalaz tear Heliah's eyes from her face, as though watching someone give a particularly dull speech, before carrying on with his day as if nothing had happened. That was when I became queen of Hagalaz, and I believe I have told you the rest…"

I stared at her in disbelief as I tried to process all this information. Akaoh, the once fearless and heartless king, had gladly handed over his throne and was now living in the secluded ruins of his old palace. I had a hard time accepting that Maheliah's story was not just some fiction.

"I am sure you have a great many questions, which I will gladly answer for you. I must insist, however, that you do not try and visit Akaoh," Maheliah warned, dragging me out of my daze.

"Why not?" I asked, surprised that she thought I would consider doing something so reckless.

"As I have just told you, he is not a pleasant person. You may think that Netis is heartless, but he is nothing compared to Akaoh. I must ask you to promise me that you will never try to find him. He could be dangerous."

"Of course, I promise…"

Deep down, I knew that I would not be able to keep that promise. I was dying to meet Akaoh. Maheliah's story had intrigued me, and I wanted to understand how someone could become so powerful, and so emotionless. Something was pushing me towards meeting him and I knew that I would not be satisfied until I had seen this mysterious being with my own eyes.

155

CHAPTER IX - NEW FRIENDS

A couple of weeks had passed since I had arrived in Hagalaz, and I was slowly adjusting to my new life. Maheliah had decided that I needed to learn to speak the Hagal language, so I had spent the past ten days studying intensively. My teachers had kept me incredibly busy, so I had not had the chance to sneak off and see Netis again since our second liaison.

Gradually, I started to understand basic sentences, and I began to practise with Maheliah, Lilhya, Nalhya and then Angel. He had come to visit me a couple of times, not only because he wanted to see me but also because Netis had asked him to, apparently. He never came inside the palace – Maheliah would not allow it – so we would always walk up to the lake together. Angel was delighted to hear me speaking their language, and he was himself a great teacher, helping me with my pronunciation and gently correcting my mistakes.

Although I was busy, and enjoying learning a new

language, my mind often drifted back to Netis, and after two weeks of not seeing him, I was struggling to focus on anything else. Knowing that there was no point in me trying to learn anything else until I had seen him, I snuck out early one morning, and made my way to Netis' palace. I knew my preoccupation with Netis was wrong, especially since I had Angel in my life, but I could not shake my desire for him. I needed to feel Netis' hands on me again.

Recognising me instantly, the palace guards silently moved aside and allowed me to enter the palace. Stepping inside, I was about to walk up the stairs towards Netis' bedroom when someone grabbed my arm, jerking my body backwards. I turned swiftly, furious that someone had touched me without my authorisation, and found myself face to face with a stranger. The man uttered a few words in the Hagal tongue, and I managed to understand that Netis was not in his bedroom, and that I should be waiting for him in the throne room.

It was the first time I had met someone inside Netis' palace other than Netis and Angel, and I felt suddenly afraid. Who was he? How did he know I was here? I tried to explain to him that I wanted to wait for Netis in his bedroom, but the man insisted that I follow him, and since I could not understand much of what he was telling me, it felt like I had no choice. Shaking his arm off me, I nodded hesitantly, signalling to him that I was willing to follow him. Nodding in response, he beckoned me down the corridor, walking a little way in front of me.

The further we walked, the more anxious I became. I had a strange feeling about this man; his smile felt off, and he looked as if he was up to no good. I knew that I was not welcome in this palace, just as I was not welcome in Maheliah's palace, but I feared that if I did not follow his commands he would call for others, and I could be trapped in a difficult situation.

Finally, we reached a door, and my guide opened it, gesturing for me to go inside. Upon entering, I realised that he had not led me to the throne room, but to the dining room instead. The room was almost identical to the dining room in Maheliah's palace, only her dining room did not feature three despicable looking men, all of whom were leering at me with wicked glints in their eyes.

As soon as I entered the room, one of the men in front of me tilted his head at the man behind me, and I felt my 'guide' grab my arms violently, while someone else blindfolded me and covered my mouth with another piece of fabric. Everything happened so quickly that I did not have time to defend myself or scream for help. I was paralysed by fear and confusion. What were they going to do to me? Kidnap me? Lock me up? Kill me instantly? My heart was beating fast as I thrashed around, trying to free myself from their grasp.

The man who had led me here turned me around, and I could feel his hot breath on my face. He tried to tie my hands in front of me, but I moved away, trying to keep myself from being restrained. I had to fight, even though I knew I would not succeed in doing much against four men. I tried to scream, but my cries were muffled by the fabric in my mouth, so I struggled instead, but more hands grabbed me, forcing my wrists together. I knew that they would probably kill me, slowly and painfully, torturing me until I was no longer able to scream. After all, it was because of me that their king and queen were quarrelling. In their eyes, killing me was the answer to ending this war.

I felt tears brimming at the corners of my eyes. I had never been so terrified in all my life, and being blindfolded only made everything worse. I was completely disorientated; I had no idea what they were going to do to me, and I would have no way of knowing what was happening until I felt the impact of their blows. I could feel the panic rising as my heart beat faster, threatening to escape from my chest in terror.

I could hear them arguing as they manhandled me, and I felt the cold hard surface of the table on my back as they forced me to lie flat. I could not understand anything – they were speaking too fast – but eventually,

159

one of them moved in front of me, as the others started to shout even louder. I felt his hand pushing down on my stomach, and the ice cold feel of a blade touching my neck. He did not say anything, but I could feel his breath on my face as he moved the blade slowly down from my throat to my chest. I tried to scream but again my voice was muffled by the fabric in my mouth. The blade cut through the top of my dress in a rapid movement, and I felt the man in front of me pulling at the fabric of my bodice. I suddenly realised what they had planned and my whole body shivered with fear.

The man's hot, sweaty hand grabbed my left breast, and I felt his face come closer to me as he whispered some unknown words in my ear. Crying bitterly, I kept on trying to escape, thrashing against his grasp. The other men all started laughing, probably happy to see me struggling so much. I felt so hopeless. There was no way I could fight my way out of this. They would all abuse me, one by one, and there was nothing I could do to stop it. I wished that they would just kill me. Even torture would be better than this.

Suddenly, the laughter stopped, and I felt the man lift himself off me. One of the men shouted something angrily in their language, but another voice cut him off, a voice that I recognised. Angel. I wanted to scream his name, but my voice was still muffled by the blindfold. He spoke again, slowly, his words crisp and clear.

"Leave her alone. Now."

The relief I felt upon hearing his voice and those words was tainted by fear: how could he possibly win against four fully-grown men? The man holding my wrists shouted something else at him and Angel answered, louder this time, his voice almost thunderous with rage. As he spoke, I heard screams of pain all around me, and the pressure on my wrists suddenly disappeared. Frantically, I removed my blindfold, but my eyesight was blurred by my residual tears. Blinking, I slowly recovered my sight, my mind simultaneously processing that the room was eerily silent.

Four men were lying on the floor, unmoving, and as I stared at their oddly twisted bodies, I finally understood what had happened. Angel had used his powers and shocked them unconscious. I turned my head in his direction, my eyes wide with fear. Angel's expression was severe and his jaw was tight with tension; I had never seen him so angry. Slowly, he walked towards me, and gently removed the piece of fabric from my mouth. I was about to say something to him, but a motion in the corner of my eye distracted me, and I turned to face the door. Netis was here.

Looking around the room in confusion, Netis settled his gaze on me, his eyes full of questions and concern. He glanced at Angel, then back at me, his gaze flickering to my naked chest. He frowned, looking at

Angel, the muscles around his eyes tightening. I glanced at Angel, and the expression on his face shocked me. He was glaring at Netis, his eyes full of loathing. I looked back at Netis, afraid that he would be angered by Angel's inappropriate glare, but his face was calm. Clearing his throat, Netis met my gaze.

"Fada, what happened?"

I did not have time to answer, for Angel, who was still glaring at Netis, spoke in my place, rapidly explaining to Netis what had happened. I could not bear the distress in his voice, so I stood up quickly, covering my naked chest with my hand, and placed my other hand gently on Angel's cheek.

"Angel, please, calm down. There's nothing to worry about anymore. You arrived before they had the time to hurt me. Look at me, I'm all right."

I brought my face towards his, laying a tender kiss on his lips, and he wrapped his arms around my shoulders, holding me close. His embrace was strong, and I could hear his heart thumping fast, yet even in his arms, I could not help but glance at Netis out of the corner of my eye. He was looking at us, his eyes pained. It surprised me; I had never imagined that Netis would suffer seeing me in the arms of another man. After all, I was certain that he did not care for me personally; he had only used me to satisfy his sexual desire. I had convinced myself that he did not even feel friendship for

162

me, let alone feelings stronger than that, so his expression confused me. Why did he look so sad?

As soon as he realised I was looking at him, he blinked, his emotionless mask returning. Frowning, his gaze became serious, and he spoke sternly to Angel. Yet again, I did not understand what was being said, but when he had finished talking, Angel looked at me with a faint smile, kissing my forehead tenderly. Squeezing my arms reassuringly, he turned and walked out of the room, leaving me alone with Netis.

As soon as Angel had left, Netis came towards me, trying but failing to mask the pain behind his eyes.

"Are you all right?" he asked, gently caressing my shoulder with his fingers.

"Angel arrived in time, that's all that matters," I managed to utter. I was still trembling, but feeling Netis' hand on my shoulder calmed me, and my heartbeat slowly returned to normal.

Resting both hands on my shoulders, Netis looked deep into my eyes, and I gazed back, trying to read his complex expression. 'The eyes are the mirror to the soul' was a saying that suited him perfectly; it was impossible not to see a soul in those deep, black eyes. Yet I was still unable to understand what he was thinking. He seemed concerned, and upset, an emotion I had never expected from him. He was a real mystery, but it felt like, during these last few minutes, I had

163

broken through the icy barrier that guarded his soul and caught a glimpse of the man beneath. I knew then that I would continue to see him, even if only to talk and be close to him. Fathoming the mystery of his soul was something I was willing to do every day, for the rest of my days.

Some of the men who had attacked me started to move, and Netis looked at them, frowning and gripping my shoulders protectively. Realising what he had done, he released me gently, before taking my hand and leading me away from the dining room, back down the corridor. Opening the main door, he spoke sharply to the two guards and they hurried inside, leaving the two of us alone.

"What did you tell Angel, before he left?" I asked, keeping his hand in mine.

"I ordered him to fetch some of the others and carry those traitors down to the prison cells."

"What will you do to them?"

"That's not something you need to worry about, Fada. Rest assured, they'll never hurt you again, I promise."

His voice was calm, but his eyes blazed with quiet rage, and he gripped my hand tighter.

I understood that their punishment would be far worse than I could imagine, and I felt safe in the knowledge that Netis would deal with them.

"Is there anything I can do for you? Why did you come here today?" he asked.

"I came to see you... to spend time with you..." I replied, blushing.

Netis moved closer to me, releasing my hand and taking my chin between his fingers. I tilted my face to meet his gaze, losing myself in his eyes. His expression was complex, a mixture of desire and sorrow, and after a few seconds, he turned away.

"You should go back to Maheliah's now. You need to rest, and get a new dress..."

His dismissal hurt; it felt like a rejection, like he did not want to see me anymore, and I felt a silent sob lodge itself painfully in my throat. Nodding silently, unable to speak, I began to walk away from him, but he took my hand gently in both of his. I turned to face him.

"Next time you come to the palace, make sure I'm here first. I have quite a busy schedule, you know. I'm not always daydreaming in my bedroom," he remarked with a smile.

His words brought a smile back to my face. Maybe he did want to see me again after all.

"I'll open a portal to Maheliah's, so you don't have to walk in the cold with your torn dress," he added, pulling me closer to him as he held his other hand in front of him and began to open the portal.

I was about to walk through it when Netis brought

his face close to mine, whispering in my ear.

"I'm truly sorry, Fada. This should never have happened to you. I promise I will never let you suffer like that again."

I stared at him, surprised by his unexpected show of compassion. I could not believe that he was apologising, especially for something that had been beyond his control. Maheliah barely thought him capable of showing any emotion that was not anger, let alone kindness, care, and compassion. It gave me hope that the two siblings might one day be able to reconcile their differences and accept one another again.

I smiled at him as I walked through the portal, arriving right in front of Maheliah's palace. I took a deep breath. I knew that Maheliah would panic when she saw the state of my dress, and given how difficult it was to get new dresses made, I hoped that this one was salvageable, or that someone in the palace would be willing to lend me something to wear for the time being.

As I entered the palace, holding my bodice together as best I could, the guardians looked at me with confusion. I felt ashamed, arriving back at the palace looking like this, and the jeering voices of the men who had attacked me were still looping around my head, intensifying my feelings of shame. I knew that I had no reason to feel this way. I had done nothing wrong, but no matter how much I told myself that this was not my

166

fault, the shame refused to fade.

As I walked up the stairs towards Maheliah's throne, she glanced up from the book she had been reading, raising her eyebrows in shock when she saw the state of me.

"Fada! What happened to you? Are you okay?" she cried, running towards me.

"I had a little trouble at Netis' palace, but I'm okay now."

"What happened? Are you hurt?"

"Maheliah, calm down, it's okay. Some men kidnapped me and tried to hurt me, but Angel arrived before they could do anything. It's okay."

"No, Fada, it's not okay. Netis should never have allowed something like this to happen to you…"

"Don't blame him, Maheliah. He wasn't there when it happened, and he apologised to me afterwards, even though it wasn't his fault."

"Netis apologised?"

"I know, I was as surprised as you are. But he was really kind to me. He even opened a portal so I didn't have to walk back here in the cold."

"He was kind? That doesn't make any sense…"

"It wasn't his fault, please don't be angry with him."

"You're right, it's my fault. I should have never allowed you to go back to his palace. It's too dangerous; you'll never go back there."

"No, Maheliah, please. Don't forbid me to see him, I'm so close to convincing him to end this war…"

"So you want to be killed after his rogues hurt you, one by one? Is that what you want, Fada?"

Maheliah's voice broke, her eyes brimming with tears. She looked so distressed by what had happened to me, and I could understand her concern. I had been terrified, but now, the whole thing seemed insignificant. They were just a group of idiots who had let their sex drive mislead them, and I knew that Netis would deal with them.

Clasping Maheliah's hands, I looked into her eyes.

"I know that you fear for my safety, but Netis will never allow anything like this to happen again. He knows that he can't trust these men, and he has promised me that he will deal with them. Besides, Angel lives in the palace; he will always be there to protect me."

"Angel may be strong, but he can't protect you against everything."

"I'm not so sure about that. He has this power… apparently it originates from another kingdom. It allows him to shoot electricity from his eyes and electrocute anyone who is a threat. He's stronger than he looks."

"I know how that power works, Fada. It can only be used when the bearer is trying to protect the most important person to them, which means you must be the switch…"

I started blushing. I had never put much thought into it, but it made sense. It was flattering, but I felt guilty. I was not sure I would ever be able to love him as completely as he loved me.

Maheliah was looking at the ceiling in silence, deep in thought. Finally, she sighed.

"Fine.... I won't prevent you from going back to Netis' palace, but you must make certain that he knows you are coming, and that he will be there when you arrive."

I smiled, hugging her tightly. Maheliah was like the mother I had never had. My own mother had died when I was born, and I had always felt envious every time I saw a mother and daughter together. I had always wanted to know what it felt like to be protected and cared for by a loving mother. Seeing my own mother look at me with admiration, or hearing her tell me how proud she was of me, had always been one of my greatest wishes, but I had made peace with the notion that this would never happen. Of course, my dad had been a wonderful father, if a little overprotective sometimes, but it was not the same thing, and I had always felt like I had a gap in my heart that needed to be filled. Now that my bond with Maheliah was becoming stronger with each passing day, I was hopeful that, eventually, she might be able to fill this void.

Maheliah told me to go up to my bedroom, informing

169

me that she would meet me there in a minute. Walking upstairs, I shut the door behind me and collapsed onto my bed, grabbing my pendant from beside my bed. I lay there, looking at the photos of my dad and brother. I wondered how they would have reacted to my current situation. My dad would almost certainly have yelled at me and forbidden me from seeing Netis again. In fact, he would probably have forbidden me from meeting Netis at all, not because he was a cruel being, but because he was a handsome man. My dad would have immediately assumed that I was meeting up with Netis for more than just conversation, and he would have hated the idea of a man like him touching me, especially given the age difference between us. Maheliah, on the other hand, appeared to not even have considered that possibility, and for that I was grateful. Keeping our relationship, if you could call it that, secret from everyone was probably for the best, especially since I had no idea how I felt about him, or how he felt about me.

I was still daydreaming when Maheliah entered my room, followed by Nalhya and Lilhya. I stood up immediately, placing the pendant back on my bedside table.

"As you know, Fada, it is very difficult for us to acquire new fabric and sew more dresses, but upon your arrival, I decided to get one of my dresses altered to fit

170

you. I wanted to save it for once you had become more familiar with this new life of yours, but given current circumstances, we cannot wait any longer."

Maheliah seemed excited by this dress, her behaviour having changed remarkably quickly. Nalhya and Lilhya undressed me carefully, before helping me into the new dress. Maheliah was looking at me with wide eyes and a massive smile on her face.

"Oh, Fada, you look absolutely gorgeous! Worthy of a great future queen," she exclaimed.

Seeing her look so happy made me smile, and as I glanced at Nalhya and Lilhya, I noticed that they looked just as delighted as Maheliah. Curious to see what had made them all so excited, I turned to look at myself in the mirror.

The white fabric was tight-fitting from my chest to my hips, becoming looser from the tops of my legs down to the floor. Just like on the other dress, there were two flounces, but these ones fanned out in a V shape from the centre of my bodice down to the floor, merging with the rest of the dress. The straps were loose and sat lightly on my arms, just above my arm bracelet. Where the two flounces met, a magnificent topaz had been sewn onto the bodice, and by the choice of that gem, I guessed that topaz was now my official Anam stone, being the same light brown as my pupils. I had never seen such a beautiful dress; it was hard to believe that it

171

was mine.

"Now no one will be in any doubt that topaz is your official personal gem," Maheliah grinned.

I turned around and hugged them all warmly, thanking them wholeheartedly. In this moment, I finally accepted who I truly was: the heir of Hagalaz. The misadventure at Netis' palace had opened my eyes to many things, and it had made me determined to show everyone that I deserved to be treated with respect. It would take some time for me to forget what had happened. Perhaps I would never forget. But regardless, I was determined to face my future with a strong mind. I was the future queen of this kingdom, and I was committed to fulfilling my destiny.

CHAPTER X - NOTHING CAN BE WITHOUT HIM

As the weeks went by, I became accustomed to living without my dad and brother, though I still missed them terribly sometimes. Getting used to life in Maheliah's palace took time, but slowly, things that had once seemed strange began to feel normal. Using a lantern was now second nature to me, and eating nothing but soup or vegetables for every meal did not feel inadequate anymore. It had been hard at first, and I sometimes still felt hungry after meals, but I would never say anything. I knew that I had to get used to this lifestyle, and quickly.

Unlike most things, getting used to the clothing was easy. On Earth, I had never been one to put any effort into my physical appearance, but here, with the help of Nalhya and Lilhya, it felt wonderful to get dressed up and do my hair. Hagal dresses were works of art, and it was nice to wear something that made me feel so beautiful. At first, I had felt deeply uncomfortable about being naked in front of the twins, but being forced to bathe in the hot springs every day quickly banished that discomfort, and I stopped trying to cover my nakedness. In the hot springs, it was pointless to try and hide my body. I was surrounded by other naked women, none of whom seemed to care about their nudity, so after the first few days I gave up, and by the end of the first week, I found myself enjoying the bathing sessions. Everyone was always so happy during this time, and the palace hierarchy did not exist in the hot springs. I was neither a lost girl from Earth, nor a princess. I was just myself.

Though I had decided to accept my status as a princess of Hagalaz, there were still days when I struggled to come to terms with that reality. Throughout my life on Earth I had either been ignored or bullied by everyone except my dad and brother, but here, everyone treated me with respect, or at least pretended to. Though they always put on a front of politeness when Maheliah was around, it was clear that Maheliah's subjects were not fond of me, and if I was left alone with them, their behaviour was always distant and cold. It saddened me that they refused to acknowledge me for who I was, but part of me understood their behaviour: in their eyes, I was the one who had destroyed their kingdom. Before I existed, everybody in Hagalaz had been united, but now,

174

since Netis and Maheliah had separated, everyone had been forced to choose a side. The kingdom was divided, and they all thought it was my fault, even though I was desperate for Netis and Maheliah to reconcile and be friends again.

Fortunately, Nalhya and Lilhya did not think like the rest of the Court, and we soon became firm friends, though it took them a while to understand that I wanted to be their equal. At first, they had been cautious around me, not wanting to say anything that might get them into trouble, but after a week of me insisting that I was not going to order them around or report them to Maheliah, they started to relax, becoming more like sisters to me than servants. We would talk and laugh together for hours, and I loved to hear them talk about their lives in Hagalaz, and they loved to listen to me talk about my previous life on Earth. Both of them desperately hoped that they would hear a soul calling to them one day, so that they could visit Earth themselves. It seemed strange to me that they were so fascinated by Earth – in my eyes, Earth was not nearly as exciting as Hagalaz – but I realised that, to them, Earth was as mysterious and foreign as Hagalaz had once been to me. It was only natural that they would be intrigued by something so unknown.

I also continued to meet up with Angel by the lake, and spending precious time with him in such a beautiful location always put a smile on my face. We usually met in the middle of the day, when the sun was reaching its zenith, and would sit and talk by the lakeside, wrapped in each other's arms, as we watched the rays of sunlight dance on the water. I adored spending time with him, and I was convinced that we were both madly in love with one another, but that did not stop me from continuing to visit Netis.

My relationships with these two men could not have been more different, and it confused me that I could desire them both at the same time. I was in love with Angel, I was sure of it, but I also yearned for Netis with a passion that I could not control. I needed to lose myself in his eyes; feel his hands on my body; experience the waves of pleasure that only he could light up inside me. When I was with him, nothing else mattered; I wanted to be with him all the time, but I also loved Angel. I had no idea what was happening to me, or why I felt like this, but no matter how many times I tried to convince myself that Angel was enough, I could not stop yearning for Netis. No matter how wrong it seemed, when I was with Netis, everything felt right.

After the first few weeks, my days all started to look the same. I woke up every morning to the sweet voices of

Nalhya and Lilhya, before heading downstairs to bathe in the hot springs. Then, once they had helped me dress and fix my hair, we would all head to breakfast, before I started my language lessons. Maheliah had informed me that all the neighbouring kingdoms spoke the same language – the Solish language – and after a couple of months, even Nalhya and Lilhya stopped speaking English to me, though my accent was still awful and my vocabulary was less than perfect.

Right after my Solish lessons, I would meet Angel by our secret place and spend a couple of hours with him, before heading back to the palace for lunch, followed by history lessons with Maheliah. Her lessons were always fascinating, and I learned many interesting things. But my favourite story of all was the tale about the curse of Hagalaz.

According to Maheliah, Hagalaz was once inhabited only by animals, until one day, thousands of years ago, when sorcerers from Earth found a way to open a portal to this land. Thrilled by their discovery, they decided to use Hagalaz as a sort of prison, banishing eleven people through the portal as a punishment for their bad behaviours. Within a year, winter came to Hagalaz, and never left, a powerful storm raging each night.

After surviving three nights by huddling together in the cavernous mountains, the prisoners feared that the storm would be the end of them unless they came up

177

with a solution. After much deliberation, they decided that their best option was to travel as far as they could, to try and find a place that was not affected by the storm.

Many hours later, they reached the shore, and met a group of sailors from another kingdom and followed them back to their settlement. There they stayed, learning the language and trading with them, using the goods they had bought with them from the mountains of Hagalaz. Realising that they could use goods from the mountains to trade with other communities, they began to set up a trading network with the surrounding kingdoms, using timber and other commodities from elsewhere to build a home for themselves in the mountains, enabling them to survive the glacial temperatures.

After a few years of prosperity, they realised that they could not bear children, which saddened them greatly. But after a few more years in Hagalaz, they began to hear the voices of souls calling to them from Earth. Eventually, one of them managed to open a portal to Earth, and they all travelled through it, hoping to stay there. But Hagalaz called to them, and they had no choice but to return with their new children.

With each new generation, the physical appearance of the people of Hagalaz and the offspring they brought back seemed to change, for the sorcerers, or perhaps something even more powerful, had cursed them, and their infertility and their gemstone eyes – which caused their people to be preyed upon by the other kingdoms – were all part of this terrible curse that had been thrown upon them. Gradually though, more of them became capable of opening portals, both within Hagalaz and on Earth, whenever they desired. This skill allowed them to grow their population, by retrieving the new lives that called to them from Earth. Thus, the people of Hagalaz survived, despite the curse, and continued to prosper.

I was drawn by the story of this curse because it was completely unbelievable, yet it explained so many things about this strange land. I was hopeful that it would be broken eventually and I yearned to see Hagalaz free and happy.

After my history lessons with Maheliah, I would walk over to Netis' palace and meet with him in his bedroom. Formalising our meetings like this ensured that Netis was always there to greet me, which made Maheliah feel less anxious about me visiting him, though had she known how our 'meetings' usually progressed, she would almost certainly have been less than happy about me being there. I always made sure that I left the palace long before nightfall, and once back at Maheliah's, I ate dinner with Maheliah and the others, before heading up to my room to read or draw before bed.

My life continued this way for several happy months, but throughout that time, I was plagued by more than just my complex relationship with Netis; Akaoh was constantly in the back of my mind. I knew that he was somewhere in Hagalaz, and for some reason, I desperately wanted to meet him. The concept of seeing this powerful, mysterious being with my own eyes haunted me. I knew that Maheliah would never allow me to talk to him, but I could not stop thinking about him, and one day, my resolve snapped.

I woke early, long before Nalhya and Lilhya usually came to wake me, and slipped out of the palace, making sure to wrap myself in a cloak to keep out the icy wind. According to Maheliah's deliberately vague instructions, the old palace was located to the west, not far from her own palace. It was not much to go on, but I reasoned that if I kept walking from the side of the palace, I would eventually find it. After all, though now in ruins, it had once been a palace… surely it would be impossible to miss?

As I trudged my way through the snow, my confidence began to falter. I knew nothing of this part of Hagalaz; there could be all manner of creatures living here… what would I do if I met one? No one had seen me leave the palace, and I was now too far away to call for help. My panic rising, I began to walk faster, shoving my way through the snowy wilderness. I need not have worried, for no more than five minutes later, I came upon what must have once been an enormous palace. Some of the walls and most of the turrets had collapsed now, but it was impossible not to imagine how vast it had once been.

I was used to everything being white in Hagalaz, even Netis' palace, yet these ruins had been built in a combination of black and rich, dark purple bricks. Gazing up in awe, I walked slowly towards the main gate, where three high columns stood, topped by black slates. A fourth column had existed in the past, but now lay on the ground, broken into pieces. Each column was decorated by a wrought iron motif, but these were barely visible now, having been destroyed by rust and the glacial winds. A giant, silver chandelier, now smashed into a thousand pieces, lay scattered in front of the entrance, alongside the remains of a massive iron throne. The giant wooden doors stood slightly ajar, held to the wall by wrought iron hinges. The long, black metal handles sprouted out of the wood like brambles, twisting to form a splendid rose where they re-joined the wood.

Bewitched by this enchanting place, I pulled gently on one of the handles and stepped inside. Most of the roof had fallen through, and shattered pieces of slate lay scattered over the floor, making it difficult to walk

181

without stabbing the soles of my feet. The walls and floor were crafted from the same dark purple stone as the outside of the palace, and apart from the shattered roof tiles, the great hall was totally empty. I could almost feel the ghosts wandering about.

I kept on walking, my gaze constantly flickering, trying to look around whilst also attempting to protect my feet from the shards of slate. After walking down what felt like an endless corridor, I noticed something gleaming to my right. Glancing across, I realised that the light was coming from a wooden door that had been left slightly ajar. Walking over to it, I discovered that it led to a ramshackle stairway, and after considering my options for a few seconds, I decided to follow the light and climb the stairs. Sunbeams filtered through the walls, helping me to distinguish where I was stepping, and as I climbed higher, I wondered what I might discover when I reached the top.

After an eternity, the stairway came to an end, and I found myself standing in front of a small wooden door. A disturbing feeling came over me; I felt like I was being watched, and I pushed the door open, trying to escape the sensation. The room behind the door was almost spherical in shape and had been crafted from the same purple stone as the rest of the palace. It had probably been dark in the past, since there were only two tiny, narrow windows, but the roof was now full of holes, letting in the early morning sunlight. A small wooden bed lay along the far wall, while a chair, still in good condition, lay on its side under the window closest to me, some roof pieces scattered next to it.

The sensation of being watched still haunted me and had now been joined by a new feeling; I had been here before… no, that was impossible… and yet the feeling of déjà vu was so strong that I could not deny the possibility, no matter how impossible it seemed. Frightened, I moved into the middle of the room, but the feeling only grew more intense, except now I was not experiencing my own emotions, but someone else's. Whoever was inside my head had been here before, and they had suffered; their screams of agony filled my head, and I covered my ears, trying to shut out the pain.

A shrill whistle sounded behind me, and I turned, but there was no one there. It happened again, and I began to panic, terrified of this invisible adversary. The room gave off a black aura, reeking of death, and though I had never been one to believe in ghosts, I felt the presence of a lost soul here. Frantically, I turned towards the door, desperate to escape, when a strange melody stopped me. The music gripped me in its embrace; I had heard this melody before, and I could not stop myself from trying to find where the sound was coming from.

I discovered a golden trunk, encrusted with gems and full of clothes. The lid was raised, yet the inside showed

183

no sign of being exposed to the elements; unlike the rest of the palace, there was no dust or snow. It seemed to have just been opened, but how? Sitting on my knees in front of it, I realised that the beautiful melody was coming from inside the trunk. Mesmerised, I lifted one of the dresses to find a gold, heart-shaped medallion hiding beneath it. The medallion was unclasped, its mechanism visible. Lifting it closer to my face, I became hypnotised by the sorrowful melody. I was certain that it was neither the first time I had seen this medallion, nor the first time I had listened to this melody. But how could I possibly have heard it before? It made no sense.

Suddenly, a scene flashed into my mind: a man with roughly chopped black hair sat on his knees, his body covered in cuts and blood. His head was being held by a man with long silver hair, and as I watched, the silver-haired man took out a long silver dagger and plunged it into the other man's chest. The scene had come and gone so quickly that I had not been able to distinguish any faces, but for some unknown reason, a wave of terrible grief consumed me. I had never experienced a pain like this; seeing that man die, whoever he was, had brought a feeling of such emptiness and loss that I felt like someone had plunged a dagger through my own heart. Tears rolled down my cheeks and I could barely breathe.

Out of nowhere, the same shrill sound as before cut

through the air, and I leapt to my feet, dropping the medallion. As it hit the floor the clasp shut tight and the melody stopped, releasing me from my internal nightmare. I turned and ran, crashing through the wooden door and almost falling down the stairs in my haste. I was frightened and confused; all I wanted to do was go back to Maheliah's palace, curl up in my soft warm bed, and try to forget the horror that I had just experienced.

Back in the great hall, everything seemed less terrifying, and as I focused my mind on trying to avoid stepping on the fractured pieces of slate, my breathing calmed. I stopped, remembering why I was here. I still needed to find Akaoh. Taking a deep breath and drying my tear-stained cheeks, I tried to calm my mind. To my right was another door, sunlight filtering softly through its aged wooden panels. Trying to forget what had just happened to me, I gathered my courage and crossed the hall, slowly pushing the door open.

A massive room came into view, scattered with giant stone blocks that had clearly fallen from the walls and the ceiling over the years as the palace had slowly disintegrated. A stone rostrum stood at the far end of the room, and in the centre of the rostrum, a large silver throne rose from the fractured stone. It looked completely out of place, not only because it remained untouched by the elements, but also because someone was sitting upon it, looking as solemn as the dark stone that made up the palace.

The man was wearing a long, hooded cloak that covered his entire body; even his face was hidden behind the dark material. All that was visible was a wrinkled, almost skeletal hand, wrapped around the handle of a black, wooden cane, which was topped by a magnificent, glittering ruby. He raised his head slightly, just enough for me to see his face. He was pale, with deep wrinkles, and his eyes were red as blood; cruel and bewitching, just as Maheliah had described them.

I walked closer to him, slowly, and he continued to gaze at me, his emotionless eyes fixed on my face. After three more careful steps, I finally plucked up the courage to speak.

"Akaoh? Sorry to bother you, I…"

"Needless to say your name. I know who you are."

His deep voice echoed around the room; it seemed to be coming from somewhere far below the ground, not from the man who sat before me. I was confused. What did he mean? How could he possibly know me?

"Fada… for the past twenty years, I have heard only this name."

He stretched his hand towards me, inviting me to sit on the ruined stairs beside the throne. I did as instructed, all the while gazing into his bewitching eyes.

"Maheliah told me about you, so I thought—"

186

"Curiosity has been the cause of much pain and sorrow in the past. Following it is not the right path."

I continued to look at him with wide eyes. He was as strange as Maheliah had suggested, and his voice was quite terrifying. Nevertheless, I could not stop looking into his eyes and listening to his every word.

"I just wanted to meet you... I have been told so much—"

"People may speak about me, but you are the one everybody is talking about. And so it shall remain, even after your departure to Eihwaz."

"Excuse me?"

Akaoh smirked. He seemed satisfied, but his words scared me. How did he know what would happen to me in the future?

"You do not like being the centre of attention, yet this is your fate. You do not have a choice."

"Are you saying you know my future?"

"I know everything about you, the entirety of your existence..." He smirked again and looked straight into my eyes. "I know about your visits to Netis, and I know how much your feelings for him torment you..."

I felt the blood drain from my face. Nobody knew about our relationship except me and Netis. Sure, the guards always made snide comments, but Netis assured me that they would never say anything to anyone. How had Akaoh found out?

"You are afraid... you believe that what you are doing is wrong, yet you cannot prevent yourself from seeing him. But this is a part of you, Fada. Your soul calls for his..."

Akaoh's words sounded like a prophecy. 'Your soul calls for his'... what did he mean by that? Being close to Netis always felt good; felt right. But I was not sure that it had anything to do with my soul.

"You seem to know everything."

"I know many things. I know that you will continue your visits to Netis, no matter how wrong it might seem..."

I hated that he was right. No matter how guilty I felt for meeting up with Netis, I knew that I would not stop. For some reason, being with him felt right; it was like something inside me could only be at peace when I was with him. Could that be what Akaoh was talking about? Was my soul the invisible force that was pulling me towards Netis, day after day?

"You believe I should continue to see Netis?"

"I do not believe anything. I am only disclosing to you what is to come."

"So, continuing to see him is my fate?"

"You finally understand."

He smirked again, a disgustingly self-satisfied smile. He looked at me like he knew I would obey his predictions, and though part of me wanted to rebel against him, I knew that I would not.

"No more words, my dear?"

"I don't know what else to say."

"Then you must go. Your future has already been decided, Fada. Go and fulfil it."

I was confused. I wanted to hear more, but I was also afraid of him, of his words. Suddenly, the horror of what had happened only moments earlier came back to haunt me, and I stood shakily to my feet, curtseying to him in the Solish manner, before walking as quickly as I could towards the door.

As soon as I had negotiated the shards of slate in the great hall, I set off in a sprint, my mind whirling with everything that had happened. I had finally met Akaoh, and he had been even more confusing and mysterious than I had anticipated. I had prepared myself to meet a strange man, old and secluded, but I had never expected anything like that. He was intriguing, and clearly very wise, but he frightened me, and I knew that if he ever commanded me to do something, I would obey his words.

I arrived back at Maheliah's palace lost in thought, still hypnotised by my encounter with Akaoh. Walking mindlessly up the main stairs, I was surprised to see Maheliah sitting on her throne, talking with Nalhya and

Lilhya, the three of them looking anxious. As soon as she saw me, Maheliah leapt to her feet.

"Fada, where were you? You weren't in your room this morning. We were about to send out a search party."

"I'm sorry to have worried you. I woke up early, so I thought I would head out and explore some of Hagalaz before breakfast. This is my future kingdom after all."

I could not tell her the truth. She would have been furious had she known that I had been to visit Akaoh.

"You're quite right, of course. I'm sorry, Fada. You have every right to go wherever you wish. I know I can be overprotective sometimes…"

I smiled. "It's okay. I know it's only because you care about me. But I'm pretty resilient, you know. You don't need to worry."

"I know, sweetheart. But Hagalaz is still unknown to you… just be careful, please? And maybe leave us a note next time if you decide to head out so early. You scared the life out of the twins!"

I smiled apologetically at Nalhya and Lilhya. "I'm sorry to have worried you."

The twins tutted their heads in unison, then grinned at me. I smiled back, and each of the twins grabbed one of my hands, pulling me along after them.

"Come on, we're late. The other women will be wondering why we're not bathing with them."

Rolling my eyes, I matched their pace, following

them down to the hot springs.

After the stress and confusion of this morning's adventure, delicately sliding into the warm water felt like a balm for my soul, and I instantly relaxed into the familiar ritual. Nalhya and Lilhya slid into the water beside me, and once we had washed our hair and scrubbed the grime from our bodies, we drifted over the edge of the springs, enjoying the warmth.

"So, Fada, where did you go this morning?" Lilhya asked.

"Oh, nowhere in particular. I wanted to discover a bit more of Hagalaz, that's all," I answered, trying to keep my face relaxed so as not to give anything away.

"Is it a tradition on Earth to visit unknown places early in the morning?" Nalhya enquired.

"No, it's just a Fada tradition," I grinned, and we collapsed into laughter.

"You're so strange, Fada."

"People used to think I was strange on Earth too."

"Must just be you then," Nalhya laughed, poking me gently in the ribs.

We chatted for a while longer, poking fun at each other and splashing around in the warm water. It made me happy, being with the two of them, and as I looked around the hot springs, I realised that everyone seemed to share that feeling. It was a peaceful time; a chance for everyone to put aside their differences and their concerns and just relax together in the warm water.

But no matter how much I was enjoying this moment, Akaoh's words still resonated in my head. I was already convinced that, no matter how hard I tried, I would not be able to stop myself from seeing Netis, and his words only confirmed that. I had never believed in such fanciful things as fate and destiny, but given the circumstances, I was suddenly unsure. Something was pulling me towards Netis, just as Akaoh had predicted, and there was nothing I could do to stop it.

CHAPTER XI - SINNING OR DOING THE RIGHT THING

Once again, I found myself outside of Netis' palace, aware that I was about to carry on with the same old mistake. The guards smirked as I approached them, and I looked down, not wanting to meet their gaze. I knew they were aware, at least in part, that something was going on between me and Netis, and I did not want to give them the satisfaction of seeing the guilty expression on my face.

Once inside, I made my way slowly up the stairs. I had walked this route so many times now, yet every step was like a stab in my stomach. I was about to betray Angel, again. I could not stop; worse still, I did not want to stop. My heartbeats sped and I took a deep breath, trying to relieve my anxiety. Why did Netis have such a hold on me?

Reaching the door, I wrapped my hand around the

silver handle, pausing for a moment. I could turn back now… end this once and for all. I sighed. I had been here before, every day for the last however many months, but the logic of turning back had never been enough. The pull was too strong. Sighing again, I pushed open the door. Netis was facing the window, his hands crossed behind his back. He turned, smiling when he saw me, and walked across the room. As soon as I met his gaze, all my doubt, guilt and confusion instantly vanished, and I smiled, shutting the door behind me.

I moved to meet him in the centre of the room, a force that I could not control drawing me towards him. He fixed his eyes on mine, full of desire, and I stared back at him with the same look, forgetting my last ounce of shame. Unconsciously, I slowly moved my face closer to his and he swiftly filled the gap, laying a passionate kiss on my lips. My hands snaked behind the back of his neck, and I pulled away, scrutinising his gaze, hoping that I might find something that would make this invisible force and my desire for him disappear. But there was nothing but his beautiful onyx eyes, gazing at me with an intensity that was impossible to resist. The last shreds of my resolve disintegrated. All I wanted now was to be here, in this moment, with him. Nothing else mattered.

His lips slid down my chin to my neck, kissing me softly, while his hands caressed my body with delicate, sensual gestures, making me sigh with pleasure. Feeling my dress softly sliding down my body, I realised that Netis must have unlaced it, but he had been so gentle that it had felt like nothing more than a caress on my back. My body was now so close to his that I wondered how we were still standing, so I pulled us over to the bed and slid my hands down to his hips as I sat on the edge. Pulling up his linen shirt, I eased it up over his head, kissing his chest.

Pulling away for a moment, I marvelled at the beauty of him. Before meeting him, I had always assumed that as a warrior his chest and arms would be bulky, but he was not like that at all. His body was lean, yet muscular, and gazing at his naked torso lit up a fire inside of me, making me want him even harder. I needed to put my hands on him; to feel the warmth of his body. Running my fingers over his chest I could feel his fast heartbeats under his soft skin, and his abs tightened with every caress.

Unlacing his trousers, I lay down on my back, still caressing his chest. He followed my gesture, looking deep into my eyes, and while my fingers were still wandering over his chest, his own gestures became more sensual, his hands alighting sensitive parts of my body. My breathing sped up as I was seized by a fit of giddiness, and I gripped his back, moaning with pleasure as he came inside me. My legs trembled; I could feel his heart beating in time with mine as his breathing became more ragged. The pleasure rose inside me, and his gaze met mine, only for a second, but it was enough for me to understand that the pleasure he felt in this moment was as strong as mine.

Feeling the pressure of his body on mine made my desire more intense, and my moans became uncontrollable shrieks of ecstasy. I had never felt so fulfilled, and I wished that he could stay inside of me forever. I moved on top of him, pulsing fast then slow, losing myself in the moment. Suddenly, I gripped his chest, a wave of heat submerging me from head to toe. My shrieks grew louder, and I was breathing heavily as my thighs tightened around his hips. It seemed like pleasure would never leave me. I directed Netis' hands towards my breasts, my entire body drowning under my passion for him, and he grasped them strongly, looking deep into my eyes, delighting in my ecstasy.

We continued to pleasure each other, moving from one position to another, but as with every good thing, this too had to end. Eventually, Netis stopped moving, letting his body relax on top of me as he recovered. Feeling the weight of his body on my back made me realise how much I belonged to him. I had fought so much for my freedom, yet I had become a prisoner to his body.

He laid down next to me, still regaining his breath,

and I rested my head on his chest, kissing and caressing it gently. I could see the sun through the window slowly descending in the sky, and I knew that I needed to leave. Usually, I had at least a couple of hours with Netis, but my history lessons had taken longer than usual that day, and I had arrived at the palace much later. I did not want to leave him yet, but I had no choice. The storm was coming; if I did not leave now, it would be too late.

Sitting upright, I slid to the edge of the bed, grabbing my dress from the floor. I felt Netis lay his hand on my shoulder, kissing my neck softly. I closed my eyes, momentarily forgetting my predicament, and turned my face towards him. He laid his lips on mine, brushing them against my cheek.

"Stay…" he whispered, his voice full of desire, taking my chin between his fingers and gazing at me.

"You know I can't stay," I whispered sadly, resting my head on his shoulder, trying to avoid his bewitching gaze. "The storm will be here soon; I have to get back."

Turning away from him, I stood up from the bed, pulling on my dress and lacing it up as best I could, before walking over to the door. Opening it, I finally plucked up the courage to glance back at Netis. He was still looking at me, but his gaze was softer now; I could tell that he genuinely wanted me to stay. I smiled softly at him before turning and leaving the room, closing the door behind me.

I walked down the stairs lost in thought, trying to imagine how Netis might be feeling now that I had gone. Perhaps he was sad that I had left, or perhaps he was already thinking about something more important than me. Had he really wanted me to stay, or had I just imagined the affection in his gaze? Still lost in thought, I wandered past the guards without paying them much attention, but as I walked away from the palace, their laughter and lewd conversation dragged me back to reality.

"Now I understand why our dear king was so desperate to have her by his side."

"She must be good to have kept his attention for this long. Can't complain though. Banging her everyday has worked wonders on his temper; I've never seen him so calm."

Their words should have annoyed me, but I did not have the energy to retaliate. It was hardly surprising that they had figured out what was going on; they saw me enter and leave the palace on a daily basis, and Netis and I weren't exactly subtle. As long as they did not tell Maheliah or Angel about our 'relationship', I did not care what the guards thought. I had too much else to worry about.

Walking towards Maheliah's palace, I once again tried to make sense of my choices. Justifying my first liaison with Netis was easy – it had been the only way to save Angel – and sleeping with him a second time had felt like a redemption for the pain I had caused him the first time. I had needed to alleviate my guilt and pleasuring him had felt like the only solution at the time. If it had only been twice, I could have understood my actions; I could have forgiven myself. But it had not only been twice, and no matter how many excuses I came up with, I could not justify those choices.

Every day I told Angel how much I loved him, and everyone around us could see how much we cared for one another. So why could I not shake this attraction to Netis? Angel had been my first love, and my first kiss; the first man I had ever been close to. Then, only days after that first kiss, I had slept with another man, in order to try and save my first love. But having sex with Netis had brought new feelings to me, new pleasures that I had never enjoyed before, and I could only reason that this was why I desired him so much. In order to break away from Netis, I simply had to control my desire. Surely it must be possible?

I was so lost in my thoughts that I barely acknowledged the palace guardians, walking up the stairs and into my room in a daze. A few moments later, Maheliah entered.

"Fada, there you are. How was Netis today? Any news for me?" she asked, sitting next to me on the bed.

I had no idea what new lie I could possibly tell her; I

felt bad for constantly making up excuses, but I had no choice. I could not tell her the truth.

"He still doesn't want to cooperate," I shrugged, unable to think of anything better to tell her.

"I see... I suppose I shouldn't be surprised. He's the most stubborn person I've ever met..."

I stopped listening to her, returning to my thoughts. Akaoh's words kept on resonating in my head, and I knew that he was right. I could not resist Netis, but I hated that I was betraying Angel. I loved him so much; he was always so sweet with me and had never done anything to hurt me. If Angel discovered what was happening between me and Netis, he would never forgive me, and I knew that I would never be able to forgive myself either. I tried to remember all the terrible things that Netis had done, but I knew that he regretted those mistakes, and would never hurt me again. I felt safe with Netis; I trusted him, and he was always charming and gentle with me. Yet I had also seen his darker side, and the way he had talked about Maheliah and Angel still pained me. But it was not enough for me to stop feeling attracted to him.

"Fada, are you listening to me?" Maheliah asked, putting an end to my daydream.

"Sorry. What were you saying?"

"I was saying that Netis should learn to be more open-minded and less selfish. He thinks about no one but himself. It's unbearable."

"Don't be so harsh on him, Maheliah. He can be kind sometimes, and I know that he has a good heart."

"You're defending him now, that's new…"

"It's just that I've seen his good side too. I know he can be gentle and understanding."

"Well, he should be like that more often. I don't recall the last time I saw that side of him. If only he was more like Angel. That boy is a gem; so sweet and respectful. You're lucky to have him."

"I know, though I have to admit, I feel like his respect for me goes a bit too far sometimes."

"What do you mean?"

"It's just that, whenever we spend time alone together, he barely touches me. He'll hold me, and kiss me occasionally, but that's all. It makes me worry that he doesn't find me attractive."

Maheliah laughed. "Oh, you worry too much, Fada. His behaviour is quite normal here."

I raised my eyebrows at her, confused.

"He's abiding by the law, Fada. That's all."

"Abiding by the law? What do you mean? What law?" I was even more confused now.

"It's one of our most ancient laws, and also one of the most ridiculous."

"What is it?"

Maheliah sighed. "It stipulates that any princess of

201

Hagalaz must share her body with the current king before she can be touched in that way by another man."

"What? But that's ridiculous. It doesn't make any sense."

"I know, it's ludicrous. The law was created in order to link each generation; since we can't procreate, the heirs to the throne are not technically legitimate. The ancients decided on this stupid law as a way to make that link."

"Does that mean that you can only become queen after sleeping with the current king?"

"No, you can become the queen, but you can't have sex with a man, no matter how in love you might be…"

I was astounded by what Maheliah was saying. How could such a law exist? And what were the implications for my own situation? I felt my muscles tense as the reality hit me. Angel would never be intimate with me; he would abide by the law and leave me untouched. He did not know that the law no longer applied to me, because I had already had sex with Netis, but in order for him to know that we could be together, I would have to tell him what I had done. How could I possibly confess such a thing to Angel? I had slept with Netis numerous times, and I knew I would not be able to lie to Angel and pretend that it had only happened once. What would Angel think of me? Would he ever forgive me? Perhaps I could convince Angel to break the law?

But then what would become of my relationship with Netis? Could I spend the rest of my life without being in Netis' arms? Perhaps I would not need his touch anymore, if I could be intimate with Angel?

"Fada, are you okay?" Maheliah asked, concerned by my silence.

"Yes, I'm fine. I just can't get over how ridiculous the law is."

"I know, but don't worry, I'll find a way for you to get around it."

"How?"

"I still don't know how, but I won't allow Netis to touch you. He would enjoy it far too much, and I could not bear to see him hurt you again."

I looked down, trying to hide my guilt. Maheliah was right, though she did not know it. Netis did enjoy being with me, and I enjoyed being with him. Though I hated to admit it, I loved feeling the weight of his body on mine, and it was exciting to feel him control his strength whenever he touched me. Being in his arms made me feel safe, protected, but every time I left him, I felt ashamed, because I had betrayed Angel yet again.

"Yes... I suppose you're right..." was the only answer I could give her.

Maheliah did not say anything else; she seemed lost in her thoughts. I suddenly remembered that she had been a princess when Akaoh was king, and an awful

203

vision filled my mind. Horrified and disgusted, I looked at her with panicked eyes.

"Wait, does that mean you had sex with Akaoh?"

"No, Fada, I did not. You needn't look so worried. I decided a long time ago that I would never indulge in such things."

"You mean you took a vow of chastity?"

"Yes, in a way. I decided that I could not let Akaoh touch me. He had raised me, and though he had never been loving, he was nonetheless like a father to me. It would have felt so wrong to even think of his hands on me. But I also think it is useless to create a new pleasure when we have so many others."

"A new pleasure?"

"Since we cannot create life, sex is only for pleasure, not for procreation. I believe we have enough pleasures in life to satisfy us already; it is useless to add another."

"Do you think, if you fell in love, you would change your mind? Have you been in love before?"

Maheliah looked down, but I caught a glimpse of unmistakable sadness in her eyes.

"No..." she answered softly.

Worried that I had hurt her feelings, I tried to think of something to say to change the subject, but she looked up and continued as if nothing had happened.

"I'm not the only one. Ever since the creation of this law, almost every princess had taken a 'vow of chastity', as you say. Most of them considered their king to be a father-like figure, making it impossible for them to imagine being touched by him in that way. I know it's different for you, because you've only just met Netis, but think of how hard it has been for all of us before you. Those men were our fathers, even though we did not share blood with them."

"What about the princess who was sent to Laguz? Did she have to give herself to her father before she got married?"

"No, it's more complicated than that. The other kingdoms don't know about this law because they don't know that we can't procreate."

"What? Why didn't you tell me about this before?"

"I felt like you needed to learn other things first, but since you're asking, let me explain. The other kingdoms don't even know about the existence of Earth; most people in our world believe that only our planet is inhabited. Not only do they have no idea that we are infertile, but they also don't know anything about the law concerning Hagal princesses."

"Why not?"

"If they knew that we could not procreate, they would see us as unworthy, and would most likely stop trading with us. They would probably also wish to go down to Earth and invade it. We cannot let that happen. We must protect our future offspring."

"But what about the princess? How did they manage to send her to Laguz and work around this law?"

"We won the war against Othalaz thanks to Laguz, and in recompense, our princess was forced to marry the prince of Laguz. Given the complex political circumstances, the princess was allowed to break our law, for in Laguz, a prince may only marry a woman who has never been touched by another man. The royal family of Laguz hoped that they would have a child together, who would then become the heir to both Laguz and Hagalaz. However, the princess would obviously never have become pregnant, so the plan was to wait for her to hear the soul of an Earthly infant, then hide her in Hagalaz until after the baby had been born, so that she could pretend that the soul she had heard was their own child. Sadly, this never happened…"

"Why not?"

"She died before hearing a soul, meaning that the kingdoms of Hagalaz and Laguz were never truly tied."

I was intrigued by this princess and saddened by her story. She seemed to have been manipulated her whole life; I wondered whether anyone had ever cared to document her side of the story.

"Can you tell me more about her, Maheliah?"

"One day, yes. Her story is quite long and complicated; there's a lot of mystery that surrounds her, and much of her story remains unknown. Perhaps once you manage to convince Netis to end this stupid war against me, I will tell you. It can be your reward," she answered, smiling.

Satisfied that, hopefully, I would one day learn more about this mysterious princess, I shifted the conversation back to the strange law.

"Why was the law about princesses accepted if no princess ever followed through with it? It seems so pointless."

"Believe me, there are many useless laws in the world, not just in Hagalaz. I have always believed that this law was not in fact instated to create a link between generations, but was instead put in place to keep the queens of Hagalaz under strict control. Indeed, it was believed by many at the time that, if they could not think about sex, the young queens would be more able to focus their minds on their queenly duties."

"What about the men then? Why should only women not be able to think about sex? What kind of misogynistic rule is that?"

"Back when the law was voted upon, only men were allowed on the council, and according to them, women let their emotions control them too much. They believed that creating such a law would prevent future queens from not doing their job properly."

"That's so stupid, how could they have been so narrow minded? Sometimes I wonder whether men just feel the need to control women purely because they're scared that those women will overpower them."

"I know, my dear, but sadly that law has been in place for centuries, and every princess has been forced to deal with it at some point in their lives."

"But didn't you say that most princesses were expected to get married?"

"Yes, but other than the princess who was sent to Laguz, most of them married men from this kingdom. Such couples were expected to sleep in separate bedrooms, but whilst the women were not permitted to have sex with their husbands, or anyone else for that matter, the men in these marriages were permitted as many mistresses as they desired."

I looked at Maheliah in horror, angered by the misogyny of this ridiculous law. Knowing that I now lived in a kingdom that had once been ruled by such men disgusted me, and I could not understand why the law had not yet been repealed. It made me all the more determined to end this war between Netis and Maheliah, so that they could agree to get rid of this ridiculous rule. I wondered whether Maheliah had ever been forced into such a marriage.

"What about you, Maheliah? How is it that you are queen and Netis is king, when you are not married to one another?"

"Netis is older than me, which means that his wife

should have been queen, but since he never married, I am queen of Hagalaz for now. And since I doubt he shall ever marry, when I eventually pass on my position, you shall be queen in my place."

My head was full of new information, and it was difficult to process everything. Governing a kingdom did not sound easy, and I knew that I would need to learn many new skills in order to become a queen as great as Maheliah.

Standing up from the bed, Maheliah explained that she had a few more things to organise before our evening bathing session, and after kissing me tenderly on the forehead, she left the room, closing the door behind her.

Collapsing onto my bed, I tried to come to terms with everything Maheliah had just told me. If the law stated that I had to sleep with Netis in order to have sex with another man, why had Netis so readily agreed to my deal to save Angel? According to Maheliah, the whole reason they were fighting was because Netis wanted to keep me by his side, so why had he not used that law as an excuse? As a tool to secure me as his property? Suddenly, I realised that Netis had not gained anything from that first liaison. He had not made a deal with me… he had done me a favour. But why?

It seemed that I was constantly discovering new things about this mysterious man. He was not as cruel and bitter as he pretended to be, and my opinion of him took a different turn that day. Suddenly, the beast was not a monster at all, but a kind-hearted prince, with a troubled past.

CHAPTER XII - TWO SOULS FOR ONE HEART

The following day, I hurried to Netis' palace as usual, barely taking notice of my surroundings. I knew this route by heart now, and as I walked the familiar path through the snow, I began to wonder whether the route between the two palaces might one day be marked by a road of some kind. I sighed internally at my foolish optimism. I would be lucky if Netis and Maheliah ever agreed to end this war; the chances of them uniting in harmony and building a 'bridge' between their two palaces was extremely unlikely.

Saddened by my harsh reality, I walked on. I had only known war and anger ever since I had arrived here, and I was desperate for a glimmer of hope, of joy. Hagalaz was a beautiful place, but nothing else was pleasant in this world. It would have been so easy for Netis and Maheliah to choose the path of peace; why had they decided on war? Sometimes I felt like everyone, both in Hagalaz and on Earth, was making life difficult for themselves on purpose. It was so easy to live happily, and I was beginning to wonder whether the people of Hagalaz and Earth enjoyed suffering. Perhaps it made them feel more alive to feel pain and anger, rather than peace and joy.

My contemplations made me think of a girl I had met as a teenager. She had every reason to be happy: loving parents with stable jobs; a beautiful house; a perfect family life; a wonderful secondary school; good friends... and yet she was always putting herself in difficult situations and inventing stories and misfortunes because she thought it made her life sound more interesting. It was as though she could not enjoy what she had without feeling that she had experienced pain. It was beyond my capacity to understand people who invented sorrow just to add excitement to their lives, and I remember being so confused and frustrated by her behaviour.

Looking back on that experience, I realised that it was exactly the same here in Hagalaz. Netis and Maheliah were fighting for no reason other than to achieve their version of happiness, their version of success. They felt it necessary for one of them to be victorious in their battle to 'own' me, when they could easily have trained me and spent time with me together.

They both felt that they had to suffer in order to have earned their 'ownership' of me, when it would have been much simpler to just accept one another's wishes and come to a compromise.

I reached the palace with these thoughts running through my head, and as usual, the two guards looked at me scornfully.

"If it isn't our little princess."

"Come for another screw with His Highness, have we?"

"Shame the king isn't one for sharing, I would love to know what it feels like with this one. But no doubt we're not good enough for her."

"At least we know where we stand. Poor Angel doesn't even realise he's got competition."

Their last words tipped me over the edge. Usually, I could ignore their lewd comments, but a lot had happened over the past few days and my nerves were strained.

"Haven't you had enough of criticising everything I do and giving your unfounded opinion on me all the time?" I snapped.

The two of them smirked.

"What are you gonna do about it, princess?"

Glaring at their smug expressions, I walked past them and pushed open the door. They were right, there was nothing I could do... unless I complained to Netis

213

about them, but I was worried that he might do more to them than they deserved. They were rude and irritating, yes, but they did not deserve to die.

Knocking on the bedroom door, I entered Netis' room without waiting for an answer. He was standing in front of his window again, and turned around slowly, greeting me with a seductive smile before turning his head back to the window. Seeing him made me forget the guards' words, and I regained my calm instantly.

"For such a busy king, you seem to spend an awful lot of time gazing out of the window. I can't imagine what could be so interesting to look at," I announced in a mocking tone.

"I would have you know that looking out of this window helps me to gather my thoughts. A king always has many matters that require thinking upon," he answered, turning to face me and smiling again.

"And what is so soothing to look at that it helps the king to focus his mind?" I asked, walking towards him.

"It's not important…"

Pulling me towards him, he gazed into my eyes, and I moved my body closer to his, before sliding to his left in order to look out of the window. He stopped me, moving his body closer to mine.

"No need to look. You wouldn't understand anyway…" he whispered, caressing my cheek with his lips.

"Why not?" I asked, caressing the back of his neck with my fingers and looking straight into his bewitching black eyes.

"Because I'm the only one who can understand... and you're not me..." he answered, before placing his hands on my back and kissing me passionately, filling my mind with his presence.

After slipping back into my dress, I lay on Netis' bed, propping myself up on my elbows as I watched him gaze contemplatively out of the window. A few minutes ago, we had been in each other's arms, regaining our breath, but now his thoughts, and mine, were elsewhere. As I lay on my front, my head resting on my forearms, I began to contemplate my life in Hagalaz, and what it had cost me. I had discovered so much during my time here, and I was grateful, but by coming to Hagalaz, I had been forced to say goodbye to the most important people in my life.

Though I tried not to, I thought of my brother and my dad often, and wondered what they thought had happened to me. They would certainly be worried, and I hated that I had been forced to leave without giving an explanation; without telling them that the sister and daughter they had always known was not the person they thought she was. But if I had told them the truth, they would have been convinced that I was losing my mind, and I was certain that my brother must be thinking that I had turned mad and had run off somewhere to live with a load of crazy people. Another, darker thought crossed my mind. What if they hated me? What if their confusion at my strange departure had turned to bitterness and anger? If I returned, would they even want to see me?

I started to panic. I needed to go back to London and explain everything to them. I needed them to know how much I loved them; that I was okay; that I was finally in a place where I belonged. I wondered what my dad's reaction would be if he could see this new life of mine. My relationship with Angel would certainly have surprised him, but he would probably be happy to see me finally in love. My mother-daughter relationship with Maheliah would definitely have upset him; my birth mother had been the love of his life, and he would have probably accused me of betraying her by forming a bond with Maheliah.

I could not imagine that he would have been particularly happy about my ambiguous relationship with Netis either. I could envision him shouting at Netis, telling him that his behaviour was unacceptable and that he was only thinking about his own pleasure. I would have had to try and explain to him that this was not exactly true, and that the whole situation was more complicated than that, but he would not have cared for my explanation, and would probably have gone for Netis, though I doubted his punches would have caused the warrior king much pain.

That image of my dad trying to attack Netis was so bizarre that I started laughing out loud, causing Netis to turn around in surprise.

"What are you laughing about?"

"Nothing, I was just daydreaming…" I giggled.

"About what? You can't just laugh out loud and not tell me why."

I understood his reaction and tried to stop my giggling, reasoning that it was probably a good idea to try and visit my dad again, rather than spending my time imagining crazy scenarios. I wanted him to know that I was alive and well; I could not tell him everything, of course, but at least he would finally know that I was okay and that he did not need to worry about me anymore.

"I was just thinking about going back to Earth. Just one t—"

"Don't even think about it," Netis interrupted in a low voice.

"But what about my dad and brother? They must be worried sick about me. I need them to know that I'm okay."

"Forget about those people and your life on Earth. None of that is your concern anymore," he continued harshly, gritting his teeth.

"Those people are my family—"

"You're a royal, Hagalaz is your family."

"But it's different for me. I grew up on Earth, with a human family. How can you not understand that?"

"You're not going back to Earth, I forbid it."

"You forbid it? How dare you talk to me like that. You don't control me. If you won't open a portal for me, I'll just ask Angel or Maheliah. I'll only be gone a few hours. I don't see why you have such a problem with this."

"You're not going back to Earth, I forbid it," he repeated.

His tone infuriated me. Why was he so against me going back to Earth? I gave him a dark look.

"Fine, I'll just ask Maheliah…"

I felt a pressure on my arm, a feeling I remembered all too well. Netis had taken hold of me, and was pulling me closer to him.

"Don't you dare ask Maheliah."

Feeling his hand on my arm reminded me of the first time I had met Netis… of the searing pain I had felt as he burned me. There was no heat coming from his hand now, but his tone and the fierceness of his grip frightened me. I could not bear to see him behaving like this.

"Let go of me!" I cried, trying to pull myself away.

"I need you to promise me that you won't go back to Earth."

"Netis, please!"

"Swear to it!" he yelled.

I could feel his hand getting warmer and my memory of our first meeting flashed through my mind. Terrified, I cried out in panic.

"Fine, I swear!"

Netis released me instantly and I pulled away from him, clutching my arm to my chest. Tears of hurt and anger were rolling down my cheeks and Netis' expression immediately changed, a look of immense sorrow and regret filling his gaze. I looked back at him furiously.

"I hate you," I spat, my voice trembling, as I fled from the room.

I could hear him calling after me, apologising profusely, but I continued to run down the stairs, forcing my way through the back door of the palace, much to the surprise of the guards. As I ran, I heard another voice calling my name. It sounded like Angel. Perhaps he had seen me running from the palace? Too angry and confused to turn back, I kept running, unable to think clearly. Netis had nearly burned my arm again, yet all I had done was contemplate seeing my family. What was wrong with me wanting to see the people on Earth that I loved and missed? It was none of his business, and I could not understand why he had reacted this way. Was he jealous? Afraid that I would never come back? Or so possessive that he could not cope with the idea of me being away from Hagalaz?

Part of me wished that I had stayed and tried to talk rationally with him, but I knew that we were both too obstinate to have a reasonable conversation. Neither of us would have been willing to compromise, and our conversation would have ended the same way regardless. It did not help that our relationship was so complex; not knowing what I truly wanted from him, or what he wanted from me, made everything more difficult. There was a connection between us, that much was clear; he seemed to understand me, and I thought that I understood him. We both felt passion for each other and seeing pleasure in his eyes made me happy. He also knew my weaknesses; how to comfort me and calm me down. I felt safe around him. And yet, from time to time, he would become the person Maheliah thought he was – violent and pitiless – and everything I thought I knew about him, and our relationship, would shatter into a million pieces.

Confused, angry and heartbroken, I ran blindly through the snowy landscape, eventually finding myself by the lakeside where Angel and I usually spent our time together. Staring out at the lake calmed my mind and strengthened my resolve. Netis did not control my life. I did not need his permission, or Maheliah's for that matter. I was a royal princess of Hagalaz; I could open a portal myself.

My face still stained with tears, I stood before the lake and held out my arm, trying to copy the hand gestures that I had seen numerous times before. After a few useless attempts, my legs began to tremble. Perhaps I was wrong, thinking that this power would come naturally to me, but I could not stop trying. Night was falling, and the icy wind was blowing colder with every passing minute. Yet I continued to stand there, trying desperately to open the portal that would bring me back to my family. They had loved me and cared for me my whole life, regardless of who I was. The people of Hagalaz were only interested in me because I would be the queen of their kingdom someday. They did not care for my feelings, or what I wanted. I needed to feel the unconditional love of my family again; I needed to know that someone loved me for just being me.

The wind was blowing stronger now, and the sun had nearly set, but I kept my arms in front of me, trying desperately to open this portal. Snowflakes began to fall heavily from the sky, and I felt my muscles tense up from the cold. Suddenly, a huge gust of wind knocked me to the ground, ripping at my hair. I tried to stand again, but the wind was too strong, and my limbs were too weak. Numb from the cold, I lay unmoving as the snow gradually covered my body, my sight growing increasingly blurry. Too exhausted to fight anymore, my senses dimmed, and I sank into a deep lethargy, the world around me taking on a dreamlike quality.

My eyes barely open, I thought I saw a shape coming towards me, but I could not distinguish its features. I felt my body rise up into the air, supported by some unknown force, and as my body left its snowy prison, I felt the sting of my frozen hair whipping at my face. My eyes drifted shut as my body was rocked gently from side to side. I could hear footsteps in the snow. Someone was walking, though I could not tell whether they were moving towards me or away from me.

In my semi-conscious state, I had no concept of time, but at some point, my hair stopped striking my face, and the sound of the footsteps changed, the crunch of snow replaced by the hollow ringing of a stone floor. My body was still in the air, being rocked gently with every footstep. Was someone carrying me? I heard a sharp sound: a woman's voice. She sounded worried, though I could not decipher her words. I felt my body descending, being placed on something soft, as a calm, deep voice answered her. A man's voice. My skin began to tingle as the cold slowly started to seep out, and I felt my soaking wet dress sliding along my body. The woman spoke again; she was angry, but the male voice remained calm as he responded. I felt a soft weight being placed on top of my body, a duvet, perhaps? It was hard to tell.

As I gradually regained consciousness, the female voice spoke again, and this time, I recognised who it was. Maheliah. She was still angry, but her voice was softer and lower now. While she was speaking, I could feel something warm moving up and down my arms, awakening my frozen muscles. The man spoke again. Netis was here. Instantly, the muscles that had just been warmed tensed up, and I was glad that most of my body still felt too numb to move. Not only was I still angry and confused, but I was also concerned about Maheliah and Netis being in the same room. What if they started fighting over me while I was too weak to intervene? Thinking about it, why were they both here together? And where was here?

My arms now restored to their normal temperature, I felt the warmth move to my shoulders, then down to my stomach and hips, gently relaxing my muscles until the top part of my body was no longer numb. I could hear Maheliah and Netis talking, and as my body warmed and my mind became clear, their words started to make sense.

"I'm sure you must be enjoying putting your hands on her like that," Maheliah hissed.

"I only want to get her warm," Netis answered in his infamously stoic voice.

There was a short pause where the only thing that could be heard was our breathing, mine being significantly weaker than theirs.

"I have such a hard time understanding this behaviour of yours, Netis..."

"I don't know what you're talking about."

"I know how you behave towards people: you're harsh and merciless, you can't deny it. Yet... you seem different with her. She's always saying how kind and caring you are; I thought she was just trying to change my opinion of you, but seeing you being so gentle with her now makes me wonder..."

"I have no reason to be unkind to her. She is sensitive and thoughtful, and though this might surprise you, she for some reason deems me worthy of her respect. She only deserves the same from me."

"That doesn't surprise me at all, actually. She always pretends not to care, but I know that she feels something for you."

"What do you mean?"

"It's hard to explain... when I talk about you, she always looks down... she seems sad to hear me speak harshly of you..."

I could hear Netis breathing more quickly now. He seemed anxious, like he was trying to control his emotions.

"… and when she comes back after being with you, she always seems lost in her thoughts, even more than usual. Every evening it's like she's barely even present, her mind entirely focused on her daydreams."

There were a few seconds of uncomfortable silence.

"Come to think of it, she never tells me much about her time spent with you. She always finds ways to evade my questions whenever I ask her what you two talk about. Perhaps you could fill me in?"

"I can't tell you anything if she doesn't want me to," Netis replied.

His voice had been calm, but his breathing still seemed ragged to me, though it could easily just be my own anxiety that I was sensing, not his. I was panicking inside, thinking about what would happen if Maheliah discovered what Netis and I really got up to during my visits. It was a relief that I was still not fully conscious, for had this conversation happened when I was more awake, Maheliah would definitely have noticed that something suspicious was going on. This was one of the main differences between me and Netis: unlike me, he could hide his feelings so easily.

After a short pause, Maheliah sighed.

"Fine, I suppose you're right. But you need to understand that she cares for you, Netis. There's nothing I can say or do to change her opinion of you…"

225

"Is it so bad that she feels affection for me?"

"No, of course not…"

Again, there was a short pause.

"Before she was born, you were kind to me…" Maheliah murmured sorrowfully. "We used to have such a strong bond…"

She sounded as though she was trying to hold back tears. I had not realised that she missed her bond with Netis this much.

"The past is the past, Maheliah. You have to forget it. As long as we disagree regarding Fada's future, we have no choice but to remain at war."

"I understand…"

Maheliah took a deep breath.

"I'll go now," she continued. "Though I understand that she needs to get warm, seeing your hands on her is unbearable for me."

I could hear her dress brushing against the floor as she walked away, and I felt a shiver go down my spine as I realised that I was now alone with Netis. I could feel his breath on my face, and slowly gathering my strength, I managed to open my eyes. My vision took a moment to return to me, but as the fog cleared, Netis' face came into view, his lips breaking into a beautiful smile as our eyes met. Seeing him so close to me, smiling so warmly, I could not help but smile back.

Lifting my head up slightly, I noticed that I had been

226

covered by a thick duvet, and as the warmth that had restored my upper body shifted to my legs, I realised that Netis had his hands under the duvet.

"What are you doing?" I asked, looking at him curiously.

"Warming you up," he said softly. "I finally found a way to use this Othal power of mine for something good." His eyes were sad as he gazed into mine. "I should never have behaved that way towards you, Fada. There are no words to express how sorry I am for the way I've treated you. You don't deserve to be spoken to the way I spoke to you, especially not by me."

His words went straight to my heart; I could almost feel his guilt, his remorse. Raising my hand weakly, I cupped his jaw, caressing his cheek with my fingertips. I could not stay angry with him for the way he had treated me. Of course, there was no excuse for that kind of behaviour, not even the fact that he had been raised by a terrible man. And yet, I wanted to give him a chance, not only because he deserved to feel cared for but also because I was a believer that there was good in everyone. The only thing that I needed to do was to find the right way to push the good straight up so that it could finally shine outside his heart too.

Smiling up at him, I realised that his hair was untied, framing his face and softening his usually austere profile. Raising my other hand, I ran my fingers through

227

the loose, ebony strands, marvelling at how beautiful he was.

"Your hair's untied."

"So is yours," he smiled.

"It suits you, you should wear it like that more often…" A thought suddenly struck me, making me giggle. "Though I suppose if you wore it down all the time, you'd have all the women of Hagalaz fawning over you like you were Don Juan or something."

"Don Juan?"

"One of the greatest lovers of all time. It's an old Spanish legend, on Earth. Don Juan is said to have seduced hundreds of women; apparently no woman could resist his undeniable charisma. According to the legend, he spent his life searching for love, but he never found it, so he used the women who lusted after him to fill the void in his soul."

"He seems a rather interesting character… though I'm not sure it's an especially accurate comparison."

"I disagree. You're extremely attractive, and undeniably charismatic, when you want to be."

Netis smiled softly, his eyes sparkling with desire, affection, and numerous other complex emotions, and I realised then that the gentleness in his face was not entirely down to his untied hair. He was not holding back his feelings as much as he had always done in the past, and my acceptance of his apology seemed to have brought joy to him. He always had such a grave look upon his face, but happiness suited him better.

Taking his hands out from beneath the duvet, he gently placed one hand on my cheek, running the fingers of his other hand through my hair, his warmth slowly drying each strand.

Shifting my body slightly, I slowly tried to push myself upright. Instantly realising what I was trying to do, Netis gently wrapped his hands around my shoulders, pulling me up into a sitting position, all the while looking deep into my eyes, his gaze full of compassion and kindness. Oh, I could have drowned under that gaze. I knew in that instant that he truly cared for me, not only because of what I meant for the future of the kingdom, but because of who I was inside.

"You know, my back still feels cold," I murmured, biting my lower lip.

Smiling seductively, he rubbed his jaw between his thumb and forefinger, tilting his head slightly, before sliding one of his hands down to my waist, pulling me close as I wrapped my arms around his neck. Resting my head on his chest, I sighed contentedly as he began to gently rub his other hand up and down my back. I hoped he understood that my back was not really cold, and that I just wanted to be in his arms. Wrapped in his embrace, a wave of wellbeing submerged me; all I wanted was to stay in his arms forever, listening to his heart beating, feeling his chest moving up and down with every breath.

Lifting my head, I laid my lips on his, the softness of his kiss enveloping me, finally confirming how I felt. I had never been able to admit it to myself before, always afraid of the consequences; always dwelling on my guilt and confusion. But now, wrapped in his arms, I knew that it was not only sexual desire that made me return to his palace, day after day; that made me unable to stop thinking about him; that filled my dreams with his face, his touch, his voice. Denial was no longer an option: I was in love with him.

Breaking our kiss, I nestled my face into the hollow of his neck, trying to come to terms with this new revelation, but Netis gently pushed against my shoulders, forcing me to look at him. It lasted only a couple of seconds, but the passion in his eyes was enough to convince me not to deny my realisation. Laying another tender kiss on my lips, he pulled me towards him, letting my head fall back onto his chest. I did not know what the future might hold, or what the consequences of this newfound love might be, but in that moment, none of those things mattered. All that mattered was how right it felt to be in his arms.

CHAPTER XIII - DON JUAN

A couple of days had passed since the incident with Netis, and Maheliah had barely spoken to me. It felt strange not talking to her, and I was desperate to ask her what was wrong, but I was afraid that she was angry with me for putting myself in danger, or worse, that she was upset about my connection with Netis. She had sounded so sad when she had spoken to Netis about my apparent affection for him, and about their broken bond, and I was worried that she thought he had replaced her with me, or that I had replaced her with him.

Of course, my relationship with Netis was completely different to the sibling relationship that they had once shared, but she did not know that. I hated the idea of her thinking that I would do something like that to her. I could never replace her with Netis, and he was certainly not trying to replace her with me. I just had to hope that she would eventually stop ignoring me and confront me about it or recognise that her jealousy was unfounded. I was desperate to go back to the way things had been before, but I was afraid to ask her directly – after all, she might be ignoring me for an entirely different reason – so I decided that it was best for me to just continue living my life as if nothing had happened.

Later that afternoon, I was lying on Netis' bed, looking at him out of the corner of my eye. He was lying on his back next to me, his face peaceful, apparently lost in his thoughts. It was rare for me to see him looking so calm and relaxed, and I could not help but scrutinise his face. My eyes travelled from his forehead all the way down to his chin, noticing how soft the curve of his nose was, and how sharp his jawline was in comparison. The corner of his mouth tilted downwards, forcing his thin lips to protrude slightly in a soft pout. The more I gazed at his face, the more beautiful he seemed to become.

"Stop staring at me, it's creepy," Netis murmured, his gaze still fixed on the ceiling.

"I didn't know you could see me. I thought I was being subtle," I giggled, covering my face with my hand, trying to hide my smile.

Netis turned his face towards mine and smiled, gazing into my eyes.

"I should teach you how to be more careful then…"

Grinning, he rolled on top of me, tickling my arms and my waist with his delicate fingers. I tried to keep my laughs back, but it was impossible. This moment with him was so magical, so perfect. I wanted to preserve this happiness forever.

Ceasing his childishness, Netis looked into my eyes and smiled softly, caressing my cheek with his right hand and bringing his face towards mine. I filled up the gap between our faces and kissed him firmly, before raising myself up to sit on top of him. Netis ran his hands down my shoulders and my back, resting them softly on my waist as I lay my head on his chest. Taking one of my hands in his, he began to play with my fingers, tracing his other hand up and down my back.

As I lay on his chest, my breathing matching the beating of his heart, I began to wonder what his life had been like before I had arrived in Hagalaz. He was a fantastic lover, even from the first time I had recognised that, and I began to wonder how many women he had encountered before me. Sex was a novelty for me; I was learning with him, and I knew that there was probably a great deal I did not know. The desire and passion in his eyes made it clear that he enjoyed my company, but I was certain that I was not providing him with as much pleasure as he must have experienced from past lovers. Sitting up, I looked down at his chest, not wanting to meet his eyes.

"Netis, may I ask you something? Promise that you won't get angry…"

He took his hand from mine and lifted it to my chin,

tilting my face to meet his gaze.

"Please don't start talking about Earth again…" he pleaded, his expression troubled.

"Don't worry, it's not about Earth," I reassured him, running my fingers over his chest.

His look of relief was instantly replaced by one of confusion. He looked at me quizzically.

"I… I was just wondering how many lovers you've had…" I murmured in a tiny voice, looking down again.

"Why did you think that question would make me angry?"

"I don't know. It's just… it's a very personal question. I was worried that you might not want to tell me…"

"Will you get angry?"

"No, of course not…"

It wasn't exactly a lie. There was no point in getting angry at him for what he had chosen to do with his body in the past. I just knew that, regardless of what his answer was, it would upset me. Imagining him having sex with somebody else was painful.

Netis remained silent. I looked up at him, trying to decipher his expression.

"You don't want to tell me?"

"It's not that. I just don't know the exact number. I'm guessing it's around one hundred, maybe more…"

"One hundred?" I exclaimed, my eyes wide.

"I thought you wanted to know," he replied with a smirk.

"I didn't expect a number that big!"

"I am fifty years old, Fada. I haven't had that many lovers for my age."

"Are you kidding me?"

"Kings and warriors are expected to have many lovers. In some kingdoms, the king will have sex with a different woman each day. The ones who are the best lovers stay in his harem; the ones that are less good get replaced."

"Wow… Don Juan would have loved to be a king in one of those kingdoms."

"Him again…" Netis laughed. "Why are you so obsessed with this legendary seducer, Fada? You talk like you're in love with him."

"Don't be ridiculous, I just love the story. He's an interesting character: ambitious, pitiless, and capable of obtaining anything, and anyone he wants. He's a lot like you, in a way."

"Is that really how you see me?"

"Well, that's what everyone says about you…"

A look of sadness flickered across his face, and he closed his eyes briefly, taking a deep breath before opening them again. He smiled, but it did not quite reach his eyes.

"Tell me his story then. I'd like to understand why

you're so fascinated by this man."

"It's quite a long story; I'll have to tell you about him another day. You're just trying to change the subject from our initial conversation."

"You're the one who started talking about your Don Juan."

"He's not my Don Juan, the only Don Juan I know is you!"

I began to laugh, and so did Netis, his smile restored to its usual brilliance. Pushing me gently, he turned us over, laying me down on the bed as he tickled me. Eventually, he stopped, lying on his back next to me.

"About our talk..." I ventured.

"You mean, about Don Juan?" Netis laughed.

"Stop it with Don Juan," I smiled, resting my head on his chest. "I mean about our conversation on lovers. You've had so many, even if you don't think so. But... have you ever been in love?"

I was looking at Netis out of the corner of my eye and I saw his smile vanish, that same sad sparkle returning to his eyes.

"You don't have to answer if you don't want to..." I murmured.

Netis was not listening to me. He sat up slowly, moving to the edge of the bed, sitting with his back to me. When he spoke, his voice was smooth and calm, but full of pain.

236

"Yes, once."

His words stabbed at my stomach, not only because of his sorrowful voice, but also because he had already loved another. I should not have been upset; I was in love with Angel, after all. But for some reason, knowing that Netis had loved someone else pierced my soul.

"What happened?" I asked in a trembling voice, trying to hide my emotions.

"She's in love with another man…"

"Oh…"

I could not think of anything else to say. His words comforted me, and for that I felt instantly ashamed. He was in agony, and I could not bear to see him suffer, but at the same time, I was selfishly happy that he had never been with this woman, whoever she was. Wracked with guilt, I tried to distract myself with questions.

"What happened to her? Is she from Hagalaz, or another kingdom?"

"It doesn't matter; it's not a very interesting story," he answered, in the same calm but painful tone, before looking deep into my eyes again. "Tell me about you now."

"What about me?" I asked, surprised.

"Have you ever been in love? Except for Angel, of course."

I stared at him, not sure how to answer. It should have been easy, after all, I had never connected with anyone on Earth. But his question made me think about how I felt towards him. Could I tell him? No, he would almost certainly have rejected my affection. And yet, I wanted him to understand.

"I don't know… I don't know if you would call it love…"

"Don Juan doesn't count you know," he laughed.

"Oh, come on! Would you shut up about your Don Juan already?"

"He's not my Don Juan, the only Don Juan that I know is you," he laughed, imitating my voice perfectly.

I felt like I should be laughing, but my smile vanished. He was right: he was the only Don Juan I knew, and he was also the man I was talking about. Netis stopped smiling, looking at me with compassion.

"Tell me about him."

"It's… it's quite hard to explain. At first, I thought that it was just attraction, but I'm starting to think that it might be more than that. When you're attracted to someone, your heart beats fast when you're around them, but with him, it's the opposite. He makes me feel calm. Content. At peace."

"Are you sure you're not in love?"

"I mean, I know what love is, but this feeling isn't the same as what I feel towards Angel. It's such a different feeling because he's different…"

"Do you still feel this way towards this man?"

"Oh no…" I lied, hoping that he would not guess that I was talking about him. "I don't know him anymore. But his hold on me is… was so powerful…"

"It sounds like love to me, Fada. I never imagined that you would talk this way about anyone but Angel."

"Forget it, it's too complicated to explain, you wouldn't understand…"

Indeed, how could he possibly understand that I was in love with Angel but that I also felt this passion for him at the same time? I wished I could have told him that he was the man I was talking about; that he was the one who I felt this unique pull towards. But how could I? Our ambiguous relationship would have become even more complicated.

Netis was about to say something when a scream from outside the palace made me jump.

"Fada! Come back home now, I won't tolerate seeing you in this palace anymore!"

The voice was Maheliah's. My pulse sped. I was naked in bed with Netis, and Maheliah was outside, so close to us. Terrified that she would enter the palace and find me with Netis, I leapt out of bed and grabbed my dress, hastily tightening the back as best I could. Netis stared at me, frowning.

"What are you doing?"

"Didn't you hear Maheliah? I have to go!"

Sprinting down the stairs, I found Maheliah standing

at the back door of the palace, the guards preventing her from coming inside. When she saw me, her face tensed even more, and she grabbed my arm, trying to force me through an open portal. Netis appeared outside at the same time, naked from the waist up. Seeing his bare chest made me blush from embarrassment, and I started to worry that Maheliah would figure out what had just happened between us.

"Who gave you the right to come to my palace and shout at Fada like she's some common slave?" Netis demanded furiously.

Maheliah released my arm harshly and walked over to Netis, looking up and down at his bare chest with anger.

"I do as I please, Netis. She won't stay here with you any longer," she answered in a grave voice, gritting her teeth.

"Who are you to decide what she can and cannot do?"

"I'm the one who's been looking after her ever since she came to Hagalaz. I am her family. She'll never be yours!"

Netis glared at Maheliah, clenching his fists, and though I was just as angry with Maheliah as he was, I still did not want Netis to hurt her. I remembered the burn of his rage all too well, and it was not a pain I would have wished on anyone, especially not Maheliah.

"Netis, please, calm down…" I pleaded, stepping closer to him, and laying my hand on his chest.

Maheliah immediately pulled me closer to her, glaring at Netis with a blind rage, before pushing me through the portal, closing behind her.

"Maheliah, what's wrong with you?" I shouted, releasing my arm from her grip. "You can't talk to me like that and order me around. I'm not your property."

"I'm your queen! That should be enough for you to obey me without questioning my intentions."

I was angry and confused; she had never used her status to force me, or anyone in her palace, to do anything before, so I did not understand why she was using it now. Distressed by her words, I ran upstairs to my room and shut the door, collapsing onto my bed. Maheliah had spoiled a magical moment between me and Netis; nothing she said or did could change that.

Lifting my head, I stared out of the window. Maheliah had spoken harshly to Netis, and I hoped that her aggression would not send him into an irrational rage. There was no reason for this to make him angrier than he already was. I felt so guilty for causing this rift between them; if their relationship had always been like this, I would not have felt so responsible, but with things as they were, I felt like everything that was wrong with this kingdom was my fault. Peace had become war; joy had turned to sadness; unity had morphed into

241

bitterness.

Maheliah always spoke of the time before the war, before she had heard my soul call to her, and I dreamed of living in that happy, peaceful time. I knew that Maheliah regretted that things had changed so much, and though she had never said so, she was certainly angry with me for turning heaven to hell. A strange thought struck me. Unlike Maheliah, Netis never spoke of the time before, and never expressed a desire to go back to the way things were before my soul had called to them both. It seemed odd to me… surely, he regretted the loss of that peaceful time as much as Maheliah did? Then again, he was probably too busy staring out of his window and contemplating the future of the kingdom to be nostalgic.

Lost in my thoughts, it took me a moment to notice that something had changed outside the window. Leaving my bed, I walked over to take a closer look. Sure enough, a dark shape was moving towards the palace. Hypnotised by the contrast of the darkness against the white snow, I watched as the shape came closer, until I eventually realised that the shape was in fact hundreds of men and women, marching forth from Netis' palace. Each of them held a dagger aloft, and I could hear their voices roaring, though I could not distinguish what they were saying. Netis was at the front of the crowd, his hand resting on the dagger that was tied to his belt. His jaw was tense, and there was a sparkle of madness in his eyes; he seemed even angrier than when I had left him an hour ago.

The reality of what was happening suddenly smacked me in the face, and I sprinted downstairs as fast as I could, hoping to warn Maheliah before it was too late. The palace was a hub of activity, and I realised that everyone was already preparing for the battle. Maheliah's voice rang out over the cacophony, her words filling me with dread.

"Everybody in ranks, I want discipline! If it's war Netis wants, war he shall have!"

Reaching the main hall, I saw everyone hurrying to form organised lines, all of them holding whatever weapons they could think to arm themselves with. I could not believe that they were about to fight against Netis' warriors. He certainly had the upper hand in this battle, for most of those with military training had followed him when the siblings had parted ways, a year before my arrival in Hagalaz.

Darting my eyes across the crowd, I spotted Nalhya and Lilhya.

"What are you doing?" I shouted, running towards them.

"We're getting ready for battle."

"But you're not warriors..."

"We've been training for the past year and a half for

this, Fada."

"But you'll die," I cried, on the verge of tears.

"If that is to be our fate, we shall do so with honour. We cannot disobey orders."

A hand grabbed my shoulder from behind, and I turned to find Maheliah glaring at me, her two beautiful emeralds full of anger.

"What are you doing here?"

"I saw the warriors coming towards the palace, so I came downstairs to warn you."

"We are already prepared, as you can see. Now go back to your room."

"No, Maheliah. Please, stop this. Let me talk to Netis. I can reason with him—"

"Shut up," she yelled, slapping me in the face. "I am still the queen. I make the decisions here. Now do as I say and go back to your room!"

I looked up at her in confusion, feeling betrayed. I could not understand why everybody was suddenly behaving this way. Maheliah and Netis argued all the time, why had this argument prompted a battle?

"Lock her up in her room and make sure she stays there," Maheliah shouted to the guardians.

The two guards came closer to me and grabbed onto my arms, walking me towards my room as I screamed and struggled to get free.

"Get off me! Why should I be the only one kept safe?

Why can't I fight side by side with my friends? You have no right to shut me away, let me go—"

"Be silent!" Maheliah shouted.

I continued to struggle as the guardians carried me up to my room, hurt by Maheliah's aggression. What had I done? Why was she acting like this? Launching me into my room, the guardians shut the door firmly behind them, and I could hear them putting something between the two handles to prevent me from escaping. I tried to open the doors nonetheless, even though I knew it was useless. All I wanted was to go out there and try to prevent this stupid battle. I knew that I could stop the fighting if I could just talk to Netis. Maheliah was making a terrible mistake by shutting me away.

Still pulling on the door, I heard voices coming from below the palace, and I ran over to the window, trying to see what was happening. Both armies were standing there, facing each other. Maheliah and Netis were in front of everyone else.

"You think you can come to my palace and take Fada without her permission?" Netis shouted furiously across the untouched snow between the armies.

"Might I remind you that you broke into her room in my palace and took her away without her permission only days after she arrived here?" Maheliah answered, in the same tone that she had used with me several minutes previously.

"That's why I'm here, Maheliah. We won't ever come to an agreement; neither of us are willing to compromise. This is the only way…"

Netis moved to the back of his army before Maheliah could answer, shouting to his warriors to start fighting. Maheliah instantly gave the command to attack, and the two armies ran forwards, screaming battle cries. Beneath raised daggers and thrown punches, bodies began to fall, the ground exchanging its white blanket of snow for a bloody red carpet.

I was trembling, helpless, unable to shift my eyes away from the massacre below. I had lived with these people for months now; I saw them every day. Seeing them fighting and dying was already unbearable, but knowing that it was because of me and that I could not do anything to stop it made it even worse. I hated myself. I had brought so much sorrow to this kingdom… I could not stay here, doing nothing, watching my people die.

I searched for Netis and found him standing behind his army, clenching his fists, his face expressionless. He was not even fighting, though neither was Maheliah, but at least she was supporting her warriors with kind words. I let my panicked eyes travel across the battlefield. The two guardians were fighting the guards who usually stood by the back entrance of Netis' palace. They were all fantastic warriors, and nobody seemed to be winning yet. I saw Lilhya and Nalhya as well, back-to-back, protecting each other as always. It was terrifying seeing those two tiny beings fighting, yet it was nothing compared to what my eyes settled on a few seconds later. Right in the middle of the crowd was Angel, his movements so swift it was almost like watching a dancer at work as he deftly stabbed his dagger at Maheliah's army. This battle was already horrifying enough, but seeing a man as sweet and kind as Angel fighting and killing people was painful beyond words.

Desperate to stop the bloodbath, I looked frantically around my room, trying to find something I could use to destroy my door, but I was in such a panic that I could not think. Staring at my dressing table, trying to gather my thoughts, I suddenly remembered the dagger that Maheliah had given to me. As a royal, I was meant to keep it on me at all times, but I could not imagine myself walking around with a dagger strapped to my thigh, hence why I kept it in the drawer instead.

Opening the drawer, I quickly grabbed the dagger, stabbing at my bedroom door over and over again. Finally, the thin wood fractured, and I dropped my blade, forcing my arm through the hole and grabbing the piece of metal that was holding the handles together. In my haste, I tore my skin against the splintered wood, but I did not care for the pain. I was too eager to escape my prison and stop the fighting.

Pushing the door open, I raced down the stairs and out of the main entrance. The battlefield looked even worse up close, and I was momentarily paralysed by the sight of so many dead bodies strewn across the ground. A movement to my left caught my eye, and I turned to see Angel battling against more of Maheliah's troops. Taking a deep breath, I threw myself into the middle of the battle, wishing that I had kept my own dagger with me to protect myself. I was still running towards Angel when a man appeared in front of me, waving his fist in the air before throwing it down onto my shoulder. I fell to the ground, screaming in pain, as the man raised his other hand, holding his dagger high whilst looking upon me with beastly eyes. I had been close to death a few times since I had arrived in Hagalaz, but this time, I truly believed that death was coming for me.

The man lowered his dagger towards me, but before I could process what was happening, he was flung aside, the punch to his jaw sending him flying. Droplets of blood rained down on my face, and I looked up to see Angel, with the man's dagger protruding from his right hip. His face was tense as he held his hand to the wound, and I stood to my feet, grabbing his falling body.

"Angel, no!"

He looked at me, opening his mouth, but his words were cut off by Netis and Maheliah, roaring at their troops to cease the attack. Everybody instantly stopped fighting, and Netis appeared by my side, frowning as he noticed my hand clutching my shoulder. He turned, the tension in his jaw visible for all to see, as he looked down at the man who had wounded Angel and me.

I could not see Netis' expression, but the man looked petrified, cowering in fear as Netis stepped towards him. Reaching down, Netis grasped the man's neck, his whole hand glowing with heat. The man desperately clung to Netis' wrist, trying to escape, but Netis was too strong. The stench of searing flesh filled the air as the man's face contorted in pain, his eyes wide with fear.

Terrified, I could only look on in silence, clinging to Angel as I tried to shut out the man's screams of agony. Seeing Netis torture this man with the same hands that he had so tenderly caressed me with earlier that day filled me with horror, and despite his wound, Angel closed our embrace, sensing how petrified I was.

After a few seconds, the man's arms went limp, and Netis threw him to the ground in disgust. Smoke drifted up from the man's charred throat, and his eyes stared blankly up to the sky, unseeing. Trembling, I buried my face into Angel's neck, my heart shattered into a thousand tiny pieces.

"The battle is over," Netis stated, his tenor voice booming across the battlefield.

Looking up, I saw him turn and open a portal, before

ushering his warriors through, some of them supporting their injured companions, others carrying the dead. As they passed through, Netis turned to face Maheliah.

"Do not think that you have won, Maheliah. This war is not over."

Maheliah gave her brother a dark look but did not answer. Turning his face towards me, Netis smiled sadly, but I could not smile back. He was nothing but a murderer to me now. Tears streaming down my face, I turned away, burying my face in Angel's neck again.

I felt Angel look up at Netis as he wrapped his arms around me, squeezing me tightly. Netis must have gestured that it was time to leave, for Angel lifted my face to look at him and smiled gently, kissing my forehead.

"I have to go now."

Unable to speak, my body still trembling with shock, I watched as Angel stood upright and slowly limped towards the portal, pressing down on his wound.

"Wait! Angel, you're wounded…"

"It's okay, Fada. I'll be all right."

He looked back at me and smiled again, before disappearing through the portal. I stared after him, watching as Netis also stepped through the shimmering doorway, turning to look back at me with sorrowful eyes. Unable to break away, I continued to watch him, staring into his soul until the portal closed for good.

Blinking at the sudden brightness of the white-grey sky, it took a moment for me to remember where I was. The scene in front of me was like something out of a horror film, the snow saturated with blood, strewn with too many lifeless bodies. This battle had been more brutal than I could ever have imagined. Hearing footsteps behind me, I turned to see Maheliah walking towards me.

"How's your shoulder?" she asked, in a soft, gentle voice.

"It's okay. Angel was there to protect me."

"Of course he was," she replied, smiling sadly and stroking my hair.

I wanted to answer, but my voice was jammed by the sight in front of me. Nalhya was on the ground, sobbing, clinging to her sister's blood-soaked body. Lilhya's eyes were closed; she could have simply been sleeping, but I knew from Nalhya's mournful cries that she was dead. I tried to run towards them, but Maheliah stopped me, pulling me into her arms and whispering gently that it was better to leave them alone. Clinging to Maheliah, I watched as Nalhya lay her sister's body delicately on the ground, tears running freely down her cheeks. I saw her reach down and grab something, and before I could process what was happening, Nalhya had lifted her sister's dagger high into the air and plunged it into her stomach, shrieking with pain as the blade passed through her.

"No, Nalhya, stop!" I cried out in a broken voice.

But it was too late. The dagger had done its job, and Nalhya's body went limp, collapsing onto her sister's corpse. I screamed, falling to the ground in despair, choking on my own tears.

My dear friends… they were gone.

CHAPTER XIV - TALKING TO FORGET

Night had fallen, and the snowstorm raged outside, erasing all evidence of the battle that had caused nothing but heartache and grief. Sitting curled up on my bed, my head resting on my knees, I stared out into the darkness, my face streaked with tears that would not stop flowing.

We had managed to salvage all the dead bodies from the battlefield and had laid them all out in the great hall, bringing basins and towels down from the washroom to clean away the blood. I had wanted to help, but Maheliah had gently informed me that it was not my role to do so. Instead, we had both stood silently in the corner, watching as each of the corpses were bathed. Seeing my friends' lifeless bodies laid out in rows on the stone had brought with it a pain that cut me right to my core. They were there, lying right next to me, and yet they were gone.

After a restless night, I trudged slowly down the

stairs, a small part of me believing that maybe, just maybe, it had all been a terrible dream. But the bodies were still lying there, and I saw Maheliah kneeling beside the twins, her head bowed in grief. I walked numbly over to join her, staring down at the twins' pale, lifeless faces. I waited, desperately hoping to see the faintest flush in their cheeks or the smallest movement, but there was nothing. They were truly gone.

Kneeling beside Maheliah, I let my head rest on her shoulder, my tears soaking through the fabric of her dress. She wrapped her arm around me, holding me upright, and we remained there, united in our grief, until Maheliah rose to her feet, kissing me gently on the top of my head. As queen, she could not dwell on her own grief for long. She had to support her subjects.

The day passed quietly and sorrowfully, with all the survivors gathering in the great hall, grieving the loss of friends and family. Maheliah comforted each group of mourners individually, her empathy and emotion never faltering, no matter how many times she spoke the same words. As evening drew near, I assumed that we would take the bodies outside and bury them beside the palace, but once every family had been comforted, Maheliah stood at the front of the hall and opened a giant portal, gesturing for us to carry the dead through with us. To my surprise, the portal brought us out in front of Netis' palace, just as the sun was setting, the glowing orb bathing the dead and living alike in its golden rays.

"Netis!" Maheliah cried in a tearful voice. "See what your stubbornness and violence have brought us. Look at these bodies. You have killed them, Netis. Your own people. They lie before you now, as a reminder of what you have done. By nightfall, snow will have covered them all, but this should not be their grave. If you have even the slightest ounce of remorse left, you will give them the burial they deserve."

Maheliah choked on her tears as she finished her speech. Then, turning to us all, she gestured for us to walk back through the portal, as the storm began to rage. Maheliah and I were the last to leave, and as I took one last look at the lifeless bodies of my friends, I understood that I had no choice but to accept that they would no longer be with me.

Sitting on my bed in Maheliah's palace, I could not stop thinking about the tragedy that had befallen us the previous day. What would happen now? Would Netis finally realise that this war was pointless? Could he be humble enough to forget his need for power? Despite everything that had happened, I did not believe that he was truly heartless, but I knew that life would be different now; I would be different. His kisses and touches would never feel the same.

I was lost in my thoughts when I noticed Maheliah peering shyly through the splintered gap in my door. Her eyes still sparkled sadly, but she smiled softly as she entered, coming to sit next to me on the bed.

"Fada, I know how hard this must be for you…" she began, her voice gentle.

"It's hard for everyone. This ridiculous battle brought pain to the whole kingdom," I answered numbly. "Everything's Netis' fault, as usual…"

"Don't blame him. It's not his fault, but mine."

"How could this be your fault? He's the one who sent his army here. You were only defending yourself."

"No, Fada, you don't understand. I pushed him too far. I know what triggers his temper, but I angered him anyway. He would have never done such a thing if I had not provoked him. You could have reasoned with him, but I locked you away, too caught up in my own jealousy and pride…"

As she spoke, tears began to roll down her cheeks. It was painful to see how guilty she felt, and I could not hold back my own tears.

"No, Maheliah, this isn't your fault. Your intention was never to kill anyone, you only did what you thought was best for your people."

"And yet half of those people are now dead; gone forever. I always wanted you to feel at home in Hagalaz,

Fada, and to find your place among our people. I was so happy to see how close you were to Nalhya and Lilhya. Your friendship was pure and honest; they truly loved you."

"I know… it's unbearable, knowing that they are gone; knowing that I will never see them again. Who will leave me next? You? Angel? I can't lose anyone else." I broke down, my body wracked by uncontrollable sobs.

"Shh, shh, Fada. It's all right. You're not going to lose anybody else, I promise."

"I just don't understand why they fought against each other. They were all united once. Why did they listen to you and Netis?"

"Because they are loyal."

"What do you mean?"

"I know loyalty to a sovereign isn't something that you are familiar with, but it's one of the foundations of our civilisation here. Netis and I are their monarchs; our people don't want to rebel against us. They swore an oath of allegiance to us, and their duty is to obey and serve us. It's a very important part of their lives. They've been raised understanding that their destiny is to serve truthfully, and to be ready to die for us and their kingdom."

I was sick and tired of constantly hearing about destiny. Why should everything be set in stone? Why should we all have a defined role and future?

Maheliah laid a kiss on my head, smiling gently as she stood up to leave.

"Maheliah, wait. There's still something I don't understand. Why did you stop me from running towards Nalhya?"

"I thought it was best to let her say her farewell to her sister alone. The love between twins is much stronger on our planet than it is on Earth. They are one soul in two different bodies. It would have been impossible for Nalhya to survive without her sister. They could not have lived without each other. Even if she had not killed herself, she would have died of sorrow soon after her sister's death. Her soul had been sawed in half; nobody could have healed her wound. As soon as her sister died, she died too."

After Maheliah had left, I curled up on my bed, thoughts and images swirling through my mind: the dead... the blood... Netis... Angel's wound... Maheliah's guilt. Staring blindly out of the window, I tried to shut everything out, tried to sleep, but it was useless.

When the sun had almost reached its zenith, I decided to get up. On a normal day, it would have been time to meet Angel, and since I could not imagine spending the rest of the day inside the palace, I reasoned that going down to the lake might at least serve as a welcome distraction.

Dressing myself felt strange, serving as a stark reminder of what I had lost. My morning routine was usually such a joyful time: just the three of us, chatting and laughing together. It would never be the same. They had left me... I would never wake up to the sound of their enchanting crystal voices again.

I finished lacing up my dress alone, in silence, before leaving for our secret place. I hoped Angel would be there. Everything else in my life was falling apart; I needed to know that he was okay.

Staring out at the frozen lake, I took a deep breath, trying to focus on the landscape and escape from the confusion of my thoughts. A few moments later, I heard footsteps in the snow, and I turned, relived to see Angel walking slowly towards me. Seeing him surrounded by snow – the blue of his eyes accentuated by the light reflecting off the frozen water – brightened the darkness in my soul. Ever since I had first met him, all those months ago, his presence had warmed my heart, and I felt like every time I saw him, I fell more deeply in love. He was beautiful and lovely; being with him was as easy as breathing.

But then I had met Netis... equally beautiful, though

his beauty was quite different. Angel was undeniably gorgeous, and his name suited him well, with his angelic loveliness and pure aquamarine eyes, whereas Netis' beauty was perhaps not as straightforward; he had a devilish comeliness about him, and it was his charisma more than his looks that made him attractive. His gaze was always stoical, and most people would assume he had no feelings at all, yet I had seen emotion behind his eyes from the moment I first met him. He reminded me of a bear, with his deep black eyes and fearsome reputation. Everyone was afraid of him, not realising that beneath his rage and anger was a broken man, sensitive and gentle, loving even. A beast with a tender heart.

Angel was more like a wolf, protective and loyal, though sometimes his gaze took on the expression of a hounded creature, struggling to break free from captivity. He constantly reminded me that he was Netis' slave, and every time I tried to tell him that this was not true, he would retort by showing me his necklace, the onyx that Netis had given to him as a child. This symbol reminded me of the bracelet I wore, and the wound beneath it. We both bore marks of ownership; I belonged to Netis just as much as Angel did.

I was dragged from my thoughts by the warmth of Angel's hand on my cheek. His gaze was concerned, so I smiled softly to reassure him, reaching up my hand and stroking his hair.

"I'm so glad you're here, Fada. I thought you might not come after what happened yesterday. How's your shoulder?"

My smile vanished, his words reminding me of the awful battle and the loss I had suffered.

"It's okay, bruised and sore, but bearable. I just can't believe how many people we lost yesterday," I answered, bowing my head.

"At least you're alive. That's all that matters."

"No, it's not," I retorted, raising my voice. "I might be alive, but Nalhya and Lilhya... they're gone, Angel. My best friends are gone..."

My voice trembled as I tried to keep my sobs back. I was so tired of everyone treating me like my life was more worthy than everyone else's. Nalhya and Lilhya might not have been princesses, but they had not deserved to die.

"I'm sorry, Fada, I didn't know. I know how close you were to them. I'm truly sorry."

"They were my closest friends... they were like sisters to me. I'll never hear their laughter again..."

"It's okay, I'm here. I'll always be here," Angel assured me, pulling me into his chest.

As I wrapped my arms around his waist and clung to him tightly, he let out a gasp of pain, making me pull away in shock. I had completely forgotten about his wound, and as I looked down, I noticed a large bandage covering the area just above his hip.

"Oh, Angel, I'm so sorry. Did I hurt you?"

"I'm okay, don't worry. I've had worse wounds before."

"Don't lie to me, I can see the pain in your eyes. Please, let me look at it…"

I moved my hand towards his bandage, but Angel stopped me.

"Don't. It's not serious, but the wound isn't pretty…"

I ignored him, gently peeling the bandage away from his skin. I heard him try to contain another gasp, confirming my suspicions: his injury was more serious than he wanted me to believe. Removing the last of the bandage, I stared down in horror. A large red cut lay just above his hip, coated in coagulated blood, the skin around it red and sore. I could only imagine how painful it was, and I could not understand how he had walked all the way from the palace with a wound like that.

Sliding my fingers delicately around the cut, I felt him shiver in response, and I looked up at him, tears in my eyes.

"This is all my fault. I'm sorry, I'm so sorry, Angel…"

"Don't apologise. None of this is your fault. If you had not stopped the fight, things would have been much worse, and I would almost certainly be dead—"

"Don't say things like that!" My voice was trembling; even the thought of what could have happened made my entire body ache. "How could Netis do this? This is all his fault. I hate him… I hate him!"

Angel pulled me back into his arms, despite his wound.

"Don't be too harsh on him. Many events led to that battle taking place; the blame is not his alone. He has cared for all of us who were wounded yesterday, and the dead have been given a respectful burial. He cleaned my wound himself, Fada. It's thanks to him that I am able to walk right now."

I stared at him. Why would Netis do such a thing? It did not make any sense.

"Well, if it wasn't for him, you would not have been injured in the first place. It's his duty to take care of you," I answered bitterly.

"Fada, please. It's not his fault. He was trying to do what he thought was best. He's not always cruel, you know."

It was ironic that Angel was the one trying to convince me of Netis' kindness: I knew better than most how affectionate and gentle Netis could be. Nevertheless, it was pleasantly surprising to hear that Netis had treated Angel well, and I felt some of my resentment melting away, though I could not forgive him fully. He may not have killed my friends with his

263

own hands, but their deaths were still his fault.

"I know he caused a lot of pain," Angel continued. "But I'm certain that he feels guilty about it."

"I don't understand why you're defending him. He's always so harsh with you."

"But he's always been there for me. He may have raised me to be a great warrior, but he has also looked after me for all these years. I am forever indebted to him for that. He's the only family I have, Fada. I care for him more than I can express."

His words stabbed me through the heart, and now more than ever, I felt the guilt of my behaviour. I had been secretly having sex with the only family Angel had ever known; I hated myself for my wickedness. People always spoke of how cruel and heartless Netis was, yet I realised in that instant that I was even worse.

"Fada, are you okay?" Angel asked, after too many seconds of silence.

"I'm fine. It's just… I need to speak to Netis. We need to talk about what happened."

"I know you're angry, Fada, but please, don't be too hard on him."

"I'll try…"

Angel did not need to worry. I knew that, even if I began my conversation with Netis angry, I would not be able to stay furious for long; my feelings for him were too strong. It frustrated me, knowing that I would almost certainly end up being kind and gentle with Netis when what I needed to be was harsh and pitiless. I hated the way he made me feel, and I hated how much power he had over me; seeing how Angel felt about him only made me feel more frustrated with myself.

Angel held my chin between his fingers and kissed me tenderly, but though I tried to enjoy the moment, my mind was already thinking about how the conversation with Netis would turn out. Slowly releasing myself from Angel's embrace, I looked up into his eyes. His gaze was soft, but instead of reassuring me, it made me feel even more guilty, and I immediately looked down, gently replacing his bandage as an excuse not to look at him.

"I have to go now, I told Netis I would help to look after the wounded," Angel murmured as he watched me fix his bandage.

"Will I see you tomorrow?"

"Always…"

He lifted my chin up and kissed me again, before standing up from the bench and walking back to the palace, leaving me alone with my thoughts once more.

The following morning, I woke up with a heavy feeling crushing my lungs. I knew I had to speak to Netis, but I dreaded seeing him, and after thinking it over, I decided to go and talk to Akaoh first. I wanted to hear his view on the whole situation, and what he thought I should do next. I knew his complex speech would make it difficult for me to understand him, but I needed to hear his advice. It was an unusual feeling for me; for as long as I could remember, I had been terrible at listening to others and obeying the rules, and I had always hated the idea of people having power over me. My freedom was too important to me, and having people tell me what I should or should not do made me feel trapped. Yet Akaoh's orders were different; they were more like prophecies, and whether I liked it or not, I felt compelled to accept everything he said.

After trudging through the snow to the abandoned palace, I entered, walking down the slate covered corridor and swiftly by-passing the door to the strange upstairs room. Akaoh was sitting in the throne room, looking as though he had not moved since the last time I had been to visit him. I walked closer, my heart pounding at the sight of this mysterious man. He had such an incredible aura around him, and it made me wonder whether he was truly human. His body seemed so weak, yet I knew that he was immensely powerful.

As I moved towards him, Akaoh raised his head and looked at me with his two glittering ruby eyes. His face was still deeply wrinkled and deathly pale, the face of a

266

wizened old man, but his gaze remained sharp and penetrating. Looking into his eyes, I tried to look regal and gracious as I bowed before him, though in truth my mind was full of fear.

"Coming back to me, young princess?" he murmured.

I could not say a word; his voice paralysed me. It sounded like it was coming from within a deep ocean gulf rather than from his shrivelled mouth.

"I shall answer your questions but remember that only a correct question will give you a correct answer." he continued, using the same lifeless tone.

"There was an awful battle…"

"You know the past, and so do I. What you seek is knowledge of your future."

"Should I reprimand Netis?" I asked bluntly.

"You lost two women whom you cherished deeply, but it was their destiny to die that day. You cannot go against fate. Everything has already been written. Reprimanding Netis will not bring your friends back…"

"I understand…" I murmured, bewitched by his words.

"Yet, you will reprimand him. This is your fate."

"But you just said that it would be useless to do so?"

"You are twisting my words, young one. Listen carefully. Reprimanding him will not bring your friends back, but you will do it anyway. Misfortune has rained

267

down on you ever since you met with him. Everything is in desolation because he cannot control his emotions, and only your words can change his behaviour."

I was compelled by his words, unable to focus on anything else.

"Blaming Netis will not bring your friends back, but it is the path you must follow to break the curse of Hagalaz."

I opened my eyes wide. Break the curse? Could it be possible? I must have misunderstood him. Surely the simple act of me blaming Netis for his actions could not break a curse as old as time?

"You must tell him how you feel. No need to raise your voice and use harsh words. Fate is all you need by your side," Akaoh continued.

Overwhelmed and confused, I nodded mutely, hoping that he might elaborate further, but Akaoh simply gave me a piercing look before dropping his head, breaking our connection. I waited for a moment, but he did not move, and I realised that our conversation was over. Making the traditional Hagal gesture of farewell, I walked backwards out of the throne room, before turning and walking away from the palace, contemplating his strange but sensible words.

There had been no need for him to advise me against raising my voice; regardless of how angry I was with Netis, I did not want my words to cause him pain.

Besides, I knew that speaking softly to him was always more effective. But I was still confused by Akaoh's words regarding the curse. I had a hard time believing that a simple talk between myself and Netis could break the curse, and I was certain that I had misunderstood. Yet I trusted his wisdom. Talking with Netis might not instantly break the curse, but there was a possibility that it would bring us one step closer to peace. It was terrifying, thinking that I was the one responsible for restoring some semblance of tranquillity to the kingdom, but regardless of how nervous I felt, I knew that confronting Netis was the right thing to do. I just had to summon up the courage to do it.

CHAPTER XV - THE BEGINNING OF THE END

Slowly walking towards Netis' palace, I tried to rationalise everything that had happened over the past few days. I was still wracked with grief, and I knew it would be difficult to calmly confront Netis when I still blamed him for the deaths of Nalhya and Lilhya. Knowing that I had lost my friends because of him was a hard pill to swallow; no one should have died that day, especially not because of something so pathetic as Netis' own childish desire to win against Maheliah. I refused to understand how Netis could be so at ease with sacrificing people for the sake of having me by his side.

Calming my breathing, I tried to push my feelings of hatred and betrayal aside. Once I was there, with him, looking into his eyes, I knew that my fury would subside, but I wanted to ensure that I was in control of my emotions before I entered the palace. I did not want to accidentally lash out before I reached Netis.

As I approached the gate, I saw that the two guards were staring at me, their expressions less than welcoming. I knew that they probably held me responsible for all the death and violence that had befallen them a few days previously, and I could not blame them. Had I never existed, Maheliah and Netis would never have had reason to argue in the first place. But it was not my fault that they had chosen to fight over me, and I needed the guards to understand that all I wanted was to end this pointless war and finally restore peace to Hagalaz.

As I took another step closer to the gate, the guards pointed their spears at me in a quick and harsh motion.

"Don't come any closer, princess. Do you honestly believe yourself welcome here after what happened?"

"Because of you, our friends are dead."

"I'm sorry for your loss," I assured them calmly. "Mine are dead too—"

"Yours?" the first guard interrupted. "How could you have any friends? You've been nothing but trouble ever since you were born, even before you came to Hagalaz. Our king and queen have been arguing for the past twenty years, and we have had no choice but to live separately from our friends and families. We have been forced to fight against the people that we love, all because of you. How could anyone be heartless enough to befriend you?"

271

"But I was given no choice; I'm just as much a pawn in this ridiculous game as you are. I was left to grow up on a planet where I did not belong, feeling different and misunderstood for as long as I can remember, and when I had finally made peace with my lot in life, someone from another world appeared in my life, told me I was a princess, and insisted that I had no choice but to leave my old life behind. How can you possibly believe that I ever wanted any of that?"

I choked down a sob. Their words had hurt me even more that I had expected, and they were proud of themselves.

"Oh look, our poor dear princess is crying because of us," the first guard sneered.

"I can see now how she succeeded in bewitching poor Angel. His life had been tied to hers for so long; by playing the victim, she only made the poor boy feel more protective over her."

I raised my head up and looked at them, disconcerted. What did they mean his life was tied to mine?

"Angel is one thing, but I can't believe our great king has fallen for her. I wonder what good he sees in her."

"Screwing her every day had clearly brainwashed him. Makes me wonder what she's hiding behind that innocent face…"

Giving each other a sly look, they turned and began

to walk towards me, brandishing their spears and glaring at me with hatred.

"I would be very careful if I were you..." came a deep, powerful voice from behind them.

The guards instantly turned as Netis appeared from the darkness of the doorway, his eyes glinting dangerously.

"Unless, of course, you wish to face the same fate as the last person who harmed her..."

The guards bent their heads and moved to the side, removing their spears from my vicinity as Netis held out his hand towards me. Looking down at his upturned palm, I crossed my arms and walked inside, making my way up the stairs without saying a word. Netis followed me, respecting my silence.

As we entered his bedroom, Netis went to shut the door behind him, but I stopped him.

"Don't. I'm only here to speak."

He immediately released the handle and walked over to me, fixing his gaze on my eyes.

"Why did you attack Maheliah's palace?" I asked abruptly. "Why, Netis? People are dead because of your pointless battle. How could you sacrifice your own people?"

"It was the only way to have you again..." he answered quietly.

"Have me? I've never been yours, Netis. I'm not

273

your slave to command. You should know by now that violence only makes me want to stay away from you. You are a great king, Netis. I don't understand why you keep making such reckless decisions."

"I will do whatever it takes to keep you by my side."

"Then why choose the path of violence? Listen to me, Netis. I know that you have a kind heart. Please, stop this stupid fight with Maheliah. I don't want anyone else to die…"

"If that idiot had not tried to kill you…" Netis closed his eyes firmly and clenched his fists. "… you would be mine now."

I looked down with a sigh and gently coaxed at his fists with my fingers, trying to unclench them. After a second or two of resistance, his hands relaxed, his fingers entwining with mine. I raised my head to meet his gaze, finding an unusual mix of sadness and wrath in his eyes.

"No, Netis, even if that man had not tried to kill me, I would not be yours now. Everyone would be dead, and you would have lost everything. You must stop waging war against Maheliah. It will only bring unhappiness to you and your people."

"Am I truly so despicable that you would rather have everyone sacrificed for you than be by my side?"

I stared at him in shock, my heart beating fast as my anger rose.

"How dare you. Is that really what you think of me? Do you truly believe that I could condone the sacrifice of hundreds of people?"

I felt my voice clamp up and I stopped, trying to hold back my tears. Netis looked at me sorrowfully, taking my hands in his, but I shook them off, moving away from him.

"No, Fada. Of course not," he murmured. "I just… I just don't understand why you despise me so much…"

His voice was so full of pain that I could not stop myself from reaching for him, resting my hands gently on his arms.

"I don't despise you, Netis."

"Then why don't you want to be by my side?" he uttered, looking deep into my eyes.

I did not know what to answer. He was right, my choice to stay with Maheliah made no sense. Not only was I constantly having to fight against my desire for Netis, but I was also separated from Angel. I should have wanted to move into Netis' palace the instant I had met him, yet something had stopped me. For a start, living under the same roof as both Angel and Netis would have made the situation I faced infinitely more complicated, and then there was Maheliah. I could not possibly imagine betraying her by leaving her side. My bond with her was now too strong to be broken.

My silence clearly meant something to Netis, for he

275

gently pulled away from me, his eyes downcast.

"I understand…"

As he pronounced these words, a wave of sadness and pain washed across his face, his eyes sparkling. He turned swiftly, trying to hide his distress, but I had seen enough.

"It's because I love you!"

I quickly put my hands over my mouth, shocked by my outburst. The words had come unbidden to my lips, but I could not undo them now. It was done. Netis knew how I really felt. My self-control was slipping through my fingers as he turned back to face me, his gaze a mixture of incomprehension, desire, affection and sorrow. Coming towards me, he placed his hand delicately on my cheek. I wanted to say something, to justify what had just happened, but I was paralysed; unable to think. He brought his face closer to mine, and I truly wanted his lips, but I knew that, if I kissed him, I would lose myself for good. Plucking up my courage, I succeeded in turning my face to the right, breaking our connection.

"No, Netis. We can't do this anymore. I still love Angel; being with you is unfair on him. He doesn't deserve that…"

Before I could process what was happening, Netis took my chin between his thumb and forefinger, forcing me to look into his eyes, before lowering his face towards mine. I knew then that I had lost, and as he slid his hand around my waist, I lifted my face, closing the gap between us. His lips were soft and gentle, and I lost myself in his embrace, enjoying the feel of his lips on mine after days of us being apart.

As I wrapped my hands around the back of his neck, pulling him closer, I heard a noise coming from the direction of the door. Still kissing Netis, I glanced over to see what it was, but what I saw made me pull away instantly. It was him… Angel. He was standing by the door, watching us, his expression flickering between shock, betrayal, and despair. He looked at me, then at Netis, then back at me, his eyes wide. Opening his mouth, he tried to say something, but he quickly closed his lips together again, clenching his jaw in distress.

My pulse was racing and my heart thumped loudly in my chest. I wanted to apologise; to tell him it had all been a mistake, but I knew that he had already seen past any pretence I could come up with. I looked desperately into his eyes, but Angel tore his face away from my gaze and ran down the stairs, his footsteps leaving a hollow echo behind. Frozen in place, I stared after him, still wrapped in Netis' arms, not knowing what to do. Eventually, the shock wore off enough for me to turn my face back towards Netis. He looked at me, his guilt and shame mirroring mine, and I shook myself out of my frozen state, leaving his embrace and following Angel down the stairs.

"Looks like our poor Angel has finally opened his eyes," the guards jeered as I ran from the palace, sprinting through the snow as quickly as I could.

I could not care less for their words. All that mattered in this instant was Angel, and I ran towards our secret place, knowing that I would find him there. As I ran, I tried to clear my mind. Should I tell him the truth about my relationship with Netis? I had to give him some kind of explanation; he needed to know why Netis had kissed me. How would he react though? Would he bear a grudge against me? Would he ever talk to me again? These questions resonated inside my head and I dreaded the answers, knowing that regardless of how he reacted our relationship would never be the same again.

I found Angel sitting on the ground, his elbows resting on his knees and his back against the bench, looking out over the lake. I stopped running and I walked slowly towards him. I was certain that he had heard me coming, but he remained seated, staring resolutely out over the frozen water. His jaw was tense, his breathing fast, and his gaze was a mix of sadness and hatred.

When I was close enough to speak to him comfortably, I stopped walking, waiting for him to say something. My heart was beating fast, and I was terrified that he would simply refuse to talk to me. I

278

hated myself for making him suffer. I wished he would just confront me, but he remained still and silent, forcing us both to endure the oppressive quiet that hung between us. Eventually, I could stand it no longer.

"Angel, please, say something…" I murmured.

He did not answer, so I crouched down next to him, looking at him with sorrow and despair.

"Angel…" I repeated, my voice trembling.

Still no answer. I sat down next to him and wrapped my hands around his arm, laying a kiss on it. I was on the verge of tears.

"Angel, please… answer me…"

With a sigh, Angel stood, leaving my embrace. Still sat on the ground, I stared up at him with tears in my eyes. He sighed again and clenched his fists, looking straight in front of him.

"I'm not angry with you, don't worry…"

His voice was calm, but a little too controlled for me to be convinced by his words, and as he turned to look back at me, I could see that his gaze was full of emotions. He seemed torn between sadness and compassion, which disturbed me as much as his words had. It scared me, his indifference. Why was he not angry with me? If he had yelled at me, I would have known that he still cared for me, but this response was like an electric shock. He could not be so stoical, not him…

Walking towards me, Angel gave me his hand, and after a moment of hesitancy, I took it, standing to my feet. I could not stop looking into his eyes. I needed him to see my shame and despair; I needed him to see that I knew how greatly I had betrayed him. I was desperate for him to shout at me, to weep… anything to show that his pain matched my own. But his gaze was stoical and understanding.

"You're the princess, Fada. It is your right… no, your duty, to be beside the king. You should never have fallen for a common slave like me in the first place."

I looked at him with despondency. His words were like stabs to my heart, and I would have preferred him to physically torture me rather than hearing those words. I was totally confused.

"Angel, what are you talking about? None of this is about what I should or should not do. My feelings for you are real, and I don't want to stop myself from feeling them. I don't care about your status. I just want you…"

"I thought you understood, Fada. You've been in Hagalaz for nearly a year now. You must know that princesses can't marry slaves. I could never be with you."

I tried to contain my sobs.

"Rules have never stopped me before, Angel. I'll be by your side as long as you want me…"

I looked down, afraid of his answer, but he took my chin between his fingers and forced me to look into his eyes.

"But I can't break the law, Fada. There will always be a law that stands between us, and I could never ask you to follow it…"

My heart exploded inside my chest. I had been dreading this moment for so long. But he had to know that the law no longer stood against us; that I had already fulfilled the terms it stipulated. He had been raised in the knowledge that not listening to laws would only bring pain and sorrow. He had already suffered under the whim of the law when he had brought me to Maheliah instead of Netis.

I wondered what would have happened if Angel had brought me to Netis when I had first arrived here… would it have ended the war, or would Maheliah have been as obstinate and obsessive as Netis? What about my relationship with Netis? Would I still have had sex with him? Would I still have fallen in love with him? Or would I have remained loyal to Angel? It was strange to think about.

I sighed. It was time to tell Angel the truth.

"What if the law didn't stand between us?"

"Fada, I could never ask you to do that—"

"But you don't need to ask me…" I paused, taking a shaky breath. "You don't need to ask me because… I've already fulfilled that law."

Angel stared at me, his eyes wide.

"What?" he whispered in a broken voice.

I could feel my tears trying to escape, but I blinked them back. Telling him everything was going to break my heart, but I had no choice. He deserved to know the truth.

"I made love to Netis," I whispered, looking down at the trampled snow.

I felt Angel's body go rigid, as if frozen, and I looked up to see him staring back at me numbly, his eyes blank and expressionless.

"I did it for you, Angel."

His eyes widened, and I started talking rapidly, desperate to make him understand.

"I know it doesn't seem to make much sense, but I promise you it was for you. To save your life, after Netis banished you. When I saw you nearly frozen to death, lying on the ground of that terrible cave, I ran to Netis with no plan whatsoever. All I knew was that I would do whatever it took to save you. We talked; I tried to reason him, but nothing worked. One thing led to another, and I realised that the only way to save you was to make love to him…"

My heart was beating frantically with panic. I needed him to understand that I had made love to Netis only to save him; I needed him to forgive me. But as I looked desperately into his eyes, I could see that he was struggling to accept my story.

"What about that kiss just now? Was that to save me too?"

Adrenaline surged through my veins as my panic rose. I realised there was no point hiding it now. I needed to tell him the truth: all of it. He had heard the hardest part already; I could only hope that the rest would be easier to swallow.

"No… it was just a kiss…" I looked down, unable to meet his gaze. "One among many others. Again and again we kissed and… made love…"

I could not bear to look at him. It was hard enough admitting the truth; seeing his aching heart through his eyes would have tipped me over the edge. I had always known that I was betraying Angel every time I went back to Netis, but to reveal everything to him made me realise the extent of my guilt.

"You made love…"

"I'm so sorry, Angel, I can't tell you how sorry I am for what I did—"

"I'm not talking about what you did. It's your words that I'm trying to understand, Fada. You 'made love' to him…"

His lifted my chin gently, forcing me to meet his gaze. His sparkling aquamarine eyes were moist with tears; his expression tortured. A single tear rolled down his cheek.

"You love him…"

I froze, shocked by my words as much as his. He was right. I had never spoken about my relationship with Netis this way before, and yet here I was, breaking the heart of my first love by unknowingly revealing my feelings. Betraying Angel with my body was one thing but giving my heart, my soul, to another man… that was something else. The reality of what I had just revealed to him hit me like a bullet, and I broke down in sobs, clinging to him.

"Please, Angel. I'm sorry. I'm so sorry, I couldn't… please, forgive me. I love you, Angel… I love you so much. Please, forget it all. I won't ever speak to Netis again; I'll do anything you ask, please just… please forgive me…"

He held my arms gently but firmly, pushing me away from him, his eyes cold.

"This behaviour is not worthy of a princess. A future queen should not be begging a common slave like me."

"Stop, stop saying you're a slave. You're not a slave, Angel. You're the man I love—"

"And yet you made love to another man…"

"I couldn't help it. Every time I… I couldn't stop it. I just wanted to talk to him, but… something always pulled me… pulled me towards him. I'm in love with you, Angel. You are the man I love, I just… I couldn't stop…"

I looked down and waited for Angel to speak, the silence hanging in the air like a dark, brooding storm cloud. I looked at him out of the corner of my eye, hoping to see a sign of forgiveness in his face, but his expression was impossible to read. After a heavy sigh, Angel spoke.

"It's okay, Fada. I understand. Please don't fear my reaction. I love you, and I always will, no matter what, and I know that you love me too. But that does not change the fact that you are the princess, and with that title comes duties and responsibilities that you must uphold. You must do what is right for your people, Fada. I'm sorry I brought you to Hagalaz; I'm sorry I took you away from your family and your freedom. No one here is free, regardless of their status: laws and hierarchy will always steal our freewill. This may be hard to hear, but you need to know that it is your duty as sovereign to put aside your own happiness for the wellbeing of your people. None of us can escape our rank. I will always be a slave, condemned to serve Netis, and you will always be a royal, who must fulfil her fate by protecting the kingdom and its people, even if that means sacrificing your own happiness. It does not matter how much you love me, because we will never be anything but a sweet fantasy. We both have to accept our reality…"

Tears rolled down my cheeks. As much as it broke

my heart to hear him say it, I knew he was right. No one could escape their fate. Angel cupped my face with his hands, looking deep into my eyes. He seemed hopeless, his ocean eyes dull and lifeless.

"I love you…" I sobbed.

"I know… but you love him more."

Bringing his face closer, he pressed his lips to mine, kissing me passionately, the strength of his kiss telling me all I needed to know. This would be the last time. Pulling him towards me, I kissed him back, desperate to cling onto our past happiness. Eventually, he removed his lips, rubbing his nose softly against mine.

"I love you, Fada. Every moment with you has brought me more happiness that I ever thought I would experience in this life. You brightened my world."

"Angel…"

I wrapped my arms around him, burying my face into his chest, and I felt his body shaking, his hot tears falling onto my hair. He held me for a moment as we both wept, before trying to pull away again. I grabbed his hands in mine, gazing at him desperately as he looked back at me, his eyes full of pain and sorrow. Bringing my hands to his lips, he laid a kiss on my knuckles, his lips trembling as more tears rolled down his cheeks. I clung to him tightly, but he gently peeled my fingers from his and turned aside, bowing his head as he walked away. I stared after him, hoping he might glance back at me;

hoping he might turn and run and hold me in his arms again. But he kept walking, and I was left alone in the cold, watching until he disappeared into the thick, winter fog.

CHAPTER XVI - BAD DECISIONS

I was alone, surrounded by nothing but the coldness of the day. Angel was gone. He hated me now, I was sure of it, and I could not blame him. I had become so cruel, hurting people's feeling constantly. It was beyond my control, yet it seemed to be the only thing I was capable of these days. I had betrayed the trust of the man I loved; I had caused my two best friends to die; my existence had cost Maheliah and Netis their friendship. I was a monster, inflicting nothing but pain and suffering upon the people I loved. Perhaps I had always been a monster; perhaps coming to Hagalaz had revealed my true self?

I could not stop thinking of Angel. His reaction and the pain in his eyes had made me realise just how much I loved him. I could never forgive myself for being this wicked to him. I knew that, regardless of what I did to try and make it up to him, he would never look at me the same way again. Our happiness had been shattered beyond repair. This place that had once been our safe haven had now witnessed our end.

I fell to the ground in despair, a cry of pure heartache breaking free, piercing the still winter air. I imagined Angel walking through the corridors of Netis' palace, passing by me with a hateful look, or ignoring me completely. It was unbearable, knowing that I had lost him forever.

I stayed on the ground for a long time, lost in my sorrow and pain, shivering as the darkness drew nearer. It was tempting to remain; to let the evening storm end my suffering. But I knew that I had caused enough pain for one day, so I wiped at my tears and pulled myself to my feet, letting my body trudge slowly back to Maheliah's palace. I wondered how Maheliah would react when she realised that I would not be meeting up with Angel anymore. She would ask me about it, certainly, but what could I say? I could not tell her that Angel was no longer in love with me because she would ask for more details, and I knew that I was not a good enough liar to create an excuse that she would believe. Should I tell her about what had been going on between myself and Netis? No, I was not courageous enough… and yet… it was the only thing I could do. I had lied to Maheliah, and Angel, and myself for far too long. It was time to admit the truth.

I had spent so long trying to convince myself that Netis did not matter to me, and even when I had admitted my feelings for him, I had still always insisted to myself that I loved Angel more. But now Angel was gone, I realised that I had been lying to myself. My life without Angel would be empty, but a life without Netis was something I simply could not imagine. I needed him, more than I could fathom. It was terrifying to admit to myself, but I could not hide any longer. I was done with the lies.

Taking a deep breath, I walked past the guardians and into Maheliah's palace, intent on telling her the truth about my relationship with Netis. Maheliah was sitting on her throne, leafing through a manuscript, but she looked up as I entered, her expression shifting to one of concern as she saw the tightness in my face and the streaks of salt on my cheeks.

"Have you been crying, my dear?" she asked gently, as she came towards me.

I smiled at her, but I could see from her face that she understood my pain.

"There's something I must tell you, Maheliah, but I would prefer it if we could talk somewhere more private."

"Of course," she replied, gesturing up the stairs, still looking at me with concern.

We walked up to my bedroom in silence, my heart

beating faster as we drew closer.

"Fada, what's going on?" Maheliah finally asked as we sat down on my bed. "Did you get hurt? Was it Netis again?"

"In a way…" I murmured, my voice trembling. "But not just him…"

"Others too?" she gasped, her eyes wide with horror.

"No, no, not at all." I took her hands in mine. "Netis is not the only one because I have also made myself suffer."

"You're making no sense at all, Fada."

Taking a deep breath, I looked down at my hands. I was about to tell her everything, and it was terrifying. I hated knowing that my life was about to change forever, and I wished that everything could just stay the same. But I knew that I could not erase the past.

"Do you remember when Netis banished Angel? When he spent the night in the cave and nearly froze to death?"

"Of course I remember. You managed to convince Netis to take him back…"

"I made love to him that day… I made love to Netis. That's how I got him to take Angel back."

Maheliah was silent, and after a long pause, I looked up, wondering why she had not said anything yet. She was staring at me, frowning, her emerald eyes full of mixed emotions.

291

"Why, Fada?"

"It was to save Angel—"

"Oh Fada, I know you're young and new to love, but surely you must know that, when you love somebody, you don't make love to someone else."

"I know, but... I've felt this connection to Netis ever since we first met. It's... I can't explain it. It's out of my control. I need to be close to him... I can't help it."

"So, this was not a one time thing, I presume?"

"No... it happened again... many times."

Maheliah looked at me with anger, and I could see in her eyes how ashamed of me she was, which made my own shame even worse.

"Angel has sacrificed himself many times to save you; to protect you. It's obvious how important you are to him, and how much he cares for you. And this is his reward? Why, Fada? Do you love him? Do you love Netis?"

I stared at her mutely, not knowing what to say.

"Do you love him?" she asked again, stressing every word.

"I... I don't know. My love for Angel is straightforward; easy. He makes me happy. The way I feel for Netis is different. When I look into his eyes, I feel understood, and his touch makes me feel alive. I am... at peace with him," I stammered, trembling.

"I can't believe you fell for him..."

"But I love Angel. My relationship with Netis only started because of that crazy deal to save Angel."

"Stop lying to yourself, Fada. If this had just been about Angel, you would have never gone back."

"I can't help it. When Netis' hands are on me, I can't think about anything else. It's like fire in my veins, but it's not just physical desire; it's not just lust. His presence it... it soothes my soul. And when I learned about that ridiculous law it made me realise that, by accepting the deal, Netis was doing me a favour, not the other way around. He knew that I would have no choice but to have sex with him if I wanted to be intimate with Angel, so he agreed to my deal to set me free from that law. After that, I could not think of him as selfish and heartless anymore."

"But Netis is selfish and heartless, Fada. He only accepted your deal to win yet another battle. He's always wanted everything, and by pretending to be kind, he has won both your body and your heart. Don't be foolish, Fada. He's incapable of loving."

I knew Maheliah was wrong. I remembered his confession that day before the battle. Those feelings he had described were not false.

"That's not true. He confessed to having loved before, and from what he said, I'm certain he still loves that woman, whoever she is."

"What are you talking about? He's never been in

293

love, believe me. He would have told me. Love has never been of interest to him; he's always been nothing more than a warrior."

"You must be wrong, Maheliah. He truly seemed in pain when he was talking about that woman. I know he was telling the truth."

"Just another swindle to get you into bed with him, I'm sure."

"But that makes no sense. I was already in bed with him when we had that conversation, it can't have been a ploy. Maybe he just didn't tell you? Maybe it happened after you two fought—"

"No! Listen to me, Fada. I'm telling you, Netis has never been in love, though sometimes I wish he would fall in love and lose it. He deserves to suffer; he deserves to feel that pain."

"How can you wish such cruel fate upon anyone? Nobody deserves that much suffering. It doesn't matter how cruel you think he is, you shouldn't wish for your own brother to go through that—"

"Then why did he make me suffer?" Maheliah clenched her fists, looking at me with fury. "Why did he kill the only man I have ever loved? Tell me that, Fada."

I stared at her in shock, my eyes wide. Netis had killed the man she loved? Why?

"Maheliah, I…"

I stood up to comfort her, but she pushed me away,

running from the room in tears, almost colliding with one of the healers who happened to be walking past. Seeing Maheliah's distress, the healer looked at me with concern and asked if I was okay, but my mind was so confused and clouded that I could barely process what she was saying. All I could do was stare blankly at her in shock. The healer walked over to me and held my arm gently.

"May I ask what happened?"

I blinked at her, trying to recover from my shock.

"Maheliah... Netis... he killed the man she loved..." I stammered.

"How did you get her to talk about it? She hasn't spoken about him since it happened."

"We were talking about Netis and she just... it just came out. Do you know when it happened?"

"Not long before she heard your soul calling to her."

My heart ached for her. She was still grieving for this man, even after twenty years.

"May I give you a piece of advice?" the healer offered.

I nodded.

"You should never mention it again. Losing her lover at the hands of Netis almost destroyed her. Bringing it up again will only open the lid of her grief. She has suffered enough."

The healer smiled at me sadly and I bowed my head,

acknowledging that I understood. She laid her hand gently on my shoulder, her gesture of kindness almost bringing me to tears, before bowing to me and leaving the room. I stared blankly after her, my mind still trying to process everything I had learned. Maheliah had been in love, and she was still grieving that man's death. I had always believed that she had never experienced anything close to love, but her confession made me realise that there were still many things I did not know about her past.

I understood now why Maheliah could not tolerate my betrayal towards Angel. She had lost the man she loved, of course she could not understand why I had broken the trust of the man I loved for the sake of another, especially when that man was the same person who had killed her true love. I could not believe that Netis had been so cruel. How could he have killed the man that Maheliah loved? Surely there was a reason for his behaviour? He could not be that heartless.

I wondered how Maheliah had managed to carry on with her life after such a terrible event. Had the same thing happened to me, I would have succumbed to my grief; I would have lost my will to live. Yet Maheliah had not only kept going, but she had also maintained her rule over Hagalaz. I had never considered Maheliah to be a strong woman, but now, my perception of her had changed. In my mind, she was no longer simply a loving mother figure who did not care for love or passion, but a resilient and courageous woman, who despite facing more pain than I could ever imagine, had not succumbed to her anger or grief, but had instead continued to rule her kingdom as a kind and generous queen.

More than ever, I wanted to spend time with Maheliah. I wanted to comfort her, to be a shoulder for her to cry on, but I feared that she probably hated me now. It was my fault that she had remembered her lost love; I was certain that I was the last person she wanted to see right now.

Alone in my room, I thought back over the events that had led to this moment. It had all started with Akaoh, convincing me that I should go and confront Netis. Why had he not warned me that all this would happen? If he was so wise, why had he not cautioned me against getting too close to Netis? All of this misery was his fault, why had he let this happen? I thought that he loved Hagalaz; that he wanted the kingdom to be at peace again. Now I wondered how peace would ever be an option.

The sun was just rising, and I had barely slept. I had spent the whole night thinking about everything that had happened the day before, and I was certain of one thing now: I needed to see Akaoh again. I needed him to

297

explain to me why he had let all these terrible things happen, and I also wanted him to tell me about Maheliah and her lost love. He was the only one I could ask such a question; the others in the palace would never tell me anything, and I did not want to ask Netis about it because I feared he would lie to me. Akaoh had no reason to hide the truth. My decision made, I set off for Akaoh's palace, determined not to linger. The old king was a dangerous being, and I had no intention of listening to his advice anymore. All I needed from him was the truth.

Akaoh was sat on his silver throne as usual, his hand holding his ruby topped cane. Without raising his head, he hissed:

"Many questions for a single answer."

I stopped walking, stung by his knowledge that I had many questions for him. I looked at him, fascinated, and sat on the ruined stairs by his side.

"I do have many questions for you, but I'm not sure there is only one answer to them."

"Open your eyes, young princess. One strong answer is often better than a hundred weak ones."

"But my questions are too different to be connected."

"Everything is connected in Hagalaz, and you, my dear, are the link."

"Why don't you just tell me what you want me to do, then?"

"Ask your questions, and you shall have the answer."

Tired of his riddles, I tried to force him to talk some sense.

"Maheliah is in pain. She is still grieving the man she lost. Is there anything I can do to help her?"

"This love had its purpose, which has been fulfilled."

"But she is suffering…"

"Ask me your questions and you shall have my answer."

"Fine. I don't understand why you told me to go and speak to Netis. He kissed me, and Angel saw it, which pained him terribly."

"It is written: Angel must suffer."

His words were unbearable. How could he say such a thing? Angel was by far the kindest and sweetest person I had ever met; he deserved happiness, not heartache. Knowing that his fate was to suffer was impossible to accept.

"You do not like my words, but that is his fate. You cannot change the future," Akaoh continued, his tone indifferent.

"But why must Angel suffer?"

"His suffering shall be the spark that lights the flames. His pain shall bring happiness to the kingdom."

I stared at him in horror. I truly wanted Hagalaz to be at peace again, but I refused to believe that Angel's pain was the only way to restore that peace. There was certainly a better solution. Akaoh seemed to think that I was the link between everything. Surely I was the one who was supposed to suffer, not Angel?

"Ask your last question, and I shall give you the answer."

How could he know that I only had one question left? He was truly the most mysterious being I had ever met. I wondered whether I even needed to ask the question out loud; he seemed to know the answer already.

"My relationship with Netis has brought nothing but sorrow and loss to the kingdom. I cannot help but think that I should stay away from him…"

Akaoh's head was still facing down, but I saw a smile slowly growing on his face. It terrified me, not only because I had never seen him smile, but also because it seemed full of cruel intentions. I looked at him, confused.

"This is indeed a rather torturing thought…" he murmured darkly.

Now I was truly afraid; everything about this situation felt wrong, and all I wanted to do was run. I tried to turn and flee from the throne room, but my feet were stuck to the ground, so I attempted to grab my legs with my arms, assuming that there was something on the floor that was stopping me from moving. But I quickly realised that my arms were just as trapped. My whole body was paralysed by an unknown force.

300

"You shall remain close to him, princess," Akaoh insisted.

Raising his head, he looked deep into my eyes, and his gaze shot through me like a laser. I could no longer look away.

"You shall remain close enough to hurt him," he continued in the same toneless voice. "He has harmed his own people; he has brought misery to Maheliah, Angel and yourself. He has corrupted and dishonoured you. His pride and vanity have caused the downfall of Hagalaz. You shall be his end."

His voice had never been so deep and strong, and hypnotised by his gaze, I felt Akaoh's every word reverberating through my skull. I had never felt so powerless.

"You shall hate him for everything that he has done to you, your loved ones and Hagalaz. You will make him pay; you will make him suffer so much that he shall beg for death before the end. It is your destiny."

His words sounded like more than just a prophecy, and I felt a wave of panic surge through my motionless body. His words kept on echoing inside my head, and with them came another strange sensation. I was not myself anymore. Someone else was inside my mind, and I could feel my soul being compacted; shoved into the tiniest space as another fought it to take its place. I pushed the intruder back, desperate to regain control. I would not let Akaoh use my body as a tool to harm Netis. Mustering all my strength, I shoved at the presence in my mind, and for a few seconds, my soul took back control.

"Stop this, Akaoh! You can't win, I won't harm Netis," I cried out, pushing the words from my mouth, trying desperately to cling on to my own body.

Akaoh opened his eyes wide, and I was instantly thrown to the ground by an invisible force. I tried to stand up, but every inch of my body was being pushed down. The pain was unbearable; it felt like my bones were being crushed by gravity, and I could not help but scream in agony.

"Not you, princess. She shall do it. Let her command you, and your pain shall fade away. Her destiny shall soon be fulfilled."

I had no idea what Akaoh was talking about, but I knew that I had to keep fighting against whatever presence had entered my body. I could not let it win; I could not let someone use my body to harm the man I loved. Desperately, I tried to hang on, pushing back against the other presence, but the pain in my body and my mind was too intense and I could not bear it any longer. Slowly, I felt my strength waning, and as the last shreds of my soul were pushed aside, I felt my body soar up into the air, before falling back to the ground again.

I felt trapped, like a tiny mouse in the corner of a

302

lion's cage. I was still inside my body, but it was not my own anymore. Terrified, I felt myself stand up from the ground and turn to face Akaoh. My lips parted, and a burning sensation seared my throat as a voice that was not my own emerged from my mouth.

"Thank you for trusting me, Akaoh. Netis shall die."

Horrified, I felt myself walk swiftly out of the throne room and back through the slate covered main hall. Voices kept resonating inside my head, but the soul that had possessed my body did not seem bothered by them, walking promptly away from the ruins towards Netis' palace. Waves of hatred coursed through my veins, and all I could feel was the soul's wrath. It desired only one thing: for Netis to suffer.

CHAPTER XVII - REPERCUSSIONS

Being separated from my body and yet still being able to see and feel everything was by far the most unusual and unsettling sensation I had ever experienced. My gestures, words and feelings were real, yet they were not mine; they all belonged to the soul that had taken over my body. I could feel the intense anger and sorrow of this soul; it was tortured, listening to nothing else but instinct. The word vengeance resonated in my head, over and over, and it soon became the only thing I could think about. I was her now.

I walked towards Netis' palace, my fury rising. I had lost everything; now it was his turn to suffer. The day I had died was the day he had been proclaimed a hero. That battlefield, sticky with my blood, had become his trophy ground. I refused to remain a lost soul, watching over him; seeing him make the same stupid decisions day after day. The battle a few days ago had been laughable. Netis, once a valiant warlord, had started the most pathetic war Hagalaz had ever seen. I had no idea how he had become so weak, but I could not let him rule our kingdom anymore. Akaoh wanted me to bring peace to Hagalaz, and I was not planning on disappointing him again.

Netis was no longer fit to be king. He had declared war on his own people and had jeopardised peace. Civil war was not the Hagal way; we had always been united, fighting together against other kingdoms and winning countless times. Netis had planned every battle during the last war against Othalaz, and we had won thanks to him. He had been a dangerous warrior and a wise warlord; he had helped Akaoh to make Hagalaz powerful again, and I had been proud of him. But since the soul of this Fada girl had called to him, he had become rash and unpredictable; weak and pathetic; a dead loss. I had fought so hard, giving my own life to bring pride to Hagalaz, but he had cast aside my sacrifice like it was nothing. My beloved kingdom was heading for disaster because of Netis, and I had no choice but to act before it fell into ruin. I had to make

305

Netis suffer for what he had done; I had to make him pay. Hagalaz would rise again thanks to me.

Giving me a body again had been a clever move by Akaoh. I was the only one who could follow his orders properly. I always had been the only one. Now, Netis would die… but I had to be quick. I did not know how long I would last in this body. It was so small and weak compared to the body I had left behind. I had been Akaoh's pride, his greatest weapon, and it had made me stronger knowing how highly he thought of me. Why had he given me such a weak body? He knew me better than anybody else; he must surely have known how much I would despise this frail frame? There must be other reasons for his choice. Akaoh never made decisions randomly. I was to make use of this body, but how? Fada was clearly not a fighter: the body was bruised, yet she had not even been part of the fight. She had a kind heart, and a pure, gentle soul; we could not have been more different. Perhaps it was for this reason that Akaoh had chosen her? Perhaps I was to use her sweetness and charm to get close to Netis? I could not let him realise that Fada was not herself. My plan had to succeed.

Arriving outside the palace, I found myself standing before two guards. They were strong, like the men I had fought all those years ago, and seeing them gave me an urge to confront them, but I had to control myself. This body was too weak to damage them, and I had to remember to behave like Fada. I was certain that she would never do anything to provoke them. Besides, these men were people of Hagalaz; I was supposed to protect them, not fight against them. Even in death, my only desire was to protect my kingdom. The only Hagal I would allow myself to kill was Netis.

The guards smirked at me scornfully.

"Looks like you finally broke Angel's heart. Poor boy is devastated. Are you proud of yourself, princess?"

I looked at them, confused. Since my death, I had only managed to leave Eihwaz a couple of times. I had no idea who this Angel was, and what Fada could possibly have done to him. But this knowledge might be of use when it came to destroying Netis, so I reasoned that I should try and discover what they meant. Putting on my loveliest voice, I spoke to them.

"What are you talking about?"

The guards looked at each other, opening their eyes wide. They seemed surprised. My voice had not been as sweet as I had expected.

"Watch your tone, princess. Don't try to play innocent with us. You know full well that your dear Angel has finally discovered your little secret. Did you honestly think you could hide the fact that you've been screwing the king forever?"

I stared at them in shock. Now I understood why

Akaoh had given me this body. Fada's relationship with Netis would make killing him easy, and the thought of it made me smile. Grinning menacingly at the guards, I made my way inside and up the stairs. I remembered Netis building these next to his chamber, so that he would be able to come and go whenever it suited him. Arriving outside his room, I knocked on the door.

"You'd better have a very good reason for disturbing me…"

I recognised his voice: low and powerful, with a touch of anger. I was impatient to see him again, so I opened the door quickly, to find him standing in front of his desk, his hands resting on the wood as he contemplated the papers that were laid in front of him. His face had barely changed, and he had the same black look in his eyes. But when he looked up at me, at Fada, his expression changed, like a fire had been lit inside his soul. A rare smile pulled at his lips and I could barely contain my surprise.

"Oh, it's you… since when did you start knocking?"

His sentence surprised me. Fada and Netis were clearly closer than I thought. Perhaps I had been wrong in thinking that their relationship was purely physical? He seemed to care for her a great deal. I smiled to myself. Killing him would be even faster. Trying to look elegant, I walked closer to him, staring into his eyes with what I hoped was a tender expression. I had never behaved like this, and it was especially uncomfortable with Netis in front of me. The man repulsed me, and I had a hard time holding back my disgust.

Netis looked at me with confusion. He was clever; I was not surprised that he had realised something was off. Aware that I needed to act fast if I was going to kill him before he realised what was happening, I hurled myself at him, kissing him fiercely. I felt disgusted by it, but I had to behave like Fada, and I supposed that kissing him was a natural behaviour for her. Netis pushed me away softly and moved away, his gaze even more confused.

"What was that about?"

Not really sure how else to proceed, I grabbed his shirt and brought myself close to him again, kissing him savagely. Surely if they were as intimate as the guards had suggested he would soon succumb to my kisses?

"Fada, please! What's wrong with you?"

His confusion was unexpected, but I did not let it stop me.

"Would you just shut up and kiss me?" I groaned.

Netis opened his eyes wide, his expression suddenly suspicious. I had completely forgotten to speak softly, and I was afraid that he might have recognised my voice. Clearing my throat, I tried to speak more softly.

"Just leave me to it…"

I kissed him again, this time more gently. I could not

bear to kiss him, especially in this way, but at the same time, it was amusing to drive him mad with this behaviour of mine. He was truly confused, yet he let me kiss him without saying another word. He was not the kind of man who would allow anyone to talk to him like that. He must care for her deeply, which would only make him suffer more when she killed him.

Grinning maliciously as I kissed Netis, I reached under the skirt of Fada's dress to grab the dagger on my thigh. I felt my leg for a couple of seconds, but I could not feel any dagger. Pushing Netis away, I raised the skirt up to look at both of my thighs, but there was no dagger to be seen. I could not believe it: how could she not have a dagger with her? The royals of Hagalaz had to wear one at all times, what was wrong with this girl? And why had Akaoh not warned me? My bare hands would have been enough to kill Netis if I had my old body, but there was no way this weak body could kill with no weapon.

"Where's that bloody dagger?" I hissed, not paying attention to my voice anymore.

"What are you talking about? You never carry your dagger with you…"

I looked at him, full of anger. I could not believe that I had kissed him uselessly. I hated this body! I had behaved like that pathetic princess for no reason, and I could not stand it. My breathing sped as I glared at

Netis. The only fight I had lost was the one that had killed me; I refused to lose this one too.

Letting my eyes wander, I settled my gaze on his own dagger, which was secured on his hip by a belt. Hurling myself at him, I pulled the dagger from its sheath and raised it above my head, screaming in rage. I was not fast enough, though, for Netis swiftly grabbed my wrist, pressing down strongly with his fingers and making me drop the dagger. This body was so weak. I had been so close to killing him, yet now I was weapon-less.

"Fada, what are you doing?" he shouted, frowning in confusion.

I threw my fist against his face in response but, yet again, Netis stopped me before I could touch him. His hand was wrapped around my fist, yet I could feel that he was controlling his strength to make sure that he would not hurt me.

"You're just a dead loss! This kingdom is better off without you!" I screamed.

He was still holding my left fist and right wrist tightly, but I threw my knee into his stomach as strongly as I could. Unlike Netis, I was not controlling my strength, and the force of this body's weight shoving into his stomach made him back down. He cared too much for his precious Fada; he could not bear the thought of hurting her, and because of his pathetic sentimentality, he had not protected himself. I was

311

certain that seeing Fada behaving like this was hurting him even more than the kick I had given him. Seeing him suffer both physically and emotionally was rewarding, and I could feel my lips pulling into a grin.

"You have destroyed my kingdom, Netis, and killed my people. You are a terrible king, and you shall pay for your mistakes. Your death will bring peace back to Hagalaz."

As I spoke, I threw my fist against his face, and to my surprise, he did not move, letting my fist punch his jaw strongly. In a matter of a seconds, he stood straight again, throwing his leg at my feet which made me fall onto my back, nearly knocking me out. This body was even weaker than I had thought, and I was too dizzy to stand on my feet again. Netis was up and strong again, holding his jaw, looking at me with anger. His other hand was clenched, and his breathing was heavy. Here I was, laying on the floor while he stood over me, back in power again. I could not stand it. With all the strength I had left, I stood up, looking at him scornfully.

"You don't even know what you're doing; you don't know anything. Is this what you call war? You, a mighty warrior, unable to harm sweet little Fada? You've become weak and easily manipulated. You're such a pathetic fool…"

I had no time to finish my sentence for Netis seized my neck with a harsh and mechanical gesture, gripping my throat tightly and pressing me against the wall. I began to tremble, and as Fada's body began to convulse, I felt her soul growing stronger. No! I could not leave now. Netis was still alive. I had failed; I could not fail! But my strength was waning as the body grew weaker, and Fada's soul slowly pushed against me, growing larger and larger until Netis vanished from my sight. I screamed with rage as Fada took back possession of her body and I was sucked away, back to Eihwaz; back to the abyss of my own loneliness...

I screamed, my eyes shut tight. My throat was on fire, and I could feel a terrible pressure on my neck, like someone was choking and burning me at the same time. I opened my eyes uneasily and found Netis staring back at me, his eyes blazing with anger. Tears started rolling down my cheeks as I realised what was happening. Why was he looking at me like that? Why was he strangling me? What had I done wrong? I remembered something taking over my body, but everything was blurry, and I could not gather my thoughts. My mind was full of images that seemed like recent memories, yet I knew that I had not done any of these things. I was confused by what was happening and having all these thoughts flashing before my eyes made me feel like I was going insane.

I heard voices whispering 'he's going to kill her, I can't believe she said all those things to him'. Panicked by their words, I laid my hands over his.

"Netis... please..." I managed, my voice weak and faint.

His gaze changed immediately, his face relaxing as he released me. I slumped to the floor, holding my throat and gasping for air. My entire body felt stiff, and as I raised my eyes, I saw dozens of people standing in the doorway, staring at me and Netis with alarm. I looked at Netis and he quickly raised his eyes to the people by the door.

"I don't need you here, get out!"

"But... we heard screams coming from your room... we thought you might need help..."

"Did I ask for your help? Be gone. Prepare everyone for battle. In a few hours' time, we go to war."

Everyone left hurriedly, glancing back at me with fear in their eyes. Nothing made sense, why were they afraid of me? And why was Netis standing in front of me with eyes full of rage.

"What's going on, Netis?" I asked, looking up at him in confusion. "Why did you tell everyone to get ready to fight? Hasn't there been enough war?"

He came closer to me, his expression bleak.

"You should have thought about that before behaving

314

the way you did…"

"What are you talking about? What have I done?"

"Don't patronise me!" he growled, grabbing my wrist. "Do you think you have the right to speak to me like that? Do you think you have power over me? Do you truly believe that you can come to me and hurt me without bearing the consequences of your actions? Your precious people would have been better off if you had stayed silent."

I stared at Netis in silence. His words made no sense at all. My memory of what had just happened was still blurry; I could not remember what the soul had said or done, but she had been cruel for sure. I could not let him think that those words and actions had come from me. He had to understand that I had not been in control of my own body.

"Netis, please, you have to listen to me. This whole situation is a misunderstanding—"

"A misunderstanding?" he interrupted. "On the contrary, everything is clear to me now. We will never be able to come to an agreement. You are too impulsive, Fada; you should have thought about your words before speaking them out loud. It's too late for apologies now; I have a battle to prepare for, and not even you can stop me this time."

"It wasn't me! I would never hurt you, Netis. I'm begging you, you've got to believe me."

315

"I can't. Not anymore…"

He walked out of his bedroom, still holding my wrist, dragging me down the stairs and out of the back gate.

"Leave," he insisted, opening a portal. "Make Maheliah aware of what your behaviour has brought upon us all. Tell her to meet me in two hours, to the east of her palace. I will be waiting for her and her army. It is time to end this once and for all."

With those words, he pushed me through the portal, leaving the memory of his merciless gaze imprinted in my mind.

I could not bring myself to enter Maheliah's palace. I had already broken her heart yesterday; I could not bear to do so again. This was all my fault. I should have never gone to meet with Akaoh. Had I stayed at home, the old king would never have had the opportunity to place another soul inside my body; that soul would never have angered Netis, and we would not be in the position where we were being forced to fight yet another pointless battle. I hated myself for the sorrow I had brought upon this kingdom.

Summoning my resolve, I entered the throne room, hoping to find Maheliah, but she was not there. Concerned, I went up to her bedroom, but she was not there either and I began to panic. Almost running through the corridors, I hurried to my bedroom, and was relieved to see that the door was open. There she was, sitting on my bed, her expression blank. My heartbeats sped as I tried to figure out what to say to her. I wondered why she was waiting for me, and I feared that she had bad news for me too, though surely her news could not be worse than what I was about to tell her?

Noticing me, Maheliah looked up, smiling sadly. I gave her the same smile and sat down next to her.

"I'm so sorry, Fada, I should have never broken down in front of you yesterday... I hope you can forgive me."

I was confused. I had not expected her to apologise; she had done nothing wrong. I had been the one who had brought up her painful memories. If anyone should be apologising, it was me. Knowing that she had recovered from her breakdown made my task even harder. How could I tell her that, in two hours' time, she would have to return to the battlefield because of me? It seemed that, whenever something good happened, something bad came up right after.

"You have done nothing wrong, Maheliah. I'm the one who needs to apologise."

She lifted one eyebrow, still staring at me, and I continued.

"I... I don't know what happened, but something... something angered Netis. There will be another battle, in two hours... Netis will be waiting for you with his

317

army, to the east of the palace. He said it was time to end this war…"

Maheliah stood up quickly. I could see how tortured she was; her jaw was tense, and her eyes kept moving rapidly from left to right. Many thoughts seemed to be rushing through her mind, and I hated that I had been the one to cause her distress.

"So be it," she said quietly, after a deep breath. "He's right. It is time to end this insane war. One of us must go—"

"No, Maheliah, don't say that. We can still prevent it; nobody needs to die. I came back to warn you, but I am going to head straight back to the palace to try and talk to Netis. I can't lose any of you."

"Go. Try to reason with him. I will not make the same mistake as last time. This war must end today, one way or another."

She swept out of my bedroom, and I hurried down the stairs after her, surprised by her assertive tone as we entered the main hall.

"My friends, Netis requests our presence once more. In two hours, we shall fight for the last time. Prepare yourselves; this battle will not be easy, but I believe in you all. Life as we know it will finally be over. This may be our last day together, but I have faith that, regardless of how the day ends, the war will end with it. Hagalaz shall finally be at peace again. Are you with me?"

"Yes!" everyone shouted in unison.

Seeing the tortured faces of my people was unbearable, and I could not believe that an entire kingdom was about to destroy itself because of me. I had to stop this fight, and end this war, before it was too late.

CHAPTER XVIII - THE END OF AN ERA

Running towards Netis' palace, I thought of Akaoh. All along I had assumed that he only wanted what was best for Hagalaz; that he wanted to restore peace to the kingdom. But by placing my trust in him, I had only made everything worse. Maheliah had forewarned me about Akaoh, about how dangerous and untrustworthy he was, but I had not listened, too determined to know the truth. Perhaps, had I heeded her warning, the terrible events that had occurred in recent days would never have happened. I realised that I had been wrong about Akaoh's intentions from the start. Peace was not what he desired for Hagalaz; all he yearned for was destruction and chaos.

My heart began to beat rapidly when I saw that there was no one guarding the back gate, and as I ran up the stairs to Netis' room, I desperately hoped that he had not yet left. Reaching his bedroom door, I frantically turned the handle, but the door would not move. Ramming my body against it, I tried to break through the wood, but I was too weak to even make a dent. My heart was in a panic, and I sprinted back down the stairs, running through the corridors of the palace and knocking on every door. But to my despair, nobody answered. My thoughts were a mess and thinking straight felt beyond my reach. I needed to concentrate. Surely someone would still be here; not everyone in the palace was a warrior.

Ceasing my frantic search for a moment, I tried to calm my breathing. If I was to have any hope of finding anyone, I needed to search more thoroughly. I needed to walk, not run. Trying to cling on to this rationality, I made my way down another corridor, and found myself at the bottom of another set of stairs. Upstairs was another corridor, and as I walked along it, I realised that every door I came across was engraved with a list of names. Stopping, I read the list on the door closest to me, and recognised one of the names. Angel. This was Angel's room.

My curiosity momentarily overriding my desperation, I opened the door, finding myself standing in some kind of dormitory. A massive window covered most of the wall in front of me, and both the right-hand and left-hand walls were lined with four simple looking beds. At the base of each bed was a small desk, each of them adorned with quills and inkwells. As I looked around, I noticed what looked like an envelope, sitting on the desk in the far-left corner. Walking towards it, I read:

To whomever finds this letter, please pass it on to our princess. I wish for her to understand.

I had never seen Angel's writing, but I was certain that this letter was from him. I took it with trembling fingers and sat on his bed. Why would he write me a letter? I feared to open it. What if he was simply too outraged to speak to me face to face? After spending a couple of seconds staring at it in my trembling hands, I took a deep breath and tore off the wax seal, unfolding the letter.

My precious Fada,

These words are for you. I want you to know what is on my mind, in the hope that your remorse will soon vanish, for I truly wish you a happy life by Netis' side. You are both so dear to me, and I know that you have always been destined to be with one another. You deserve to be happy.

For as long as I can remember, my only duty has been to serve you. I never knew the man who heard my soul, and spent my early years being cared for by nurses, like

322

many of us slaves. I was five years old when Netis took me under his wing. He never told me why he chose me, only that it was my fate to be his slave. My entire military education was focused on finding you and bringing you to Hagalaz. If it were not for you, I would have probably died young; most slaves do not make it past ten years old, for the harsh conditions of Hagalaz make it difficult to survive without adequate protection. Netis gave my life purpose, and thanks to him, I grew up in a palace. I had warm food... a soft bed... friends. None of this would have been possible without you.

I may have suffered over the years, but meeting you has been the most precious event of my existence. Looking at you from afar, seeing what a passionate and kind-hearted person you were, made me fall for you even before saying a single word to you. But that day when I saw you at the museum, I could no longer resist, and although introducing myself to you was scary, it was worth it. When I saw you standing in the middle of a crowd of people, drawing that bracelet with such a concentrated gaze, I knew that I was doomed. I had already fallen for you, Fada, and spending those next few months with you on Earth made my love for you grow even stronger. Those were the happiest days of my life; I never imagined I would experience such happiness. I must confess that, sometimes, I forgot you were our princess and that I was meant to bring you to

323

Hagalaz, because that beautiful smile of yours made me forget who I was too. But Netis grew impatient, and when he ordered me to bring you to Hagalaz, my happiness vanished, because I knew that I was about to destroy yours. I would bring you to Netis; you would train to become a strong warrior and a wise heir to the throne. There would no longer be any room left for me in your life.

I knew I would have to bear terrible consequences, but I never regretted bringing you to Maheliah instead of Netis. Your happiness has always been my weakness, and imagining how unhappy you would be, living the life Netis had planned for you, was unbearable. Even to this day, I do not regret breaking Netis' order that day. You were already my meaning in life; as long as you were safe and happy, so was I.

Who else but you could break my heart; you are the only one who ever owned it. After that night in the cave at Maheliah's palace, I truly believed that it would be the end of me, and frankly, I was ready to die. My lifetime mission had been completed; you were a princess, and I was a slave, what else could I expect from life? But you took the decision to save me, and in doing so, gave me a terrible burden to carry. Had I known that Netis only allowed me to live because you had given yourself to him, I would have ended my own life earlier. When you told me what you had done, it

324

made me realise how much you love me, but also how much you love Netis.

People talked in the palace; they were always telling me that your relationship with Netis was more than diplomatic talks, but I refused to believe it. I could not imagine you being attracted to such a man. I care for Netis more than I can express, and although he has been kind and caring towards me from time to time, I never saw him as a loving person. I believed that he would never bring you anything that you needed. But that was my mistake. I was standing behind his bedroom doorway long before your kiss that day. I saw the way he softly touched your arms, and how pure his gaze was upon you. During that kiss, all I saw was the way you looked at him, and the way he looked at you. I have never seen him look at anyone this way. He loves you, Fada. It pains me to say it, but he truly does, and you love him too; you should stop denying it. It hurts me to acknowledge it, but I have to accept the truth. You two are made for each other, and I am in the way. I have no doubt of your love for me, but the way you stared into his eyes made me realise that I will never be enough. The way you look at me is loving and caring, but when you look at Netis, it's like everything clicks into place. It is a look of completeness, of wholeness. When you are together, you are one.

That is why I need to leave. You don't need me the

way you need him, and when I am gone, you will finally see clearly that your love for Netis is meant to be, and that he is your fate, not me. I am not angry with you, Fada, how could I be? I do not know what is waiting for me on the other side, but I hope I will be able to leave Eihwaz from time to time to look over you and see what a wonderful queen you have become. I have no doubt that your future will be bright, and that you have found your happiness already. You will have to brave many challenges, but I shall be looking upon you always.

Your love for me was the highlight of my short life. I will die, yes, but my mind is at rest knowing that it will bring you close to your happiness and life's purpose. You brought a new vision of life to me, and thanks to you, I discovered what it means to love so deeply that dying for you seems like a fair end.

Forever yours,
Angel

My heart had stopped. Every inch of my body was trembling, and fat, hot tears were pouring from my eyes. Angel was going to die. For me. The letter crinkled between my fingers and my tears fell onto the ink, blurring his words. I had never experienced anything like this before. My heart was crushed, and I could barely breathe. I had to do something; I could not allow Angel to die today.

Shoving Angel's letter into my corset I leapt to my feet and ran out of the palace as fast as I could. I knew exactly where to run, for I had no doubt of Angel's whereabouts. He wanted to die because of me; our secret place would be his chosen grave.

Snowflakes were falling heavily, and I ran faster, desperate to reach him in time. Turning the corner, I arrived at the lakeside, and as I ran, I perceived a shape on the ground next to the rock bench. The heavy snow made it hard to distinguish, but as I drew closer, the shape became clearer. I stopped, my breath catching in my throat. No... no... it could not be him...

Throwing myself onto the ground I crawled towards him, choking on my own tears as my body began to tremble, my chest heaving with heavy sobs. His body lay on the ground, with his dagger protruding through his abdomen. His face seemed peaceful, but the blood rolling down his torso, seeping into the snowy ground, erased any hope I had. He had left me. Forever.

I shook him, crying his name and hoping to bring life back to him, but his eyes remained empty. I held him strongly in my arms, letting my suffering submerge me entirely. I realised that I would never see his smile again; his ocean eyes would no longer bring happiness to my heart; I would never feel the warmth of his arms around my body. He had saved me so many times, and I had hurt him too many times... He had thought his action would bring me happiness, but how could I be happy now? The world seemed empty without him. How could he do this to me? How could he leave me? I needed him! No physical pain had ever made me feel the agony I felt in this moment. My entire body was aching, and it felt like my heart was being crushed and stabbed at the same time. Even breathing had become a torture. I deserved to feel this much pain. I had killed him. This was all because of me.

I lay down next to his lifeless body, holding his hand and resting my head in the hollow of his neck. My tears would not stop. I wanted to stay like this forever; I wanted to die by his side and follow him to wherever he was now. Soon, the snow began to cover both our bodies, and laying beneath this icy shroud, I felt as dead as him.

I understood neither his actions nor his words. How could he have thought that his death would bring me happiness? His single action had killed not only him, but my hopes and dreams too. I wanted nothing but for my soul to follow his. I wanted to feel his kiss on my lips; see the blue of his eyes looking deep into mine; see him smile because of something I said or did. His gaze, his voice and his touch haunted me, but the more I thought about him, the more unbearable my pain became. My mind kept wandering through the memories of him, and I could feel the warmth of his body next to mine, his breathing on my head and his heartbeat on my hand. But none of it was real. Next to me was a cold, empty body. Angel's beautiful soul was no longer by my side.

The sound of marching and the shouts of warriors dragged me from my slumber. The battle was about to begin. Soon, more people would die because of me. I raised my head slowly, opening my eyes. My sight was blurry, but I never stopped looking at Angel's face. I could not leave him like this, staring blankly at the sky. Gently, I closed his eyelids and laid a kiss on his frozen lips, moving my hand towards his dagger. Still kissing him, I pulled the dagger out of his abdomen, holding it with a trembling hand as more tears fell onto his frozen body. Raising my face softly, I rested my forehead on his, caressing his cheek. Between two sobs I painfully whispered 'I love you', before dragging myself to my feet, still looking at his beautiful face. I moved away from him, walking backwards for a couple of steps. I could not stop staring at him, but I had to. I could not stay here and die in his arms… my death could not be in vain.

Dying by his side would have been the sweetest of deaths, but even if I still had a hard time accepting it, I was a princess. I had responsibilities and duties towards my people. I could not leave Hagalaz in such a state, and I needed to bring peace back once and for all. To do so, there was only one solution: I needed to die in front of them all.

I started walking towards the battle, gripping Angel's dagger. My thoughts drifted; I wondered what my life would have been like if I had never met Angel… if I had remained on Earth. I doubted things would have changed. Life would have remained the same as it had always been, dull and loveless. I would have grown up to be a mere shadow of my true self, and I would not have known that I could ever feel differently. Although a year in Hagalaz had brought me more pain than I had ever experienced during my twenty years on Earth, I was still glad that I had been brought here. I would have never found love on Earth, and the boredom of Earthly life would surely have killed me anyway.

Another vision appeared in my mind. I was sitting on a silver throne, dressed all in white, with a majestic look on my face. Netis was sitting next to me, his gaze cold and ruthless. I shivered. Imagining myself as a heartless queen was too much to bear. Something bonded me to Netis, and I knew how sweet and charming he could be, but in this instant, I could only recall his cruelty and coldness. Right now, all my love was directed to the man who was lying lifeless on the ground behind me. I could not think of Netis with beautiful thoughts.

As I was approaching the battlefield, I saw myself resting my hands on the bridge that stood above the frozen lake, contemplating my reflection. My long white hair floated in the air, and my forehead was creased with deep wrinkles. Behind me, holding me in his arms, his hair as white as mine and his face still perfect, despite the time that had passed, was Angel. As I turned to face him, his lips touched mine, and the two of us fell peacefully into a deep, endless slumber. I shook myself. It was nothing but an illusion. None of these visions would ever become a reality. The only future I could see for myself was about to end.

In front of me, Netis and Maheliah were facing each other, their armies standing behind them, ready to fight. As soon as the warriors saw me, they began to whisper my name, and soon, that whisper became a wave of sound. Netis and Maheliah turned their faces towards me, their angry features quickly shifting to expressions of confusion. I could only imagine how I looked; my eyes red from weeping, my cheeks stained with tears, and my white dress sullied with blood. I stopped walking when I reached the midpoint between the two of them. Netis was now to my right; Maheliah to my left. She started to walk closer to me, but I stopped her, staring at her with anger.

"Fighting… is this the only thing you can do? I dreamed of a peaceful world; bringing happiness to Hagalaz had always been my main purpose. But I see now that I will never live in the world you once described to me, Maheliah. I wish things could be different, but they won't be, not as long as I'm alive…"

"Fada, what are you talking about?" Maheliah whispered, tears in her eyes.

"I'm talking about these useless battles; this useless death…" I broke down. The thought of Angel's dead body covered in snow came back to me, and it was unbearable. "One of my biggest dreams was to visit the other kingdoms, to see with my own eyes the oceans and mountains of this world. But this cannot be my fate, I know that now. I was born to suffer. Dying young and unhappy is the only suitable end for me…"

"Fada, please, put down the dagger," Maheliah pleaded, her voice panicked.

"Why should I do that? Peace must come back to Hagalaz. I won't see it myself, but at least I can restore peace for all of you. Why should I continue to live in this world which isn't mine? I have never belonged: not here; not on Earth…"

I turned to look at Netis. His lips were trembling, his eyes shining brightly with sorrow. Seeing him on the verge of tears was a first, and the pain in his eyes almost made me waver. But I held strong to my resolve and turned back to Maheliah, wiping my tears away with the back of my hand.

"I'm so sorry Maheliah, I should have listened to you. It's all my fault… I shouldn't have gone to Akaoh… I never told you because I knew you would not approve, and I understand why now. He tricked me into thinking I should listen to his advice, which I did. But because of him, I made one bad decision after another, and now Angel is dead…"

My tears were unstoppable now, and the pain in my chest seemed to grow larger with every word. I took another look at Netis; his eyes were wide and his mouth hung open in shock.

"Angel is dead because of me… Akaoh warned me that Angel would suffer, that it was his fate to suffer, but I never thought that he would end his own life. I suppose, in the end, Akaoh was right… Angel had to suffer. Only his death could have confirmed my thoughts regarding my own fate."

I looked at the dagger in my hand, still covered with Angel's blood, and I squeezed it strongly as another sob took hold of me. I raised my eyes to Netis.

"I beg you to forgive me, Netis. Let me leave in peace, knowing that I do not hate you. The one who slandered you was not me; I do not know who she was, but Akaoh forced her soul inside of me. She took control of my body; she wanted to kill you. I have never felt such rage as she felt towards you. I am only grateful that she did not succeed. I could never hurt you, Netis, please believe me. I could never hurt you…"

My breath caught in my throat, and I looked away, turning towards Maheliah.

"You've been like a mother to me ever since we met, Maheliah. I will never forget your kindness. I love you, and I know that you will do whatever is necessary to rule this kingdom as a kind and righteous queen. I was never meant to take your place; you are the true queen Hagalaz deserves, not me…"

I turned back to Netis, my voice weak as I gazed into his sorrowful eyes.

"I feel like I should not be saying these words to you, Netis, not after what just happened to Angel. But you need to know how I feel. I love you, Netis… I hate myself for it, but I can't help it. I have felt connected to you since the instant we met. You have not always been lovable, yet even at your worst, I had this force pushing me towards you. I have never understood this sensation that draws me towards you, and I am certain that love is not the only reason, but it seems it will remain a mystery to me always…"

I could not look at him any longer; the pain in his eyes made me want to fling myself into his arms and stay with him forever. It would have been so easy to give in, to let my determination falter. But I knew that I could not stay.

"War began because of me. It will end thanks to me…"

Gripping the dagger with both hands, I held it out in front of me and in a short, swift motion, plunged it into my abdomen. I heard Maheliah and Netis cry out as I fell to the ground, and almost instantly, they were both by my side. Netis wrapped his arms around my body and pulled me into his chest, holding me as I had held Angel only moments before. I looked into his eyes, my heart aching, knowing that I would never look into those deep black onyxes ever again. My last breath of life was for him, this being whom would forever be a mystery to me. I closed my eyes, waiting for my soul to leave my body as Netis held me tightly, the man I had learned to love through passion and sincerity. Regardless of the bad decisions I had made, I was leaving knowing that I had always been true to myself.

But the suffering did not stop. It was still painful, oh so painful. My heart was beating rapidly, bashing against my chest like a drum. Where was Angel? Why was I still lying in Netis' arms? The pain... why was there so much pain?

EPILOGUE

He put his hands on me and it felt right, it always had. *Him*... he had been on my mind ever since we met and being reunited with him after all these misadventures was such bliss. I hoped I would never have to stay this long away from him again, and that we were back together for good now. I had no doubt regarding my feelings for him, and everything that had happened over the past few days only confirmed that he was the only one for me, and that I could not bear the thought of having another man touching me.

I had never been one to believe in fate, yet ever since I had arrived in Hagalaz, everything that had happened to me had seemed to have a purpose. With each event came a lot of questions, which ultimately led to more events and more questions. I finally had the answer to the most important one though: I was one to believe in fate now. How could I not? Everything had been written for me and it was perfectly clear that I had never had control of anything that had happened to me over the years. But in this instant, I was happy, and I thanked fate for bringing me close to him again. Right now, none of my past troubles mattered and my suffering seemed to be gone entirely. I was calm, and breathing had never felt easier. Being in his arms had always done that to me. It had been many months since I had felt his embrace, but I had not forgotten it, though I had not allowed myself to think of it because it had been too painful. But now, after everything I had been through and learned along the way, I was ready to feel him again, now and always…

BV - #0043 - 090322 - C0 - 198/129/19 - PB - 9781803780313 - Gloss Lamination